I was silenced by his mouth on mine as he pulled me into his arms.

It was no sweet kiss of seduction, no chaste, heavenly kiss. It was full and openmouthed and carnal, and I stood frozen in shock as he put one arm around my waist, pulling me up against his hard body, while the other caught my chin, his long fingers cradling my face.

I'd been kissed before, of course. But never like this, with an almost cosmic sense of urgency and longing. I could feel my nipples harden against the lace of my bra, the clutch of longing in my belly. Who the hell was I trying to fool? I was turned on, every time he was in the room.

"Stop thinking," he said, his voice hot. "I want you. All right? I don't want to—you're nothing but trouble. I wish I could just walk away from you. But I can't."

RAZIEL

The first book in Kristina Douglas's captivating debut series

THE FALLEN

This title is also available as an eBook

THE FALLEN

RAZIEL

KRISTINA DOUGLAS

Pocket Books

New York   London   Toronto   Sydney

Pocket Books
A Division of Simon & Schuster, Inc.
1230 Avenue of the Americas
New York, NY 10020

This book is a work of fiction. Names, characters, places, and incidents either are products of the author's imagination or are used fictitiously. Any resemblance to actual events or locales or persons, living or dead, is entirely coincidental.

First Pocket Books paperback edition February 2011

POCKET and colophon are registered trademarks of Simon & Schuster, Inc.

For information about special discounts for bulk purchases, please contact Simon & Schuster Special Sales at 1-866-506-1949 or business@simonandschuster.com.

The Simon & Schuster Speakers Bureau can bring authors to your live event. For more information or to book an event, contact the Simon & Schuster Speakers Bureau at 1-866-248-3049 or visit our website at www.simonspeakers.com.

Designed by Jacquelynne Hudson
Cover design by Lisa Litwack
Cover illustration by Craig White

Manufactured in the United States of America

10 9 8 7 6 5 4 3 2

ISBN 978-1-4391-9192-7
ISBN 978-1-4391-9194-1 (ebook)

For Abby and Jane.
One kicks my butt, one keeps me sane.
Together it works. Smooch.

RAZIEL

IN THE BEGINNING

I AM RAZIEL, ONE OF THE TWENTY fallen angels spoken of by Enoch in the old books. I live in the hidden world of Sheol, with the other Fallen, where no one knows of our existence, and we have lived that way since the fall, millennia ago. I should have known there would be trouble on the horizon. I could feel it in my blood, and there is nothing more powerful than blood. I had taught myself to ignore those feelings, just as I had taught myself to ignore everything that conspired to betray me. Had I listened, things might have been different.

I rose that day, in the beginning, stretching out my wings to the feeble light of early morning. A storm was coming; I felt it throbbing in my veins, in my bones. For now the healing ocean was calm, the tide coming in, and the mist was thick and warm, an enveloping embrace, but the violence of nature hung heavy in the air.

Nature? Or Uriel?

I had slept outside again. Fallen asleep in one of the wooden chairs, nursing a Jack Daniel's, one of the many pleasures of this last century or so. Too many Jacks, if truth be told. I hadn't wanted this morning to come, but then, I was not a fan of mornings. Just one more day in exile, with no hope of . . . what? Escape? Return? I could never return. I had seen too much, done too much.

I was bound here, as were the others. For years, so many years that they'd ceased to exist, lost in the mists of time, I had lived alone on this earth under a curse that would never be lifted.

Existence had been easier when I'd had a mate. But I'd lost too many over the years, and the pain, the love, were simply part of our curse. As long as I kept aloof, I could deprive Uriel of that one bit of torture. Celibacy was a small price to pay.

I'd discovered that the longer I went without sex, the easier it was to endure, and occasional physical matings had sufficed. Until a few days ago, when the need for a female had suddenly come roaring back, first in my rebellious dreams, then in my waking hours. Nothing I did could dispel the feeling—a hot, blistering need that couldn't be filled.

At least the women around me were all bonded.

My hunger wasn't so strong that it crossed those lines—I could look at the wives, both plain and beautiful, and feel nothing. I needed someone who existed in dreams only.

As long as she stayed there, I could concentrate on other things.

I folded my wings back around me and reached for my shirt. I had a job today, much as I hated it. It was my turn, and it was the only reason the détente existed. As long as we followed Uriel's orders, there was an uneasy peace.

I and the other Fallen took turns ferrying souls to their destiny. Death-takers, Uriel called us.

And that's what we were. Death-takers, blood-eaters, fallen angels doomed to eternal life.

I moved toward the great house slowly as the sun rose over the mountains. I put my hand on the cast-iron doorknob, then paused, turning to look back at the ocean, the roiling salt sea that called to me as surely as the mysterious siren female who haunted my dreams.

It was time for someone to die.

I AM URIEL THE MOST high, the archangel who never fell, who never failed, who serves the Lord in his awful majesty, smiting sinners, turning wicked cities to rubble and curious women to pillars of salt. I am his most trusted servant, his emissary, his voice in the wilderness, his hand on the sword. If need be, I will consume this wicked, wicked world with fire and start anew. Fire to scourge everything, then flood to follow and replenish the land.

I am not God. I am merely his appointed one, to assure his judgment is carried out. And I am waiting.

The Highest One is infallible, or I would judge the Fallen to be a most grievous mistake and smite them from existence. They have been damned to eternal torment, and yet they do not suffer. It is the will of the Most Holy that they live out their endless existence, forced to survive by despicable means, and yet they know joy. Somehow, despite the black curses laid upon them, they know joy.

But sooner or later, they will go too far. They will join the First, the Bringer of Light, the Rebel, in the boundless depths of the earth, locked in silence and solitude throughout the end of time.

I am Uriel. Repent and beware.

CHAPTER
ONE

I WAS RUNNING LATE, WHICH WAS NO surprise. I always seemed to be in a rush—there was a meeting with my editors halfway across Manhattan, I had a deposit to make before the end of the business day, my shoes were killing me, and I was so hungry I could have eaten the glass and metal desk I'd been allotted at my temp job at the Pitt Foundation.

I could handle most of those things—I was nothing if not adaptable. People were used to my tendency to show up late; the secretary over at MacSimmons Publishers was wise enough to schedule my appointments and then tell me they were half an hour earlier. It was a little game we played—unfortunately, since I now knew the rules, I'd arrive an hour late, ruining her careful arrangements.

Tant pis. They could work around me—I was reliable in all other matters. I'd never been late with a manuscript, and my work seldom needed more than minimal revision. They were lucky to have me, even if biblical murder mysteries weren't a big money-maker, particularly when written in a smart-ass tone. *Solomon's Poisoner* had done even better than the previous books. Of course, you had to put that in perspective. Agatha Christie I was not. But if they weren't making money they wouldn't be buying me, and I wasn't going to worry about it.

I had just enough time to make it to the bank, and I could even manage a small detour to grab a hot dog from a street vendor, but there wasn't a damned thing I could do about my stupid shoes.

Vanity, my uptight mother would have said—not that she ever left the confines of her born-again Idaho fortress to see me. Hildegarde Watson trusted nothing and no one, and she'd retreated to a compound filled with other fundamentalist loonies where even her own sinful daughter wasn't welcome. *Thank God.* I didn't need my mother to tell me how shallow I was. I embraced it.

The four-inch heels made my legs look fantastic, which I considered worth any amount of pain. On top of that, they raised me to a more imposing height than my measly five foot three, an advantage with obstreperous middle-aged male editors who liked to treat me like a cute little girl.

However, the damned stilettos hurt like crazy, and I hadn't been smart enough to leave a more comfortable pair at my temp job. I'd been hobbling around all day without even a Band-Aid to protect my poor wounded foot.

I'd feel sorry for myself if I hadn't done it on purpose. I'd learned early on that the best way to accomplish anything was to grit your teeth and fight your way through it with the best grace you could muster, and wearing those damned shoes, which had cost me almost a hundred and eighty dollars, discounted, was the only way I'd ever get comfortable in them. Besides, it was Friday—I had every intention of spending the weekend with my feet up, working on my new book, *Ruth's Revenge.* By Monday the blisters would have healed enough, and if I could just tough it out for two more days, I'd be used to them. Beauty was worth the pain, no matter what my mother said.

Maybe sometime I'd be able to support myself with my writing and not have to deal with temp jobs. Snarky mysteries set on debunking the Judeo-Christian Old Testament weren't high on the public's interest meter, the occasional blockbuster Vatican thriller aside. For now, I had no choice but to supplement my meager income, making my weekends even more precious.

"Shouldn't you be heading out, Allie?" Elena, my

overworked supervisor, glanced over at me. "You won't have time to get to the bank if you don't leave now."

Crap. Two months and already Elena had pegged me as someone chronically late. "I won't be back," I called out as I hobbled toward the elevator. Elena waved absently good-bye, and moments later I was alone in the elevator, starting the sixty-three-floor descent.

I could risk taking off my shoes, just for a few moments of blessed relief, but with my luck someone would immediately join me and I'd have to shove them back on again. I leaned against the wall, trying to shift my weight from one foot to the other. Great legs, I reminded myself.

Out the sixty-third-floor windows, the sun had been shining brightly. The moment I moved through the lobby's automatic door to the sidewalk, I heard a loud crash of thunder, and I looked up to see dark clouds churning overhead. The storm seemed to have come out of nowhere.

It was a cool October afternoon, with Halloween only a few days off. The sidewalks were busy as usual, and the bank was across the street. I could always walk and eat a hot dog at the same time, I thought, heading over to the luncheon cart. I'd done it often enough.

With my luck there had to be a line. I bounced

nervously, shifting my weight, and the man in front of me turned around.

I'd lived in New York long enough to make it a habit not to look at people on the street. Here in mid-town, most of the women were taller, thinner, and better dressed than I was, and I didn't like feeling inadequate. I never made eye contact with anyone, not even with Harvey the hot-dog man, who'd served me daily for the last two months.

So why was I looking up, way up, into a pair of eyes that were . . . God, what color were they? A strange shade between black and gray, shot with stria-tions of light so that they almost looked silver. I was probably making a fool of myself, but I couldn't help it. Never in my life had I seen eyes that color, though that shouldn't surprise me since I avoided looking in the first place.

But even more astonishing, those eyes were watch-ing me thoughtfully. Beautiful eyes in a beautiful face, I realized belatedly. I didn't like men who were too attractive, and that term was mild when it came to the man looking down at me, despite my four-inch heels.

He was almost angelically handsome, with his high cheekbones, his aquiline nose, his streaked brown and golden hair. It was precisely the tawny shade I'd tried to get my colorist to replicate, and she'd always fallen woefully short.

"Who does your hair?" I blurted out, trying to startle him out of his abstraction.

"I am as God made me," he said, and his voice was as beautiful as his face. Low-pitched and musical, the kind of voice to seduce a saint. "With a few modifications," he added, with a twist of dark humor I couldn't understand.

His gorgeous hair was too long—I hated long hair on men. On him it looked perfect, as did the dark leather jacket, the black jeans, the dark shirt.

Not proper city wear, I thought, trying to summon up disapproval and failing because he looked so damned good. "Since you don't seem in any kind of hurry and I am, do you suppose you could let me go ahead of you?"

There was another crash of thunder, echoing through the cement and steel canyons around us, and I flinched. Thunderstorms in the city made me nervous—they seemed so *there*. It always seemed like the lightning snaking down between the high buildings would find me an easier target. The man didn't even blink. He glanced across the street, as if calculating something.

"It's almost three o'clock," he said. "If you want your deposit to go in today, you'll need to skip that hot dog."

I froze. "What deposit?" I demanded, completely paranoid. God, what was I doing holding a conversation with a strange man? I should never have paid any attention to him. I could have lived without the hot dog.

"You're holding a bank deposit bag," he said mildly.

Oh. Yeah. I laughed nervously. I should have been ashamed of my paranoia, but for some reason it hadn't even begun to dissipate. I allowed myself another furtive glance up at the stranger.

To hell with the hot dog—my best bet was to get away from this too-attractive stranger, drop off the deposit, and hope to God I could find a taxi to get me across town to my meeting. I was already ten minutes late.

He was still watching me. "You're right," I said. Another crash of thunder, and the clouds opened up.

And I was wearing a red silk suit that I couldn't really afford, even on clearance from Saks. Vanity again. Without a backward glance, I stepped out into the street, which was momentarily free of traffic.

It happened in slow motion, it happened in the blink of an eye. One of my high heels snapped, my ankle twisted, and the sudden rain was turning the garbage on the street into a river of filth. I slipped, going down on one knee, and I could feel my stockings shred, my skirt rip, my carefully arranged hair plastered limp and wet around my ears.

I looked up, and there it was, a crosstown bus

ready to smack into me. Another crack of thunder, the bright white sizzle of lightning, and everything went calm and still. Just for a moment.

And then it was a blur of noise and action. I could hear people screaming, and to my astonishment money was floating through the air like autumn leaves, swirling downward in the heavy rain. The bus had come to a stop, slanted across the street, and horns were honking, people were cursing, and in the distance I could hear the scream of sirens. Pretty damned fast response for New York, I thought absently.

The man was standing beside me, the beautiful one from the hot-dog stand. He was just finishing a chili dog, entirely at ease, and I remembered I was famished. If I was going to get held up by a bus accident, I might as well get a chili dog. But for some reason, I didn't want to turn around.

"What happened?" I asked him. He was tall enough to see over the crowds of people clustered around the front of the bus. "Did someone get hurt?"

"Yes," he said in that rich, luscious voice. "Someone was killed."

I started toward the crowd, curious, but he caught my arm. "You don't want to go there," he said. "There's no need to go through that."

Go through what? I thought, annoyed, staring at the crowd. I glanced back up at the stranger, and I had the odd feeling that he'd gotten taller. I suddenly realized my feet didn't hurt anymore, and I looked down. It was an odd, disorienting sensation. I was barefoot, and if I didn't know it was impossible, I would have said there was thick green grass beneath my feet.

I glanced back up at the rain-drenched accident scene in front of me, and time seemed to have moved in an odd, erratic shift. The ambulance had arrived, as well as the police, and people were being herded out of the way. I thought I caught a glimpse of the victim—just the brief sight of *my* leg, wearing *my* shoe, the heel broken off.

"No," said the man beside me, and he put a hand on my arm before I could move away.

The bright light was blinding, dazzling, and I was in a tunnel, light whizzing past me, the only sound the whoosh of space moving at a dizzying speed. *Space Mountain,* I thought, but this was no Disney ride.

It stopped as abruptly as it had begun, and I felt sick. I was disoriented and out of breath; I looked around me, trying to get my bearings.

The man still held my arm loosely, and I yanked it free, stumbling away from him. We were in the woods, in some sort of clearing at the base of a cliff, and it was already growing dark. The sick feeling in my stomach began to spread to the rest of my body.

I took a deep breath. Everything felt odd, as if this were a movie set. Things looked right, but everything seemed artificial, no smells, no sensation of touch. It was all illusion. It was wrong.

I wiggled my feet, then realized I was still barefoot. My hair hung down past my shoulders, which made no sense since I had short hair. I tugged at a strand, and saw that instead of its carefully streaked and striated color, it was brown again, the plain, ordinary brown I'd spent a fortune trying to disguise, the same plain, ordinary brown as my eyes. My clothes were different as well, and the change wasn't for the better. Baggy, shapeless, colorless, they were as unprepossessing as a shroud.

I fought my way through the mists of confusion—my mind felt as if it were filled with cotton candy. Something was wrong. Something was very wrong.

"Don't struggle," the man beside me said in a remote voice. "It only makes it worse. If you've lived a good life, you have nothing to be afraid of."

I looked at him in horror. Lightning split open the sky, followed by thunder that shook the earth. The solid rock face in front of us began to groan, a deep, rending sound that echoed to the heavens. It started to crack apart, and I remembered something from Christian theology about stones moving and Christ rising from the dead. The only problem was that I was Jewish, as my fundamentalist Christian mother had been for most of her life, and I was nonobservant at that. I didn't think rising from the dead was what was going on here.

"The bus," I said flatly. "I got hit by the bus. I'm dead, aren't I?"

"Yes."

I controlled my instinctive flinch. Clearly he didn't believe in cushioning blows. "And who does that make you? Mr. Jordan?"

He looked blank, and I stared at him. "You're an angel," I clarified. "One who's made a mistake. You know, like in the movie? I shouldn't be dead."

"There is no mistake," he said, and took my arm again.

I sure as hell wasn't going quietly. "Are you an angel?" I demanded. He didn't feel like one. He felt like a man, a distinctly real man, and why the hell was I suddenly feeling alert, alive, aroused, when according to him I was dead?

His eyes were oblique, half-closed. "Among other things."

Kicking him in the shin and running like hell seemed an excellent plan, but I was barefoot and my body wasn't feeling cooperative. As angry and desperate as I was, I still seemed to want him to touch me, even when I knew he had nothing good in mind. Angels didn't have sex, did they? They didn't even have sexual organs, according to the movie *Dogma*. I found myself glancing at his crotch, then quickly pulled my gaze away. What the hell was I doing check-ing out an angel's package when I was about to die?

Oh, yeah, I'd forgotten—I was already dead. And all my will seemed to have vanished. He drew me toward the crack in the wall, and I knew with sudden clarity it would close behind me like something out of a cheesy movie, leaving no trace that I'd ever lived. Once I went through, it would all be over.

"This is as far as I go," he said, his rich, warm voice like music. And with a gentle tug on my arm, he propelled me forward, pushing me into the chasm.

CHAPTER
TWO

THE WOMAN WAS FIGHTING ME. I could feel resistance in her arm, something I couldn't remember feeling before in any of the countless people I'd brought on this journey. She was strong, this one. But Uriel, the ruler of all the heavens, was infallible, or so he had managed to convince just about everyone, so this couldn't be a mistake, no matter what it felt like.

She was just like so many others I had brought here. People stripped of their artifice, shocked and needy, while I herded them on to their next life like a shepherd of old, not wasting much thought on the entire process. These humans were simply moving through the stages of existence, and it was in their nature to fight it. Just as it was my job to ease their passage and see them on their way.

But this woman was different. I knew it, whether

I wanted to admit it or not. She should have been anonymous, like all the others. Instead I stared down at her, trying to see what eluded me. She was nothing special. With her face stripped free of makeup and her hair down around her shoulders, she looked like a thousand others. The baggy clothes she now wore hid her body, but it didn't matter. I didn't care about women, in particular human women. I'd sworn off them for eternity, or for as long as Uriel kept me alive. This one should have been as interesting to me as a goldfish.

Instead I reacted to her as if she somehow mattered. Perhaps Azazel was right, and swearing off women and sex had been a bad idea. Celibacy was an unhealthy state for all creatures great and small, he'd argued. It was even worse for the Fallen. Our kind need sex as much as we need blood, and I was intent on keeping away from both. And instead of things getting easier, this woman was resisting.

I paid no attention to my hunger—it had nothing to do with her, and I could ignore it as I'd been ignoring it for so long. But she was somehow able to fight back when no one else could, and that was something I couldn't ignore.

There was no question—Allegra Watson was supposed to be here. I had stood and waited as she stepped in front of the bus, moving in to scoop her up at the moment of death and not a second before.

I never lingered. There was no need for her to suffer—her fate had been ordained and there were no last-minute reprieves. I had watched the bus smash into her, waiting just long enough to feel her life force flicker out. And then it was over.

Some argued when I brought them away. In general, lawyers were the biggest pain in my ass, also stockbrokers. They cursed me—but then, they weren't heading where Allie Watson was heading. Lawyers and stockbrokers and politicians uniformly went to hell, and I never minded escorting them. I took them to the darkside, pushing them over the cliff without a moment's regret.

It always shocked them, those who were banished. First they couldn't believe they could actually die, and when hell loomed up they were astonished, indignant.

"I don't believe in hell," many of them had said, and I always tried to resist the impulse to tell them that hell believed in *them*. Sometimes I even succeeded.

"You're a goddamned angel," one had said, never realizing quite how accurate he was. "Why are you sending me to hell?"

I never bothered to give them the straight answer. That they deserved it, that their lives had been filled with despicable, unforgivable things. I didn't care enough.

Goddamned angel, indeed. What else would a fallen angel be, a creature cursed by God and his administrator, the archangel Uriel? As man had developed and free will had come into play, the Supreme Being had all but disappeared, abandoning those in heaven and hell and everywhere in between, leaving Uriel to carry out his orders, enforce his powerful will. Uriel, the last of the great archangels to resist temptation, pride, and lust, the only one not to tumble to earth.

The curse on my kind had been clear: eternal life accompanied by eternal damnation. "And ye shall have no peace nor forgiveness of sin: and inasmuch as they delight themselves in their children, / The murder of their beloved ones shall they see, and over the destruction of their children shall they lament, and shall make supplication unto eternity, but mercy and peace shall ye not attain."

We were the outcasts, the eaters of blood. We were the Fallen, living our eternity by the rules laid out.

But there were the others, the flesh-eaters, who had come after us. The soldier angels who were sent to punish us instead fell as well. They were unable to feel, and driven mad by it. The Nephilim, who tore living flesh and devoured it, were a horror unlike anything ever seen before on the earth, and the sounds of their screams in the darkness rained terror on those left behind, those of us in the half-life.

We had taken one half of the curse: to live forever

while we watched our women die, and to become eaters of blood. While the Nephilim knew hunger of the darkest kind, a hunger for flesh that could only be fed with death and terror.

This had been our lot. Two of the oldest earthly taboos—eating human flesh and drinking human blood. Neither could survive without it, though we Fallen had learned to regulate our fierce needs, as well as the other needs that drove us—that had driven us from grace in the beginning, before time had been counted.

In the end the Fallen had made peace with Uriel. In return for the task of collecting souls, we were allowed at least a measure of autonomy. Uriel had been determined to wipe the Fallen from the face of this earth, but the Supreme Being had, for once, intervened, staying our execution. And while there were no reversals of the curses already in place, there would be no new ones levied against us. For what little joy that brought us.

As long as we continued our job, the status quo would remain. The Nephilim would still hunt us by night, rending, tearing, devouring.

The Fallen would live by day as well, fed by sex and blood, with those needs kept under fierce control.

And Allie Watson was just one more soul to be delivered to Uriel before I could return to our hidden place. Do the job and get back before too much time elapsed. The duties of a fallen angel were not onerous, and I had never failed. Never been tempted. There had even been a time when I rushed to get back to the woman I loved.

But there had been too many women. There would be no more. I had one reason and one reason alone to hurry back.

I couldn't stand humans.

This particular creature was no different, though I couldn't understand how she had the strength to resist my resolve, even the small amount of resistance I felt beneath my grip. Her skin was soft, which was a distraction. I didn't want to think about her skin, or the unmistakable fear in her rich brown eyes. I could have reassured her, but I'd never been tempted to intervene before, and I wasn't about to make an exception for this woman. I wanted to, which bothered me. I wanted to do more than that. My hands shook with need.

I looked down into her panicked face and I wanted to comfort, and I wanted to feed, and I wanted to fuck. All of the needs I kept locked away. She didn't need anything from me. If she did, she'd have to make do without.

But the stronger her panic, the stronger my hunger, and I gave in to the safest of my urges. "Don't be afraid," I said, using the voice given to me to soothe frightened creatures. "It will be fine." And I pulled her forward, spinning her out into the darkness and releasing her as I stepped back.

It was only at the last minute I saw the flames. I heard her scream, and I grabbed for her without thinking, dragging her back. I felt the deadly fire sear my flesh, and I knew then what had been waiting for me, out there in the darkness. Fire was death to my kind, and the flame had leapt to my flesh like a hungry lover. I pulled the woman out of the dark and hungry maw that should have been what humans referred to as heaven, and I sealed my own trip to a hell that would have no end.

We tumbled backward, onto the ground with her soft body sprawled on top of mine, and I was instantly hard, my rebellious flesh overruling everything I'd been trying to tell it for decades, overshadowing the pain as a pure, unspeakable lust flamed through me, only to be banished a moment later.

An inhuman howl of rage echoed up from the flames. A moment later the rocks slid closed with a hideous grinding noise, and there was nothing but silence.

I couldn't move. The agony in my arm was unspeakable, wiping out my momentary reaction to the woman's soft body sprawled across mine, and I could almost be glad. The flames were out, but I knew what fire did to my kind. A slow, agonizing death.

It was one of the few things that could kill us, that

and the traditional ways of disposing of blood-eaters. Beheading could kill us as surely as it would kill a human.

So would the minor burn on my arm.

If I'd only stopped to think, I would have let her go. Who knew how she'd spent her short life, what crimes she'd committed, what misery she'd inflicted on others? It wasn't my place to judge, merely to transport. Why hadn't I remembered that and let her fall?

But even as I felt the pain leaching away any semblance of common sense, I couldn't help but remember I'd brought any number of innocent souls to this very place, seemingly good people, cast them forth, assured them that they were going to the place of peace they'd earned. Instead it had been hell, the same hell to which I'd taken the lawyers and stockbrokers. This was no temporary glitch. I knew Uriel too well. Hell and its fiery pit were Uriel's constructions, and I knew, instinctively, that we'd been offered no alternative when we'd delivered our charges. I had been dooming the innocent ones to eternal damnation, unknowing.

The sin of pride, Uriel would have said placidly, with great sorrow. The cosmic hypocrite would shake his head over me and my many failings. To question the word of the Supreme Being and the emissary he'd chosen to enforce it was an act of paramount sacrilege.

In other words, do what you're told and don't ask questions. Our failure to do that was why we had fallen in the first place. And I had done more than question—I had just contravened the word. I was in deep shit.

Night was falling around us. The woman rolled off me, scrambling away as if I were Uriel himself. I tried to find my voice, to say something to reassure her, but the pain was too fierce. The best I could do was grit my teeth to keep from screaming in agony.

She was halfway across the clearing, huddled on the ground, watching me in dawning disbelief and horror. Too late I realized my lips were drawn back in a silent scream, and she could see my elongated fangs.

"What in God's name are you?" Her voice was little more than a choked gasp of horror.

I ignored her question—I had more important things to deal with. I had to gather my self-control or I was doomed. If I didn't, I wouldn't be able to save myself at this point, and I couldn't save her either, not that I particularly cared. She had gotten me into this mess in the first place.

She was going to have to help get me out of it, whether she wanted to or not. I shuddered, forcing the agony back down my throat. In a few minutes I wouldn't be able to do even that much; a few minutes longer and I would be unconscious. By morning I would probably be dead.

Did I care? I wasn't sure it mattered one way or the other. But I didn't want to leave her behind, where the Nephilim could get her. I'd rather finish her myself before they tore her body into pieces while she screamed for help that would never come.

I sucked in a deep bite of air, steeling myself. "Need . . . to make a . . . fire," I managed, feeling the dizziness pressing against my brain, feeling the darkness closing in. I could hear the monsters out in the night forest, the low, guttural growling of the Nephilim. They would rip her apart in front of me, and I would be paralyzed, unable to do anything but listen to her screams as they ate her alive.

Things were beginning to fade, and the nothingness called to me, a siren song so tempting that I wanted to let go, to drift into that lovely place, the warm, sweet place where the pain stopped. I managed to look over at her—she was curled in on herself, unmoving. Probably whimpering, I thought dizzily. Useless human, who probably belonged in hell anyway.

And then she lifted her head, staring at me, and I could read her thoughts easily. She was going to make a run for it, and I couldn't blame her. She wouldn't last five minutes out there in the darkness, but with luck I'd be unconscious by the time they began ripping her flesh from her bones. I didn't want to hear the sounds of her screams as she died.

One more try, and then I'd let go. I tried to rise, to pull the last ounce of strength from my poisoned body, struggling to warn her. "Do not . . ." I said. "You need a fire . . . to scare them away."

She rose, first to her knees, then to her bare feet, and I sank back. There was nothing else I could do. She was frightened, and she would run—

"And how am I supposed to start a fire?" she said, her voice caustic. "I don't have any matches and I'm not exactly the camping type."

I could just manage to choke out the words. "Leaves," I gasped. "Twigs. Branches."

To my glazed surprise, she began gathering the fuel from nearby, and within a few minutes she had a neat little pile, with branches and logs on the side. The last of the twilight was slowly fading, and I could hear them beyond the clearing, the odd, shuffling noise they made, the terrible reek of decaying flesh and old blood.

She was looking at me, expectant, impatient. "Fire?" she prompted.

"My . . . arm," I barely choked out. The last ounce of energy faded, and blessed darkness rushed in. And my last thought was now it was up to her. I had done everything I could.

And the night closed down around us.

THREE

E'D PASSED OUT. I STARED down at him, torn. I should leave him, I thought. I didn't owe him anything, and if I had any sense at all I'd get the hell out of there and leave him to fend for himself.

But I could hear those noises out in the darkness, and they made my blood run cold. They sounded like some kind of wild animal, and in truth I'd never been Outdoors Girl. My idea of roughing it was going without makeup. If those creatures out there liked to eat meat, then they had dinner stretched out on the ground, waiting for them. It even smelled as if he were already slightly charbroiled. I didn't owe him anything. So what if he'd pulled me back from the jaws of hell . . . or whatever it was? He was the one who'd pushed me there in the first place. Besides, he'd only gotten slightly singed, and he was acting like it was third-degree burns over most of his body. He was a drama queen, and after my mother and my last boyfriend, I'd had enough of those to last me a lifetime.

Hell, who was I kidding? Whether he deserved it or not, I wasn't going to leave him as food for wolves or whatever they were. I couldn't do that to a fellow human being—if that was what he was. Though I still didn't have the faintest idea how I was going to start the damned fire.

I edged closer, looking down at him. He was unconscious, and in the stillness the unearthly beauty of his face was almost as disturbing as the unmistakable evidence of fangs his grimace of pain had exposed. Was he a vampire? An angel? A fiend from hell or a creature of God?

"Shit," I muttered, kneeling beside him to get a closer look at the burn on his arm. The skin was smooth, glowing slightly, but there were no blisters, no burned flesh. He was nothing more than a big baby. I reached out to shake him, then yanked my arm back with another "Shit," as I realized that beneath the smooth skin fire burned.

That was impossible. It looked as if coals were glowing deep under the skin, and the eerie glow was putting out impressive amounts of heat.

There was a shuffling noise in the underbrush, and I froze. My comatose abductor/savior wasn't the highest priority. The danger in the darkness beyond was worse. Whatever was out there was evil, ancient, and soulless, something foul and indescribable. I could feel it in the pit of my stomach, a nameless dread like something out of a Stephen King novel.

This was just wrong. I wrote cozy mysteries, not horror novels. What was I doing in the equivalent of a Japanese horror movie? Not that there'd been any blood as yet. But I could smell it on the night air, and it sickened me.

I glanced back at the small pile of twigs and grasses that I'd assembled. My fingertips were scorched, and on impulse I scooped up some dried leaves and touched them against his arm.

They burst into flames, and I dropped them, startled; they fell onto the makeshift pyre, igniting it.

The fire was bright, flames shooting upward into the sky. But darkness had closed in around us, and the monsters were still waiting.

I put more leaves on top of the fire, adding twigs and branches, listening to the reassuring crackle as they caught. It was only common sense, using fire to scare away the carnivorous predators in the darkness. Even cavemen had done it. Of course, cavemen hadn't started fires from the scorched skin of a fanged creature, but I was handling things the best I could. Hell, maybe saber-toothed tigers had had fire beneath their pelts as well. Anything was possible.

I rose, turning back to my own personal saber-toothed tiger. We were too close to the fire, close enough that my companion would go up in flames if we stayed there. If I could pull him back against the rock face, we might be safe, and it would be easier to defend only one side of the clearing. I reached under his arms and tugged at his shoulders.

"Come on, Dracula," I muttered. "You're too big for me to move on my own. I gotta have some help here."

He didn't stir. I looked down at him, frustrated. He wasn't huge, more long-limbed and elegant than bulky; and while I didn't waste my limited time and money chasing after the perfect body in one of the many fitness clubs in Manhattan, I was strong enough. I should have been able to drag him a short distance away from the fire. Nothing was making any sense, and all the possible explanations put him in a fairly nasty light. Even so, I couldn't just let him die.

I couldn't get a good enough grip on his body, so I caught hold of his jacket and yanked. He was unexpectedly heavy, though it shouldn't have surprised me—the man had towered over my meager five foot three, and I'd felt the crushing strength in his hand as he'd propelled me toward the . . .

I couldn't remember. Five minutes later, and I couldn't remember a damned thing. I didn't know how he'd managed to get burned, or what he'd been trying to do. It was a blank. Everything was a blank. The last thing I remembered was stepping off the curb outside the office building on my way to meet with my editors.

They were going to be pissed as hell that I'd stood them up again.

How much time had passed since then? Days, weeks, months? The short, sassy hairstyle I'd spent a fortune on was now an unruly mane hanging down to my shoulders, and I could see that it was its original mousy brown instead of the tawny, streaked blond I'd gone for. That certainly couldn't have happened in a matter of hours. How long had I been gone?

His heavy body finally began to budge, and I dragged him as far as I could until he let out a piercing cry of pain. I let him be, squatting beside him, staring at his burned flesh. It was the weirdest thing—it seemed like he had flames beneath his skin, as if his bones were made of burning coals.

His entire body was radiating heat, but apart from his arm he wasn't painful to touch. The night had grown sharply colder, and the shapeless thing I was wearing wasn't made for late autumn nights. My patient shivered as I put more wood on the fire. Thank God I'd grabbed an armload. The nighttime marauders seemed to have gone, but there was no guarantee they wouldn't return if I were fool enough to let the fire go out. Wolves didn't actually attack people, did they? But who said they were wolves?

It was going to be a long night.

I sat back on my heels, studying him. Who was he, and what the hell had he done to me? There had to be a reasonable explanation for what had appeared to be fangs. There were crazies out there who filed their teeth to points so they could resemble vampires—I'd seen it on one of the rotting-corpse television shows like *CSI* or *Bones*.

I could certainly see why some people would want to dress up like vampires. After all, bloodsuckers were hot and elegant; they dressed well and clearly had a lot of sex, if all the fiction was to be believed. They also didn't exist.

But this particular man didn't need to dress up or pretend to be anything he wasn't. He was hot, in every sense of the word. I snickered at the notion. No one was around to appreciate my feeble wit, but I'd always managed to amuse myself.

"So what's up with you?" I demanded of his unconscious figure. "What are we doing here? Did you abduct me?" Wishful thinking on my part. This was a man who clearly had no need to kidnap women. All he had to do was snap his fingers, and they'd be lining up around the block.

I had no illusions about my own charms. I was no troll, and I cleaned up pretty well, but next to this man I was clearly only ordinary. All the gym memberships in the world couldn't seem to get rid of the unwanted ten pounds that hugged my hips. With the right clothes, hair, and makeup I was someone to reckon with, but even so I'd never be in this man's league. Right now, dressed in sackcloth and ashes, I probably looked like a bag lady.

Not that I cared. My only company was passed out, presumably for the night. I leaned back, stretching my legs out in front of me, then realized I was leaning against the stone wall. I scrambled away from it, thoroughly creeped out. Hadn't it split open, revealing some kind of horror . . . ? No, that was impossible.

And yet, where had the fire come from? It seemed to me I could remember flames, like the flames of hell, before he pulled me back again—no, the night must be sending my imagination into overdrive.

Smoke billowed up into the inky-blue sky, and I shivered again, wrapping my arms around my body in a useless attempt to warm myself. I could feel the thin, loose clothing beneath my fingers—it was little wonder I was freezing. And there was a delicious source of heat lying at my feet.

He was nothing special, apart from his rather spectacular good looks. And I lived in the Village—I saw any number of beautiful men on a daily basis and they never made me weak in the knees. Of course, in the Village most of the men would be patently unavailable, but that didn't mean I couldn't appreciate them. I seriously lusted after Russell Crowe, and he was just as unlikely to find his way into my bed.

This man wasn't my type. I liked rugged men, a little on the beefy side, with broad shoulders, and average height so they didn't make me feel small and inconsequential. I hated being loomed over, and if I could have found a boyfriend shorter than my five foot three, I would have grabbed him.

He had dark gold eyelashes fanned out against his high cheekbones. Even unconscious, he was still clearly in pain. If only I could remember how the hell I'd ended up here with him, I might figure a way out of it. But my mind was a blank, and all I could do was sit next to the unknown man at my feet and worry.

I put my hand on his hot forehead, brushing a lock of his hair away, and he muttered something beneath his breath.

"Hush," I murmured. "Hush, now. We'll find help in the morning if you're not better." I could hike out of this place and find the police as well as a hospital, and maybe come up with some solid answers.

But in the meantime I was freezing and he was warm and I wasn't going anywhere. And while I couldn't remember how he'd been hurt, any more than I could remember how the hell I'd ended up here, I had the unmistakable conviction that he'd been wounded trying to help me. So I owed him.

I lay down beside him, the ground cold and hard beneath me despite my natural padding. I'd always wondered why metal chairs hurt my butt when I clearly carried my own built-in cushion—if I had to have those extra pounds, I ought to have had some benefits.

I inched closer to the living furnace beside me, leaning against the comforting, solid feel of him. The dangerous heat sank into my bones, and I let out a blissful sigh.

He moaned, restless, and suddenly moved, rolling onto his side and putting his good arm around me. I was pressed up against him, and he was hot. Too hot. Burning up.

But for some crazy reason, he felt so safe. He lay back, still holding me, and I went with him, letting my head rest against his shoulder. For the moment there was nothing I could do to rescue us. For the moment I could close my eyes, listening to the wild creatures out there in the darkness, and know that I was safe.

I could remember nothing; it was all lost and fuzzy. I was like that fish in *Finding Nemo*—two seconds later and the thought was gone. I only knew one thing. Lying in this man's arms was good, and there was no place else I wanted to be. Not back in my apartment in the Village, not doing any of the thousand empty things that had seemed so important just a short time ago. This was where I belonged.

Beyond in the darkness, the hungry creatures howled their rage.

And I closed my eyes and slept.

CHAPTER

FOUR

AZAZEL LOOKED OUT AT THE sky from his perch atop the high cliff. His only company was the occasional night bird—the rest of the Fallen knew well enough to leave him alone at times like these. He could be very dangerous when roused.

He closed his eyes, trying to concentrate on Raziel. He had gone out for a routine pickup—should have been back hours ago. But there was no sign of him.

He had been with Raziel since the beginning of time. They were brothers, though born from no woman's womb. He had always known when Raziel was in any kind of trouble, but right now that connection was blocked.

There could be any number of reasons. Raziel could turn off the mental connection anytime he wanted to, and he often did. During his jobs. During sex. Though Raziel had sworn he would never bond again, and his brief sexual encounters were rare.

He could be underground, or caught in an electrical storm. Strange atmospheric conditions sometimes interfered with the strong bond that lay between them.

Or he could be dead.

No, that was unthinkable. He would know if Raziel had died—they were too much a part of each other, from back in the mists of prehistory.

He closed his eyes, breathing in deeply, searching for the smell of him, the merest trace of him. He sent his questioning mind in each direction, and finally he felt it. The faintest spark of life—he was barely holding on. He wasn't strong enough to signal for help, but Azazel sensed he wasn't alone. Whoever was with him might be able to help. All he or she had to do was ask.

Unless Raziel's companion was the one who had brought him close to death in the first place.

Azazel's eyes flew open. There were others in their hidden stronghold who had different gifts. Someone else might be able to narrow down where Raziel was. And if they were to have a chance of saving him, he would need help.

He looked out over the stormy ocean, the thick mists of daylight moving in, the mists that kept them hidden from everyone. Their home was tucked away on the northwest coast of North America, between the United States and Canada, shrouded in shadows and fog. Sheol was safety, secrecy, literally "the hidden place." A place where they could dwell in peace until Uriel sent one of them out to collect one of the infrequent souls that actually required guidance.

Sheol had been in its current location for hundreds of years. A physical place that sheltered both the Fallen and their human wives, it could still be moved if Azazel deemed it necessary.

But there was no way to shield it from Uriel's inimical gaze. He would find them, as the Nephilim would, and the uneasy détente would continue.

They had no choice. The Fallen lived precariously, doomed to eternal life, to watch their mates age and die while they stayed young. Cursed to become a feared and hated monstrosity.

By day they were free. And they'd learned to harness their blazing need, to control it and use it. No one outside the community would understand, and he didn't expect them to. Ignorance was safer. They would keep their secrets, whatever the price.

He rose, his wings spreading out behind him, and soared down to the rocky outcropping in front of the great house. By the time he landed, the others had gathered, Raphael and Michael, Gabriel and Sammael.

"Where is he?" Azazel demanded roughly. "We cannot lose him."

"We can't lose any of us," Gabriel said somberly. "He's been betrayed."

Michael snarled, his dangerous anger barely in check. "Who the fuck betrayed him? Why hasn't Uriel looked out for him?"

Tamlel was the last to join them in front of the dawn-struck sea. They were the oldest of the Fallen still left on earth, the guardians, the protectors. Only Sammael was newer. "I don't know where he is," he said, his slow, deep voice leaden. "I don't know if we'll be in time. He is very weak. If I could just get a fix on him . . ."

Azazel hid his reaction behind a cold, unemotional exterior. If Tam couldn't find him, there was no hope. Tamlel's gifts were specific but strong. If one of the Fallen was lost, he could find him, until the very last spark of life was extinguished. If the energy was too weak even for Tam, then Raziel was doomed.

Unless someone found him and called for help, he would die, countless millennia after he'd first come into existence. The Fallen were not even given the comfort of death, but something far more terrifying.

Falling had made them close to human. The curses that accompanied that fall from grace might have finally caught up with Raziel. No hope of redemption, not even the dubious blessing of Uriel's hell. Just an eternity of agonized nothingness.

Azazel shut his eyes, pain lancing through him. There had been so many losses, endless losses, so few of the original left. This might be one loss too many.

And then he lifted his head, and he could feel the light enter his body again. "I think I hear her," he said softly.

FIVE

I T WAS ALMOST DAWN, AND THE MAN next to me was dying. His body felt as if it were on fire, and the coals had spread beneath his skin, emanating an unearthly red glow that lit the darkness after the fire had finally died out. He hadn't made a sound in hours; even his moans had been silenced. Sometime in the night he'd released his hold on me, and the heat from his skin had become unbearable. I wondered why his clothes hadn't burst into flames.

I'd done what I could to cool him down—I'd managed to strip the leather jacket from him and put it beneath his head as a makeshift pillow, then unfastened his denim shirt and pulled it free from his jeans, opening it to the cool night air, feeling oddly guilty about it. The skin on his chest and stomach was smooth, with just a faint tracing of golden hair.

Human, I'd thought, and laughed at myself for thinking anything else. I'd reached out a hand to touch him, unconsciously drawn, and yanked my hand back, burned.

His mouth was a grim line of pain. At least I was spared the disquieting view of those disturbing teeth. I must have been hallucinating, and no wonder. I didn't know where I was, *when* I was, or how I'd even got here, and the night had been filled with the terrifying sounds of predators. No wonder I was imagining things.

Even now my brain wasn't working properly. One thing was clear—I wouldn't have come here on my own. So it was only logical to assume this man had brought me here; and being a city girl, I wouldn't have come willingly. While I liked a pretty face as much as the next female, I was preternaturally wary.

So why was I so determined to protect this man? This man who didn't seem to be quite human, teeth or not? The glow of fire beneath his skin was far from normal. Yet I knew that I had to keep him alive, I had to stay with him.

The first light of dawn was beginning to spread over the tall trees that guarded the clearing. Whatever foul things had lurked in the bushes were long gone, and there was nothing keeping me here. I could walk out of this forest—it couldn't go on forever. The man was dying; there was nothing else I could do for him except see if I could find help. I should save myself, and if he survived, fine. It wasn't my business.

But it was. I moved closer to him, as close as I could get to the ferocious heat that burned deep inside his bones. "It serves you right," I whispered, wishing I dared put my hand on him, to push the tangled hair away from his face without getting scorched.

Except that he'd been hurt pulling me back from whatever horror I'd somehow imagined behind what was most definitely solid rock. I couldn't remember, but that much I knew. He'd been trying to save me, and for that I owed him something.

I edged closer to him, and the heat seared me. I felt tears form in my eyes, and blinked them away impatiently. Crying wouldn't do any good. If I leaned over and let them fall on him, they would sizzle and evaporate like water on a skillet.

"Oh, hell," I muttered disgustedly, wiping them away. "You shouldn't have to die, no matter what you did to me." I moved closer, and my face felt sunburned. "God help me, don't fucking die on me," I said desperately.

The sudden flash of light was blinding, thunder shaking the ground, and I was thrown back against the stone wall. Panic swept through me—what if it opened again; what if this time he couldn't save me? I scrambled away from it, then turned to look for the dying man, and I knew I was hallucinating again. His body was surrounded by a circle of tall figures, shrouded in mist, and there were wings everywhere. Maybe he'd died. They must be angels coming to take him . . . where?

One of them picked him up effortlessly, impervious to the heat of his flesh. I was frozen, unable to move. Sure, he was dead and on his way to heaven, but I had no strong desire to accompany him. I wanted to live.

But I could feel eyes on me, and I wondered if I could run for it. And I wondered if I really wanted to.

"Bring her." The words weren't spoken out loud; they seemed to vibrate inside my head. I was prepared to fight, prepared to run before I let them put their hands on me, before I let it happen all over again . . . but there was nothing but a blinding white light, followed by dark silence, as a blackness deep and dark as death pulled in about me.

"Shit," I said weakly. And I was gone.

I WAS COLD. AND DAMP. I could hear a strange sound, a rushing noise almost like the ocean, but there was no ocean in the forest, was there? I really didn't want to move, even though I was lying somewhere hard and wet, the dampness seeping through my clothes and into my bones. In my Swiss cheese of a memory, it felt as if every time I opened my eyes things had gotten worse. This time I was going to stay put with my eyes tightly shut—it was a lot safer that way.

I licked my lips and tasted salt. There were voices in the distance, a low, muffled chant in a language older than time.

Keep your eyes closed, goddamn it. This had all been one hellacious nightmare, and clearly it wasn't time to wake up. Once I could feel my comfortable bed and my five-hundred-thread-count cotton sheets beneath me, then it would be safe to wake up. Right now consciousness was nothing but more trouble, and I had had enough.

But all my self-discipline had been reserved for my writing, and when it came to anything else, like denying my curiosity, I had the willpower of a rabbit. I decided to open my eyes just a slit to verify that, yes, I really was lying in wet sand at the edge of a rocky beach. And out in the waves the men stood waist-deep in the water, holding the body of my . . . my what? My kidnapper? My savior? It didn't matter what the hell he was, he was mine.

He wasn't dead. I knew this as I struggled to my feet, my whole body feeling as if it had been kicked around by monkeys. He wasn't dead—yet they were letting him sink beneath the surface as they chanted some kind of garbled nonsense. They were letting him drown, burying him in the sea, and I was not going to let that happen, not after working so hard to keep him alive last night.

I'm not sure whether I said something, screamed "No!" as I raced toward them. Out into the icy water, shoving past them as they let his body go, diving for him before he could sink beneath the turbulent waves.

It was only when my hand touched him beneath the water, felt him turn and his hand catch mine, that I conveniently remembered that I had never learned to swim.

The words came out of nowhere, dancing in my head:

> Full fathom five thy father lies:
> Of his bones are coral made;
> Those are pearls that were his eyes:
> Nothing of him that doth fade,
> But doth suffer a sea-change
> Into something rich and strange.

The words were muzzy, dreamlike, but now I was the one sinking. What an idiot I'd been, diving after him. I was going to die after all, and it was no one's fault but mine. I should have known I'd hear Shakespeare when I died.

I would suffer a sea change, entwined with the demon lover beneath the cold salt sea, and I welcomed it, dazed, when his mouth closed over mine beneath the briny surface, his breath flowing into me, my body plastered against his as I felt life return. A moment later I found myself propelled to the surface, still trapped in the dead man's arms. The dead man who had pulled his mouth away, and was looking down at me from those strange, silvery-black eyes.

Then we were standing waist-deep in the ocean, the waves breaking against us, and he was holding on to me as he looked to the men who had brought him here, a dazed, questioning expression on his face.

Which was basically how I was feeling. A sort of a sodden WTF, and the only thing familiar to hold on to was this man beside me.

"She called for help," one of the men said from the shore. "You told us to bring her."

The man threw back his head and laughed, unexpected and unguarded, and relief washed through me. His teeth were white and even. I'd been imagining the fangs, of course. Vampires weren't real. I couldn't believe I even remembered that particular hallucination.

He scooped me up in his arms, and I rested my face against his wet chest as he carried me out of the surf, not quite sure why. The footing must have been uneven, yet he carried me without a misstep, almost gliding over the rough sand. I'd never been carried in my life—despite my short stature I was built upon generous lines, and no one had ever been romantic enough to scoop me up and carry me to bed.

Of course, that wasn't what this man was doing. Come to think of it, what the hell *was* he doing? I looked up at a huge stone building set on the edge of the sea, and I squirmed, trying to get down. He ignored me. That, at least, felt familiar.

He didn't put me down, and I found I knew him well enough not to expect that he would. He'd kissed me. Sort of. He'd put his cold, wet mouth on mine and breathed life into me, when he was the one who'd been on the verge of death.

"You wanna put me down?" I demanded in a reasonable voice. Not that I expected him to be reasonable, but it was worth a try. He said nothing, and I struggled, but his grip never tightened. It didn't need to; it was loose but unbreakable. "Who the fuck are you?" I demanded irritably. "*What* are you?"

He didn't answer, of course. The other men came up to us, and I had the oddest sense that they were surrounded by some kind of haze or aura. It must be a reaction to the salt water. No matter how hard I tried to focus, things stayed as hazy as my memory.

"We can get rid of her now, Raziel, before it's too late," one with a cold, deep voice said. "She has no more need of you, nor you of her."

The language sounded oddly old-fashioned, and I tried to turn my head to see who was speaking; but Raziel, the man who was holding me, simply pushed my face against his chest. "What about the Grace? Surely that would work."

There was a moment's silence, one that didn't seem to bode well for my future. With my foggy brain, he was the only thing familiar, and I panicked, reaching up and tugging at his open shirt. "Don't let them take me." I sounded pathetic, but there was nothing I could do about it. I'd swallowed some salt water before Raziel grabbed me, and my voice was raw.

He glanced down at me, and I knew that look. It was as if he knew everything about me, had read my diaries, peeked into my fantasies. It was unnerving. But then he nodded.

"I will keep her, Azazel," he said. "At least for now."

Better than nothing, I thought, not precisely flattered. I was tempted to argue, just for the sake of it and because he'd sounded so damned grudging, but I had no idea where I might go, and I didn't trust those other men who'd tried to drown my companion.

At least for the moment, as long as he held me, nothing could harm me. I could deal with the rest of it when it happened.

For now, I was safe.

CHAPTER

SIX

HAD I LOST MY MIND? "I WILL keep her." Ridiculous. I had no use for a human.

It was early evening. I'd spent most of the day in the pool, letting the seawater wash my battered body, healing the pain that still spiked through me.

Azazel was looking at me. "What are we going to do with the woman? Now is not the time to bring someone new into Sheol, particularly someone with no set purpose. Uriel moves closer, and the Nephilim are at our very doorstep. We can't waste time with inconsequentials."

"Where is she?" I said, stalling for time, my voice cool as I stretched out on the black leather sofa. The searing agony was gone, but my body ached as if I had run a marathon and then been trampled by a herd of goats.

"Sarah has her. She and the other women will take care of her, calm her fears."

"Will they tell her the truth?" I wasn't sure that was a good idea. The woman was smart, fearless, and just the kind of woman to fight the status quo. The kind of woman who would drive me to insanity and beyond with her ways.

"She probably knows already. At least part of it. What she remembers, that is," Azazel said in the icy voice that terrified most of our brethren and managed to roll off my back. We'd been through too much together for him to intimidate me.

"We can always make her forget," I said. "She has been with me so long the Grace would have to be very strong. She'd be confused for weeks. But it would work. She's already forgotten what happened when I first took her."

"But where will she go, old friend? She died yesterday. Her body has already been cremated."

"Shit," I said, thoroughly annoyed. "I thought she was Jewish."

"You know that some of them no longer follow the old ways."

Typical of humankind. They were always so hypocritical when it came to their faith, choosing what they cared to follow, ignoring anything that was inconvenient. It was little wonder the Supreme Being had washed his hands of them, leaving a heartless bastard like Uriel in his place. "If they are going to be devout enough to bury her immediately, they should at least keep her body intact," I said, trying not to growl. "We could have worked with that."

"Where is she going to go?" Azazel persisted. "You have no use for a human female. Unless you've changed your mind?"

I knew that was coming. "I haven't. I won't bond again, and I have no current need for sex. And if I were stupid enough to change my mind, it wouldn't be with someone like her."

"What's wrong with her?"

I closed my eyes for a moment. I could see her, smart, questioning, undeniably luscious. "She's just wrong," I said stubbornly.

Azazel was watching me too closely, and I shifted so he couldn't see my face. "Then why did you save her?" he said in what for him was a reasonable voice. "Why did you tell us to bring her?"

"How should I know? A moment of insanity. It's not as if I remember anything that was going on—I was almost dead. Are you sure I did? I could barely speak."

"Yes. I heard you."

Damn. Azazel never lied. Even if I couldn't say the words out loud, Azazel would hear me and follow my wishes. If I'd told them to keep her, I must have had some reason, but damned if I could think of what it was. "Just one more thing to deal with, then. And I have no idea what the hell is going on, only that Uriel has been lying to us."

"And that surprises you? His power is infinite. As long as free will exists, Uriel is in charge, to heal or hurt anyone as he sees fit. Just because he told us the good ones are moving on is no guarantee that we aren't taking them straight to hell. Children, babies, young lovers, grandmothers . . . It was foolish of us not to realize he would do this. Uriel is a cruel and mighty judge."

"Uriel is a pain in my ass."

"You'd best watch out," Azazel warned. "You never know when he might be listening."

I rose, stretching my iridescent blue wings against the twilight sky, glittering against the purple and pink hues that saturated our misty world. "You're a pain in the ass, Uriel," I said again, raising my voice so there could be no confusion as to who was tossing out the insults. "You're a spiteful, vindictive, lying pain in the ass, and if the Supreme Being knew what you were doing, how you were interpreting the laws, you would be in deep shit." I loved cursing. That was one thing I actually liked about humans—their language. The rich expressiveness of the words, sacred and profane, that everyone outside of Sheol seemed to use. The way the forbidden words danced on my tongue. Not to mention the fury I knew I was causing Uriel.

Azazel was unamused. "Why are you asking for

trouble? We already have enough as it is. What are you going to do with her?"

He was right. Our lives were precarious enough, balanced between Uriel's powerful hatred and the unspeakable dangers of the Nephilim, and now I had brought our entire family closer to devastation because of one stupid, quixotic gesture. I sank back down on the old leather sofa, momentarily distracted by the feel of it beneath me. Its coolness soothed my damaged body.

"Asking me over and over won't get you an answer any sooner—it will just annoy me," I grumbled. "I expect I'll find someplace to send her. Somewhere far away, and Uriel will have more important reasons to come after us."

"And you're sure you have no interest in mating with her?" Azazel said carefully.

"I don't even want to fuck her." I watched Azazel wince. Not that he had any problem with the word—he just knew I was courting trouble. Uriel hated words as much as he hated so many other things of the human world, including sex and blood, and I did my level best to annoy him whenever I could. After all, our sentence was eternity, and the one remaining archangel couldn't kill.

"She will have to stay here for now," Azazel said finally. "Sarah will know what to do with her. She's the wisest of us all."

"Of course she is. She's the Source." I didn't bother keeping the sarcasm out of my voice. There were times when Azazel treated us all like idiots.

"I will remind you that I am your leader. I can take everything away from you, every gift, every power," Azazel said, his voice like ice.

I ignored his empty threat. We'd been raised up together, lived together, fallen together, been cursed together. There was no way he was going to cow me. "Leaving you short one soldier if the Nephilim decide to engage, or if Uriel sends the Host down on us as he always threatens. But feel free to try it. You could banish me as well. . . ."

Azazel made a noise very much like a growl. "You know I would never do that."

"I'm touched."

"The Nephilim are too dangerous. They outnumber us, and they're all mad."

I laughed. No sentiment for Azazel. I was just another soldier. "Why the hell can't they be like the others? Unable to harm us. Uriel's heavenly forces cannot attack us. The Nephilim were once like them—"

"They were before they fell," Azazel interrupted me. "When will you learn to stop fighting against the forces that cannot be beaten? There are times when you are your own worst enemy. You have no one to blame but yourself for this current mess. Get rid of the girl, and we'll concentrate on what matters."

I laughed bitterly. "I blame Uriel. He led me to believe I was taking her to heaven. How many people have I tossed into the mouth of hell for him, thinking they were returning to paradise? Paradise!" I was filled with disgust, both for Uriel and for my own unwitting complicity.

"So this is about the woman?" Azazel said.

I shrugged off the ridiculous idea. "Of course not. I don't like being manipulated."

"Then don't think about it. There is nothing we can do except not let him trick us again. And you still haven't answered my question. What are you going to do with her? We have no place to put her—Sheol is not made for visitors."

"She can go in my rooms until we decide. I sleep outside half the time anyway."

Azazel looked at me for a long moment. "Are you certain she isn't your mate?"

"How many times do I have to tell you? I will not take a mate ever again." I kept my voice neutral, but Azazel knew me too well.

"You can stop as soon as I believe you. In the meantime, how are you feeling?"

That question was too stupid to answer, so I just looked at him.

"It has been months since you've fed," he continued. "I'll tell Sarah."

That was the last thing I wanted. "No! I'm in no mood for all that fuss. Do not say a word—

"I don't need to," Azazel said. "You know Sarah can feel your need even before you do." He came closer. "You're weak, and you know it. You'd be worthless if we were attacked. I'm willing to respect your ridiculous wishes as long as they don't hurt the community. Having you this weak puts us all in jeopardy."

I knew I wasn't going to be able to talk him out of it. And he was right—after the last twenty-four hours, I was barely able to lift my head, much less fly. "Not the full ceremony," I grumbled.

"I will tell her to make it very short. Then you need to sleep. Though if the woman is in your rooms—"

"I can find a place," I said sharply.

Azazel looked at me with the wise eyes of an old friend. "Are you certain Uriel wasn't right? What do you know of her and the crimes she may have committed? Perhaps you risked everything and saved her for no reason. It would make things much simpler if I finished the job you started."

"Keep your hands off her!" I said, suddenly furious. I took a deep breath. "She saved me. We keep her here until we decide what to do with her."

Azazel stared at me for a long, annoying moment, then nodded. "As you have spoken," he said formally. "Come with me to Sarah before you collapse."

I didn't want to move, any more than I wanted to admit that Azazel was right. I wanted to close my eyes and disappear. If I'd had the energy, I would have risen and soared away from everything. But right then I could barely summon up enough energy to walk. I needed to feed, and until I did I was useless.

Once I fed and recovered, I would know what to do with the unwanted woman, would find a place to leave her. Until then I had no choice but to obey Azazel, no matter how much it galled me.

WHEN I AWOKE THE ROOM was dark, and I lay perfectly still, clinging to the vain, eternal hope that this had all been a nightmare. I already knew I was shit out of luck, and I opened my eyes reluctantly, knowing this bizarro world was going to continue.

The women had been very kind. The man, Raziel, had carried me into this huge old house and then unceremoniously dumped me, disappearing before I realized what was going on. The women had gathered around me, making the kinds of soothing noises that always made me nervous, and they herded me up to some rooms where they fed me, bathed me, and cosseted me, deftly deflecting any of my questions, all under the capable direction of the woman named Sarah.

And an extraordinary woman she was. Over six

feet tall, she was one of those ageless women who might be anywhere between forty and sixty, with the serene grace and lean, agile body that probably came from decades of yoga. The kind of woman who made me feel lumpy and inadequate. The practice of yoga always seemed to suggest a moral superiority rather than a physical conditioning, and I mentally promised myself that I'd drag out the yoga DVDs that were still shrink-wrapped, sitting on my bookshelves.

No, I wouldn't. I wasn't going home. That was one thing I knew, amidst all the vast holes in my memory. There was no returning to my comfortable life in the Village. Just as well—I couldn't really afford that apartment, but it had been so gorgeous that I'd gladly beggared myself for the chance to live there.

Well, maybe if I was going to stay, I'd have Sarah teach me yoga. If it made me look as good as she did at her age, it was clearly worth the effort.

Sarah had silver hair in one long, thick braid, wise blue eyes, and a rich, comforting voice, and when she'd eventually dismissed the other women, some half dozen between the ages of twenty and forty, she'd sat by my bed until I slept. My questions would be answered soon enough, Sarah had said. For now I should rest.

Which I was quite happy to do. The night before had been endless, lying huddled against Raziel's blazing body, trying to get comfortable with sticks and rocks and hard earth digging into my soft flesh. Maybe if I slept long enough, this nightmare would be over.

No such luck. When I awoke I was alone, and hungry again. I sat up, waiting for my eyes to grow accustomed to the darkness. I was wearing soft clothes, a loose-fitting white dress of some sort, and I remembered the embarrassing battle I'd had with the Stepford wives when they wanted to bathe me. A battle I'd lost.

I touched my hair, finding it freshly washed but still that disconcerting length. I hadn't worn my hair that long since I'd attended that lousy high school outside of Hartford, after I'd been kicked out of my expensive boarding school. Not that that was my fault. It had been the one fundamentalist Christian boarding school in the entire liberal, anarchistic, blaspheming state of Connecticut. Clearly I was going to break out as soon as I could.

Always in trouble, my mother had said in disgust, praying over me loudly. I always got the feeling that she never prayed for me in private—that her loud exhortations were for my benefit and mine alone. I was a miserable daughter, she told me, always spitting in the face of society, always talking too much and pushing against the status quo. Was that what had got me here? And where the hell was *here*?

I swung my legs over the side of the bed, feeling dizzy for a moment. There were shoes on the floor, and I slipped my feet into them, then winced, kicking them off again as I rubbed my heel. I had a blister there, left from those miserable shoes—

That was flat-out impossible. A blister healed in a few days, but it took months to grow my hair this long. Months that I couldn't remember. Maybe I hadn't lost huge blocks of time after all. The idea was reassuring, but it held its own kind of freakiness. None of this was making any sense, and I needed it to, quite desperately.

Sarah would tell me the truth if I asked. Unlike the man, she wouldn't just brush off my questions, ignore my doubts. The warmth and truth of Sarah was palpable, soothing. I needed to find her.

I didn't bother searching for a light beside the high bed; I didn't bother with the shoes. The door was ajar, a sliver of light beckoning, and I started toward it, feeling only slightly uneasy. I'd seen those movies, read those books. Hell, written those books, where the stupid heroine in her virginal white goes wandering where she shouldn't, and the homicidal maniac appears out of nowhere, complete with a butcher knife or an ax or a fish spike.

I shivered. People got murdered in their beds, too. Staying put wasn't going to get me anywhere.

The outer room was empty. Hours ago this had

been filled with women. Now it was abandoned, thank God, leaving me to my own devices, to find my own answers.

I looked down at my flowing white dress. Yup, virgin sacrifice stuff, all right. At least I was a far cry from a virgin—if they wanted to cut out my heart as an offering to the gods, the gods were going to be mighty pissed. Though in truth, that part *was* virginal. I'd had sex, but my heart had never been touched.

All the women had been similarly dressed, in some variant of flowing white clothes. They all had long hair, loose and natural, and they'd been warm, welcoming. Stepford wives. Had I been abducted into some kind of cult? Next thing I knew we'd be singing hymns and drinking Kool-Aid.

I shivered again. The women hadn't looked like mind-sucked idiots. My imagination was running away with me, and no wonder. Somewhere along the way I'd fallen down the rabbit hole, and nothing made sense anymore.

The hallway was as deserted as the rooms, a mixed blessing. On the one hand, I didn't want to be shepherded back to the bedroom with a bunch of platitudes. On the other, I didn't know where the hell I was going, or whether Freddy Krueger was about to appear.

I looked around me. The interior of the house was interesting—it look like an old California lodge from long ago, with bronze art-deco sconces on the wall that made me think of Hollywood in the 1930s. There were overstuffed leather chairs and mission-style tables at various intervals down the long hall, with an ancient Persian runner in the center of the highly buffed floor, and a sudden horrifying suspicion came to me.

Things were bizarre enough already—if I'd somehow managed to travel through time, back eighty years to the early part of the last century, I would be extremely annoyed. That was the problem with time travel—no one ever asked if you'd be interested. Just a flash of lightning and you were gone.

I remembered a flash of lightning, on a New York street. The vision was swift and fleeting, and then I was back in this weird old house, looking for serial killers.

No, time travel was out of the question. I simply refused to consider the possibility. It was as absurd as some of the half-remembered fantasies that played in the back of my mind. Wings? A body with fire beneath the skin? A vampire?

I became aware of a sound, quiet, muffled, a soft chanting not unlike the voices I'd heard on the beach—the sound those men had made as they'd tried to drown my rescuer and I'd gone splashing into the surf like a complete idiot to save him. I listened carefully, trying to make out the words. It bore no resemblance to any language I'd ever heard, just a strange, almost melodic thread of noise.

Well, if they were getting ready for a virgin sacrifice, at least they weren't planning to slice and dice me. Besides, there was something infinitely soothing about those voices, something that drew me toward them.

I began to move down the halls, silent on my bare feet, and at each juncture I took a turn unerringly. Me, who could never find my way through the haphazard streets of the Village no matter how long I'd lived there. I didn't stop to question it—I just kept going. Maybe I'd been given superpowers, like a decent sense of direction. Anything was possible.

The sound never grew louder, never softened. I could hear it inside my head, feel it underneath my skin; and when I finally stopped outside an ornately carved set of double doors, I knew I'd found answers.

I paused. Something stopped me from going farther, just for the moment. So unlike me—I was a woman who always wanted straight answers, no matter how painful, and I knew that answers lay beyond those heavy doors, beneath the steady, almost musical chant that emanated from behind them. I had never been the type to hesitate—what the hell was wrong with me?

I pushed open the doors and froze.

It looked like some strange sort of temple, though

clearly not for any religion I was familiar with. There was no cross, no ark to hold the Torah. Only the cluster of people in the center of the cavernous room lit by a strange, unearthly glow.

My eyes focused on Sarah, sitting in a chair that seemed like a cross between a throne and a La-Z-Boy. Sarah's calm blue eyes had been closed in a look of meditation, but they opened and turned to mine, almost as if she'd heard my clumsy entrance above the soft chanting.

She smiled gently that serene, sweet smile that seemed to bestow a blessing on everyone around her, and the others must have realized that I was there, for the chanting stopped abruptly and the men moved back.

He knelt beside Sarah. I knew who he was immediately, even in the candlelight. I knew the sun-shot hair, the rough grace. His head was bent over Sarah's outstretched wrist, but I must have made some kind of noise, and he lifted his face to stare at me.

I could see the blood at his mouth, the elongated fangs, the pulsing veins at Sarah's slender wrist, and I know I let out the most girly shriek of horror.

And then I ran, letting the heavy doors slam shut behind me.

CHAPTER

SEVEN

I MADE IT AS FAR AS THE GRASS IN front of the house before I went sprawling face-first. I hit the rough sand on my knees and elbows, sliding, and ended up at the very edge of the water, breathless, my arms over my head as if I were ducking from a hurricane. It was impossible. Flat-out impossible.

Someone must have drugged me. That was the only reasonable explanation for what I thought I'd just seen, for the craziness that shot such holes in my memory. But if I was still drugged, who and what could I trust? I rolled onto my back, still gasping for breath as I stared up at the house. Parts of it stuck out at strange angles, like a bureau with the drawers pulled out at varying degrees. The sun was setting behind me, reflecting off the windows, rendering them golden and opaque. Someone inside was looking down at me. If the house even existed, if the ocean existed, if I existed.

It was the oddest feeling: I couldn't trust anything, my eyes, my ears—even the rich salty smell of the ocean could be part of some bizarre hallucination that had started God knows when. I stared up at the darkening sky, trying to pull in what few things I remembered. I could still feel the man's hands on me as he'd tried to throw me into some deep, bottomless hole. So, serial killer, right? But he'd pulled me back. Serial killer with a conscience?

But maybe he hadn't pulled me back after all. Maybe this was what death was like—a long, strange, trippy hallucination with vampires and men with wings—

Men with wings? Where had that come from? I briefly considered sitting up, then decided against it. I was just fine where I was. Sprawled on the rocky beach, I kept a lower profile. I could just stay this way, listening to the soft hush of the ocean, until the drugs wore off or I woke up or whatever.

Or discovered I was in hell, or heaven, or somewhere in between. Sitting up meant I'd have to do something, and right then I just didn't have the energy.

The setting sun was blotted out for a moment, and I looked up to see the man standing over me. Raziel, had they called him? Strange name, just another part of the nightmare that had started with his hands on me.

"How long are you going to lie there?" He had such a beautiful voice, the kind that could lure angels to their doom; yet the words were calm and emotionless. "It's cold and the tide's coming in, plus there's a nasty riptide that could pull you out to sea before anyone realized what had happened. You may as well get up—running isn't going to change things."

The sunset was gilding him, a nimbus of color around his tall body. I made myself relax. Not a vampire, then. I knew the rules—they couldn't be in the sun.

I hadn't realized I'd spoken the words out loud. Not until he answered me.

"You're an expert on vampires now, are you?" he said.

I considered not rising, but lying sprawled in front of him definitely put me at a disadvantage, so I sat up, ignoring the shriek of my stiff muscles. I glared at him. "No, I'm not. I don't believe in them, and if you and your friends are into that kind of scene, then you can count me out. I want to go home."

He was looking at me with detached interest. "'Kind of scene'?" he echoed.

There was no blood on his mouth now. Maybe I'd imagined it. My brain still didn't seem be holding two thoughts together. "I'm not a complete idiot," I said in a cranky voice. "I know there's an entire sub-culture of people who like to pretend they're vampires. They file their teeth to points, they hang out in Goth clubs, they drink blood, they dress in Edwardian clothes . . ." My voice trailed off. Black jeans and a worn black denim shirt didn't equal Edwardian finery and we both knew it, though I was willing to bet he'd look pretty damned gorgeous in a white puffy shirt. Considering that he looked pretty damned gorgeous already.

"I don't see a Goth club anywhere," he said. "No one around here would pretend to be a vampire."

"So what was that I walked in on a few minutes ago?"

"Allie?" Sarah came up behind him before he could answer, almost as tall, with another of the men just behind her. "What's wrong?"

"You know what's wrong," I said, feeling cranky despite the fact that I liked Sarah. "I saw him."

"Saw him what?"

I looked at her narrow wrists: blue-veined, delicate, and unmarred. I pulled my knees up close to my body, hugging them. "Who *are* you people?" I demanded in a frustrated moan.

"Come back to the house, Sarah," the other man said impatiently. "This is Raziel's mess—it's up to him to deal with it." There was an oddly proprietary tone to his voice.

"In a moment," Sarah said, kneeling next to me and putting her hand on my arm. "I don't want you to be afraid, child. No one is going to hurt you."

I wasn't as sure as she was, either about Raziel or about the other man. He was as tall as Raziel, with jet-black hair, cold blue eyes, and a merciless expression on his face. "I want to go home," I said again, feeling like a fretful, stubborn child.

The other man swore. "Raziel, do something about this. That, or let me clean up the mess you've made."

"Give her a minute, Azazel," Sarah said over her shoulder. "She's shocked and frightened, and no wonder, with the two of you stomping around, being mysterious. If Raziel won't give her some simple answers, then I will."

"Woman," Azazel said in an icy voice, "I want you upstairs in bed."

"Husband," Sarah replied sweetly, "I'll be there when I'm damned well ready."

Well, that was definitely weird. Azazel had to be in his early to mid-thirties; Sarah was likely in her fifties and probably older. It was hardly surprising—Sarah was a beautiful woman—but most of the men I knew liked nubile young chicklets. At the ripe old age of thirty, I'd already been dumped once for someone younger and more pliant.

"She's going to come inside," Raziel said, making it clear there were no options. That's what he thought. My eyes narrowed, looking up at him.

"And just where is she going?" the other man demanded.

"My rooms," Raziel said. "I don't see that we have any other choice."

"She's certainly not coming with us," Azazel snapped.

Sarah rose, a graceful, fluid motion that made me desperately envious. If I got back home, I was definitely going to start going to yoga. *When,* not if. I wasn't giving them any choice in the matter. I wanted my life back.

"Go with Raziel, child," she said. "He's not going to hurt you. In fact, he's been looking out for you. When he wasn't dying of fire poisoning," she added with a mischievous glance at him. "Go with him, and he'll answer any questions you have."

"The hell I will," Raziel said. "I'll take her to my rooms and leave her there until I figure out—"

"You'll do what Sarah says," Azazel said, his soft voice chilling.

Raziel shot the other man a disgruntled look. And then he crossed the sand to me, holding out his hand.

I stared at it, not moving. Now was not the time to notice that he had strong, beautiful hands. Or that everything about him was beautiful, almost supernaturally so. I didn't like pretty men, damn it. Though

God knows I wasn't sure if I'd ever seen anyone quite as gorgeous as he was.

"Don't make me carry you," he said in a warning voice.

Azazel and Sarah were already heading into the house, his arm around her waist. For a moment I considered scrambling to my feet and running after them; but reasonable or not, Azazel terrified me even more than this inexplicable man.

I needed to get up, not loll there like a Victorian heroine. The only problem was that my knees felt like spaghetti. I'm as tough as the next woman, tougher maybe, but I'd been through a hell of a lot in the last . . . whatever. There was a limit to how much I could handle. I tried to rise, but he ended up putting his hands on my arms and hauling me up anyway. He released me quickly enough, and started back toward the odd house, clearly expecting me to follow like a dutiful third-world bride.

The hell with that. I looked around me for some kind of escape and came up with a flat zero, unless I wanted to pull a Virginia Woolf and walk into the sea. There was no place else for me to go. The tide was coming in, and beyond the house all was misty darkness and forest. Besides, I was finally going to get some answers to my questions, wasn't I?

I just managed to catch up with him. His long legs ate up the distance, but after a shaky start I managed a brisk trot. "You needn't be so grumpy," I said, trying not to huff and puff. "It's your fault I'm here."

"In case you don't remember, I was unconscious when they brought me back."

"That's up to interpretation," I said. "I can't argue, since I seem to have huge gaps in my memory. What do you think they should have done, then? Left me in the forest? With those wild animals out there in the dark?"

He frowned. How could a man have a beautiful frown? "No," he said. "They shouldn't have left you."

"And what the hell were we doing there in the first place? What in God's name is happening to me?" I hated the plaintive note in my voice, but honestly I couldn't help it. I could be all Strong Modern Woman most of the time, but right now I was tired, cranky, and totally defeated.

He didn't answer. I hadn't really expected him to. "Are you hungry?" he said instead.

As a distraction, it was an effective one. I suddenly remembered I was famished. "Yes. Why don't you take me to McDonald's and we can hash this out?" I figured that was unlikely but worth a try.

"No McDonald's," he said. "No restaurants at all, but we have people who cook. Tell me what you want and they'll bring it to us."

"Just like that?" I said caustically. Not that I

believed him, but if that was true, this might very well be paradise.

"Just like that."

I decided to be difficult, simply because I could. Besides, my need for comfort food had become critical. "Meat loaf, mashed potatoes, gravy, corn, strawberry shortcake for dessert. And a nice Beringer cabernet."

"You want champagne with your strawberries? Red wine is a little heavy for dessert."

He was being sarcastic, of course, but I simply nodded. "Of course. Moët, I think. No need to go overboard with Dom Pérignon."

He said nothing, walking into the house. I took one last longing glance outside. Nowhere to go. Until I found out what the fuck was going on, I was stuck.

In a place with, supposedly, limitless, effortless food and a beautiful man who'd kissed me. I supposed things could be worse.

I had to run to catch up with him. He made no effort to adjust his stride to mine, and I was damned if I was going to complain. It was taking forever to get to his rooms—we went through a maze of hallways, and up so many stairs I was ready to fling myself down on the polished wood floors, gasping and panting like a landed fish.

"How much farther?" I gasped, clinging to the thick, carved handrail.

He was watching me out of narrowed eyes. "One more flight. My rooms are at the top of the building."

"They would be," I said in a dire voice. "And I don't suppose you believe in things like elevators?"

"We don't need them," he said.

No wonder Sarah was so lean and fit at fifty-something. She didn't need yoga, she just needed these stairs.

"Sarah isn't fifty-something," Raziel said.

I froze. "That time I didn't say it out loud."

"No, you didn't. You're very easy to read. Most humans are."

Most humans? WTF?

"Wait until we get to my rooms."

I hadn't said anything that time either. I was getting seriously creeped out by this situation. It didn't matter how much food I got or how pretty he was, this was just plain weird. The kiss had been nice, from what I could remember, but I wasn't sure kisses were enough to—

"I'm not going to kiss you again. I didn't kiss you in the first place—you were drowning. I gave you breath."

This was just . . . wrong. Clearly silence wasn't silence to the creature I was following, so I quickly changed the subject, trying not to think about the cool salt taste of his mouth on mine. "Then how old is Sarah? She's married to Aza—what's his name?"

"Azazel," he said. "Yes, they are married; at least, that's as close a definition as most people could understand. And I don't know how old Sarah is, nor do I care."

I looked at him with astonishment. "She's got to be at least twenty years older than he is. And he's, what . . . thirty-five? Cool."

"He's older than she is," he said in a dry voice. "And you might think twice about passing judgment on someone like Sarah."

If Azazel was older than Sarah, then I was the Virgin Mary. "I'm not passing judgment," I said rapidly, following him down the hallway toward another miserable, cock-sucking, goddamned, motherfucking flight of stairs. "I meant it. Too often it's men who have younger lovers. I heartily approve of boy toys."

"You think Azazel is a boy toy? He'll be entertained by the notion."

"Christ, don't tell him I said that! I expect by this time their marriage is more platonic than anything else."

He looked amused, which was even more annoying. "I believe they have a vigorous sex life, though I can ask Azazel to tell you all about it if you prefer."

"No need," I said hastily. "It's none of my business."

"No, it is not," he said in that odd, half-formal way of speaking.

I looked up at the steep flight of stairs. It was the last one, he'd said. Of course it had to be the steepest and longest. I took a deep breath, steeling myself. I could make it. If it killed me, I was going to make it.

"What do her children think of her new husband?" If I kept him talking he might not notice how long it was taking me to get up the stairs.

"She has no children, and Azazel isn't her new husband. He's her only one."

I thought back to Sarah's gentle, tender concern. "That's a shame," I said. "She would have been a wonderful mother."

"Yes." It was one word, but there was a wealth of meaning beneath it.

Suddenly I thought back to the stretch of beach in front of the house, the wide expanse of lawn. With no toys, no games littering the beach. Something felt off about the place. "Where do the children live around here?" I asked, uneasy.

"Children?"

"The women who were with Sarah—she said they were other wives. Some of them were quite young; there must be children."

"There are no children here."

"That goes against whatever crazy cult you have going on here? You send the children away?" I was righteously infuriated, and it gave me energy. And the end of the stairs was in sight, thank God. I was ready to fling myself on the top landing with a weeping cry of "Land!"

"The women here don't have children."

"Why not?" Shit, it wasn't the top of the stairs, it was just a landing. I faltered, turning the corner, looking at what simply had to be the last flight. Maybe. I wanted to cry, and I never cried.

Before I realized what he was going to do, he'd scooped me up in his arms and started up the final flight of stairs.

I was too shocked to struggle. His arms were like iron bands, his body hard and cold and uncomfortable; for a bare second I considered arguing, then thought better of it. Anything was better than walking.

"You know, if it weren't for the stairs, I could manage it with no problem," I said, keeping myself as stiff as he was.

He snorted, saying nothing. When he reached the top of the stairs he dumped me on my feet, seconds before I could demand that he let me down. The hallway was shorter than the lower ones, with only one double door in the center of it. *I must be near the top of this damned skyscraper,* I thought, remembering those cantilevered shelves that stretched over the ocean.

He'd left me again, already pushing open one of the doors, and once again I followed him, resentful as hell until I stepped into the dimly lit apartment. The door closed behind me automatically, and I caught my breath in wonder.

It was like being on the prow of a ship. The front of the room was a bank of windows looking out over the night-black sea. Several of them were open, and I could smell the rich briny scent of it, hear the sound of the waves as they lapped against the rocks below. There were seagulls in the distance, and I breathed a small sigh of relief. At least something in this crazy place was normal.

"Sit down," he said.

He was standing in the shadows. There were two mission-style sofas in the room, upholstered in white linen, and a low table between them. With a covered tray on top, a bucket of ice with a bottle of champagne waiting, and a bottle of red wine open to one side.

I stared at the table mistrustfully. "Shit," I said. I knew without question that there would be meat loaf and mashed potatoes beneath the domed cover. "How did you manage that?"

"Sit down and eat," he said. "I'm tired and I want to go to bed."

I stiffened. "And what does your wanting to go to bed have to do with me?"

Such a pretty mouth, such a sour smile. "Since I don't intend to be anywhere near you when I go to bed, I won't be around to answer your incessant questions. So if you want answers, sit down."

"You're an asshole." I took a seat and pulled the cover off the tray. The smell of meat loaf was enough to make me moan with pleasure. Ignoring him, I started in on it, only looking up when I realized he'd poured me a glass of the red wine and pushed it toward me.

Way to make me feel like a mannerless glutton, I thought dismally.

"Mannerly," he said.

"What?"

"Mannerly glutton. You haven't drooled or dropped food or—"

I dropped my fork. "Stop that! I don't know how you do it, but stop it!"

He took a sip from his own glass of wine, leaning back against the cushions of the opposite couch with a weary sigh. "Sorry," he muttered. "It's rude of me."

"You bet your ass," I snapped. Of all the mental assaults of the day, his invasion of my thoughts felt somehow worse than anything else. I ought to be able to have my errant thoughts be private. Particularly when looking at Raziel made them so very errant. When he wasn't annoying me.

But I'd better behave. "I'm sorry. I'm being rude as well. Did you want some of this?" I gestured toward the decimated meat loaf.

He shook his head. "I don't eat meat."

It was my turn to snort. "Yes you do. You ate a hot dog." I paused. "How do I know that? When was I around you when you were eating hot dogs?"

"I don't eat meat when I'm in Sheol," he said.

"Is that what this place is called? Isn't that another word for hell?"

"It means 'the hidden place,'" he said. "And you're not in hell."

I stopped shoveling food in my face long enough to drink some wine, hoping it might calm me down. I looked up to realize that Raziel was watching me out of his strange black and silver eyes, watching me too closely, and unfortunately it wasn't with unbridled lust.

"I want to go home," I said abruptly, pushing away the tray.

"You haven't had your strawberry shortcake yet," he said. "I'll open the champagne—"

"I don't want any champagne, I want to go home."

"You can't. You don't have a home anymore."

"Why not? How long have I been gone?"

He turned his attention to his glass of wine. "From New York? A day and a half."

I stared at him blankly. "That's impossible. How can my hair have grown this long in a day and a half?"

"You still have blisters on your feet from those shoes, don't you?"

I didn't need to touch my heel to check. The blisters were still there. "If I've only been gone for a day, then my apartment must still be there. I want to go back."

"YOU CAN'T."

"Why not?"

"You're dead."

"Crap," I said.

EIGHT

I SET THE WINEGLASS DOWN ON THE table very carefully, pleased to see my hand wasn't shaking at all. It wasn't as if I hadn't suspected as much—after all, I was no dummy. Men with wings, fires of hell, bloodsuckers. One moment I was in New York City, minding my own business, ogling a gorgeous man at the hot-dog stand, and the next I'd fallen down the rabbit hole. It didn't mean I was going to give up without a fight. "How is that even possible?" My voice was hoarse but, apart from that, entirely calm. I'd learned to hide my reactions and emotions from my mother, Saint Hildegarde.

"You think you were immortal?" Raziel said. "Everyone dies sooner or later. In your case, it was a combination of those idiot shoes of yours and a cross-town bus."

Okay. I sat back, the meat loaf sitting like a lump

in the pit of my stomach, floating in a pool of gravy grease. "What were you doing there? You were there before I crossed the street. You were ahead of me at the hot-dog stand. I remember now." I stared at him, thoroughly unsettled. "I remember everything now. Why? Why do I remember now when I couldn't before?"

"I lifted what we call the Grace. It's one of the gifts we have, the ability to make someone forget things. You wanted to remember, so I lifted it."

"You should call it what it is: a mind-fuck," I said, feeling definitely peevish. "What were you doing there? What am I doing here?"

"I was there to collect you."

I let myself melt off the seat down onto the floor, needing something solid beneath me. I wasn't going to hyperventilate. I hadn't had a panic attack since I was a teenager, dealing with my mother's attempts to save me from the devil. Guess Mom failed, because it looked as if I'd gone to the devil after all, if Raziel's fangs and blood-sucking tendencies were anything to go by. *Calm,* I reminded myself. The sound of the sea would soothe me if I could just concentrate on it for a moment or two.

The danger passed, and I sat straight, rallying. "And exactly what were you—"

"Be quiet and I'll tell you what you need to know," he said irritably. "Your time was over. My job is to collect people and ferry them to the next . . . plane of existence. You weren't supposed to fight me. No one does."

I was freezing, colder than when I'd been lying on the wet sand. "What can I say, I fight everyone," I said glumly.

"I believe it. As annoying as you are, I was still fairly certain that you're an innocent, and I—"

"Depends on how you define *innocent*."

He glared at me, and I subsided. "I assumed I was taking you to . . . what you might call heaven. Unfortunately I was wrong, and at the last minute I became foolishly sentimental and pulled you back."

"From the jaws of hell," I supplied. "My sainted mother would be so pleased."

He didn't react to that. He probably knew all about my crazy-ass mother. Was probably best friends with her, being an angel. No, he was a bloodsucker as well—she wouldn't countenance that. "In a word, yes," he said.

"Then maybe I shouldn't be quite so cranky with you." I made an effort to be fair. If he'd saved me from eternal damnation, then I supposed he deserved his props. "Then what happened? You got sick?"

He looked disgusted at the thought. "We can't tolerate fire. In particular hellfire, but we don't like any kind of flame. The women here have to tend the candles and fires when we need them. I got singed pulling you back, and it poisoned my blood. It would have killed me if you hadn't asked for help."

That was news to me. "Really? Who did I ask for help?"

"I don't know—I was unconscious at the time. I imagine you asked God."

Considering that I'd always had mixed feelings about the existence of God, I kind of doubted that. If God had created my born-again mother, he had a very nasty sense of humor. "And God sent them? The men who brought you—brought us back here?"

"God doesn't involve himself in the day-to-day business of life. Not since free will was invented. But if you asked God for help, Azazel would have heard you, and he's the one who came to get us."

"Azazel, Sarah's husband? I doubt it. He hates me."

"Azazel doesn't hate anyone. Though if he heard you being rude about Sarah—"

"I wasn't rude, I was envious," I said. "So they came and found us and brought us here. How?"

He took a sip of wine, stalling.

"How?"

"You know, this is going to take an eternity if you don't manage to infer anything on your own," he said.

"All right, I'll *infer* up the wazoo and you can tell me if I'm wrong or right. I'm *inferring* that you're . . .

God, some kind of angel. If your job is to collect people and ferry them to the next existence, then that's
usually the work of angels, isn't it? At least according
to Judeo-Christian mythology."

"Judeo-Christian mythology is often quite accurate. Angels escort the souls of the dead in Islam and
the Viking religion as well."

"So is that what you are? A fucking angel? Is that
what all of you are?"

"Yes."

Somehow I was expecting more of an argument. "I
don't believe you," I said flatly.

He let out a sigh of sheer exasperation. "You're
the one who came up with it."

The problem was, I *did* believe him. It all made
sense, in a crazy-ass way. Which meant all my slightly
atheistic suppositions were now out the window,
and my mother had been right. That was even more
depressing than being dead. "And how did they
bring us here from the woods? They flew, didn't
they?"

"I told you, I was unconscious at the time. But yes,
I imagine they flew."

"They have wings."

"Yes."

"You have wings."

"Yes."

That was too much. "I don't see them."

"You'll have to take it on faith," he grumbled. "I'm not about to offer a demonstration."

"So—"

"Just be quiet for a few minutes, would you?" he snapped.

"You're not very nice for an angel," I muttered.

"Who says angels are supposed to be nice? Look, it's simple. You died in a bus accident. I was supposed to take you to heaven. For some reason you were heading for hell, I experienced a moment of insanity and pulled you back, and now you're stuck. You can't go back. You're dead, and your body has already been cremated, so I can't return you even if I thought it might be possible. Right now you're here in Sheol with a family of angels and their wives, and you're going to have to put up with it until I figure out what I can do with you."

"This doesn't make sense. If I'm dead and cremated, why am I here?" I looked down at my all-too-corporeal self. "I'm real, my body is real." I reached up and hugged myself, and his eyes went to my breasts. Real breasts that responded to his look, wanted his touch.

I was losing my mind. First off, I didn't want him touching me. Secondly, last time I checked, my breasts were incapable of thinking. *I* was the one who wanted him to touch me.

I was insane.

"On this plane you exist and your body is real.

Not on the mortal plane." He pulled his gaze away from my body, a relief.

"So I'm stuck here with a bunch of Stepford wives. Aren't there any girl angels?"

"No."

"Well, fuck that! Hasn't God heard of women's lib?"

"God hasn't heard of anything—he's not involved. Free will, remember?"

"Male chauvinist asshole."

"God isn't male."

"Well, he sure as hell isn't female," I snapped. Not that I should have wasted the energy. Judeo-Christian theology was patriarchal and male-centric? Surprise, surprise.

"True enough."

"So you live here together in this happy little commune and ferry people to heaven and hell. Isn't that too big a job for the bunch of you? How many people die every minute of every day?"

"One point seventy-eight per second, one hundred and seven per minute, six thousand four hundred and eight per hour, nearly one hundred and fifty-four thousand per day, fifty-six—"

Oh, God. I had to be rescued by a pedant. "No need to get literal—I get the picture. Aren't you a little bit overworked?"

"Most people don't need an escort." He poured

himself another glass of wine, then gestured with the bottle toward mine. I shook my head. I was already too rattled—I didn't need alcohol making things worse.

"Why did I need one? I'm no one important, no great villainous mastermind. Don't tell me—it's because of my mother."

He looked blank for a moment; then realization dawned. Of course he knew about my mother. "Your mother has nothing to do with it. I expect someone will be escorting her to hell sooner or later."

I'm afraid I was a bad enough daughter to chuckle at the thought. Maybe that's why I'd been sent to hell.

"I don't know why I was sent to get you any more than you do," he went on in his slightly formal way. "Why did Uriel decide you were to go to hell instead of heaven?"

"Uriel? He's one of the four archangels, isn't he? What's he got to say about it?"

I'd managed to surprise him. "How do you know about the four archangels? Most people aren't that familiar with biblical history."

"I know more than you think," I said. "It's part of my job."

"What's your job?" He looked blank. "I've forgotten—"

"I'm a writer. A novelist."

"Maybe that explains why you were going to hell," Raziel said in a wry voice.

"Shut up," I said genially. "What's Uriel got to do with who needs an escort or not? I don't remember much of anything specific about him—wasn't he the archangel of redemption?"

He was staring at me, momentarily forgetting I annoyed him. "Among other things. How do you know these things?"

"I told you."

"Remind me—what do you write?"

I didn't bother to disguise my irritation. He remembered my crackpot mother, but my life's work was easily forgotten. "Old Testament mysteries," I said in a testy voice. "They're tongue-in-cheek, of course, and a little sarcastic, but—"

"There's your answer. Uriel is as pitiless as a demon, and he has no sense of humor."

"I got sentenced to hell for writing murder mysteries?" I demanded, incensed.

"Probably. Unless you have other dark secrets. Have you killed anyone? Erected false idols? Committed adultery? Consorted with demons?"

"Not until today," I muttered.

"I'm not a demon."

"Close enough. I know what I saw downstairs. You may be an angel, but you're a vampire as well." My head was about to explode.

"We're not vampires. Vampires don't exist. We're blood-eaters."

I'm afraid I rolled my eyes at such nit-picking. "Whatever. I'm not saying I believe you. I'm trying to keep an open mind about it."

"How broad-minded of you," he said, his voice acidic.

"Besides, you're not very nice for an angel," I observed. "I thought angels were supposed to be sweet and, er . . . angelic."

"You're thinking in modern terms. An angel is just as likely to be the instrument of divine justice with a flaming sword to smite the unworthy."

"And what kind of angel are you, precisely?"

"Fallen."

I should have gotten past being shocked by now. "Fallen?" I repeated, no doubt sounding a little slow on the uptake.

"I think you've heard enough for now," he said. "Humans have a limited capacity to absorb this sort of thing."

"Who the hell are you to tell me what I can or cannot absorb? You haven't even begun to explain the blood and Sarah and—"

He gestured with one beautiful, elegant hand. It was a strong hand, which surprised me. Angels didn't do any manual labor, did they? So they ferried people to heaven and hell—that didn't require any particular strength. And what—

It was like someone had turned out the lights. Suddenly I was drifting in a cocoon, soundless, lightless, no sharp edges or uneven surfaces. I struggled for just a moment, because it felt like death, and I didn't want to find myself in even worse trouble; then I heard Raziel's rich, golden voice in my head: "Let go, Allie. Just let go."

So I did.

I LOOKED AT HER, NOT moving. I didn't want her here, didn't want her anywhere around me. She'd slid farther down on the floor, her head resting against the seat cushion of the couch, and she looked . . . delicious. That is, if I were someone else. She was not what I needed. I poured myself another glass of wine and leaned back, surveying her as dispassionately as I could.

Which was easier said than done. For all the distance I was putting between us, I couldn't ignore the fact that she'd saved my life, as surely as I'd saved her from Uriel's pit of hell; and the unfortunate truth was that we were bound together, whether I wanted it or not. I most definitely didn't want it, and the timing couldn't have been worse.

I was thinking too much, forgetting the rule of blind obedience, the rule that Uriel tried to force down our throats, usually with little success. If I'd just tossed her and left, my life would be much simpler, and the Fallen wouldn't be bracing for angelic retribution on top of everything else.

It was just as well she didn't know much about Uriel. There was no doubt he was one scary mother-fucker, and she was probably scared enough as it was.

Though she hadn't looked scared. She'd simply taken in the information I'd given her, with no drama, no hysterics. I was used to a little more Sturm und Drang when I told people they were dead. She'd just blinked her warm brown eyes and said, "Crap."

I stretched out on the other couch, looking at her. I was feeling better than I'd felt in months. Azazel was right, damn it. I'd needed the Source, rich blood filling all the empty places inside my body, repairing the broken parts, bringing me back to life. A little too much life, in fact. Because I wanted to fuck Allie Watson.

Hear that, Uriel? I sent the thought outward. *Fuck and motherfuck. Deal with it.*

She stirred, almost as if she could read my mind. Impossible—that Grace was given only to a bonded mate. I could read her anytime I wanted to, but there was no way she could know what I was thinking.

I shouldn't bother trying to feel her thoughts. I was already too attached to her, whether I liked it or not. One thing was certain—I was not going to have sex with her, even if I wanted to. Hands off from now on, at least while she was awake.

Old Testament mysteries. I snorted. No wonder Uriel had judged her. She was just lucky it had been my turn. She wouldn't have stood a chance with Azazel or any of the others—they would have tossed her without a second glance.

Which would have been a shame, I thought lazily, watching the rise and fall of her breasts beneath the loose white clothes Sarah had provided for her. She'd saved me last night in the forest. If she hadn't listened, if she'd run, the Nephilim would have ripped her apart and then devoured my paralyzed body.

But she had stayed. And then, when she thought the Fallen were drowning me, she'd raced into the water to try to save me. I still couldn't understand why.

She would have drowned if I hadn't breathed into her, filling her with . . . That knowledge was making me uneasy, unhappy. Aroused that she held my breath inside her body. The feeling was erotic, explicit, and powerful. She held my breath, my very essence, as intense a bond as if she held my semen, my blood. I was inside her, and in return a part of her claimed me, owned me. I was irrevocably tied to her, and I hated it. I was hard just thinking about it, and obsessed by it, and I had to break her hold.

I should have insisted on waiting for the renewal ceremony until after she'd been dealt with. In my depleted state, I would have been impervious to the allure of a human female.

Not just any human female. Even at my most vulnerable moments, I'd been able to resist the most beautiful, sexual women I'd been chosen to escort. Unfortunately, I wasn't feeling at all resistant to the current albatross around my neck. I was feeling . . . lustful.

This wasn't normal. Why her, why now? Things were already in a mess, and I'd vowed not to risk bonding with a woman again.

Which meant my only sex was with myself, a quick, soulless release that kept me from exploding in rage and frustration. Or with some anonymous human looking for a night of pleasure. A night I made sure she never remembered.

Neither did I.

Every woman in our hidden kingdom was mated, bonded to one of us. There were no offspring to grow up and carry on the tradition. The only way a woman entered Sheol was as a bonded mate, so I was shit out of luck if I wanted someone new, which must please Uriel. Anything that caused pain and discomfort to the Fallen brought Uriel . . . satisfaction. I was fairly certain he was incapable of feeling joy.

But right now I was too tired, too edgy, to come up with any possible solution to the problem of Allie Watson.

I couldn't even leave her for the night. By putting her to sleep, I'd claimed a certain responsibility for her, at least until she woke up, anywhere from six to twenty-four hours from now. Even if her sleep had been normal, I couldn't leave her alone up here, not until I'd extracted a promise of good behavior on her part. I couldn't risk her running off again—the sea might take her, or if she managed to find the borders of our kingdom, the Nephilim would be waiting.

There was only one bed, and I was damned if I was going to give it to her. She would likely sleep at least eight hours. She'd slid farther, so that she was lying on the floor half beneath the coffee table, her head on the thick white carpet. She'd be fine where she was.

I drained my wine and headed toward the bedroom. I pushed open the row of windows that fronted the sea and took a deep, calming breath of air. Even in the dead of winter with snow swirling down, I kept the windows open. We were impervious to cold—the heat of our bodies automatically adjusted. The sound of the ocean waves was soothing, and the cool night air reminded me that I was alive. I needed that reminder of the simple things that made up my life.

I stripped off my clothes and slid beneath the cool silk sheets. My arm still throbbed where the poison had entered, but the rest of me had healed properly, thanks to the salt water and Sarah's blood. My arm and my cock throbbed—and both were Allie Watson's fault.

I closed my eyes, determined to fall asleep.

I couldn't. I kept picturing her on the floor, dead

to the world. She'd had a rough couple of days as well. I knew she'd curled up next to me on the hard ground the night before—I'd been dimly aware of it through the haze of pain, and I'd been comforted.

After an hour I gave up, climbing out of the bed I'd longed for and heading for the door. At the last minute I paused and pulled on a pair of jeans. Nudity wasn't something that meant much in Sheol, and I didn't care about preserving her modesty. It was my own temptation I was trying to avoid. Even silk boxers or pajama pants were too thin, too easy to slip out of. These jeans had buttons, not a zipper, and it would take a major effort to get them off. Give me time enough to think twice about making such a foolish move.

I pushed the door open and walked back into the living room. It was lit only by the fitful moonlight reflected off the sea, and she was just a huddled shape in the shadows. I went over and scooped her up in my arms. She was heavier than some, though not enough to notice—her weight was no more trouble than carrying a loaf of bread would be for a human. I carried her into the bedroom and carefully set her down on the bed.

She needed to build up her stamina—she hadn't been able to run very far, and she'd been breathless after only three flights of stairs. She was a pampered city girl, not used to actually moving.

She had a beautiful body. Her breasts were full, enticing, and her hips flared out from a well-defined waist. By current standards, she'd be considered maybe ten to fifteen pounds overweight. By the tastes of the Renaissance, she'd be considered scrawny.

The Renaissance had been one of my favorite periods. I'd enjoyed myself tremendously—the art, the music, the creativity that seemed to wash over everyone.

And the women. Full and lush and beautiful. I'd sampled a great many of them before I made the mistake of falling in love with one, only to lose her. I would have had no choice but to watch my beloved Rafaela age; back then, foolishly, I would have welcomed the chance. But she'd run from me, certain I wouldn't want her when she looked decades older than I did. She died before I found her again.

Too many women, too many losses, each bit of pain a boon to my enemy, Uriel. I wouldn't go through that again.

If Allie Watson was going to stay—and right now I couldn't think of any other option—then she would have to learn to manage all those stairs. Sheol wasn't set up for guests, and for now she was my responsibility. I couldn't afford to coddle her.

The tangy salt breeze from the ocean rumpled my

hair, and I remembered that humans were more susceptible to the cold. I pulled the sheet up over her—probably a good idea anyway.

And then I lay down beside her. It was a big bed, and she wasn't going to shift in her sleep, migrate over to my side. She'd lie perfectly still until that particular Grace wore off. As long as my dreams didn't move me toward her, I'd be safe.

And even if they did, I'd wake up long before I could do anything about it.

I hoped the Grace would last the full twenty-four hours—I needed as much time as possible to deal with the situation. Not that she'd consider this particular comatose sleep a Grace, but that was the all-encompassing term for any of the extraordinary things we were capable of doing. The Grace of deep sleep was one of the least harmful. The Grace to cloud the minds of humans could have much more long-lasting consequences.

I stretched out, closing my eyes. She should smell of the flowered soap the women here used in the baths. She should smell like all the other women, but she didn't. She had her own sweet, erotic scent underlying the flowers, something that made her subtly different. Something that kept me awake as my exhausted mind conjured all sorts of sexual possibilities.

I glanced over at her comatose figure. She looked

younger, prettier, when she was asleep. Sweeter, when I knew she was anything but. She was a time bomb, nothing but trouble, yet somehow I'd gotten tied up with her.

I propped myself up on one elbow, looking down at her. Could I take my breath back from her, loosening the hold she seemed to have over me?

I moved my mouth over hers, not quite touching, and sucked her soft breath into my lungs. And then I bridged the small distance and rested my open mouth against her lips, caught by the sudden urge to taste her.

I sank back on the bed, cursing my own stupidity. I'd felt myself inside her, felt my breath in her body, the inescapable connection. In trying to take it back from her, I'd simply brought her into *my* body, completing the circle. I could feel her breath inside me now, curling in my lungs, spreading out into the blood that coursed through me.

I threw one arm over my eyes. Uriel would be laughing now. As if things weren't bad enough, I'd just made them quantitatively worse.

I couldn't think straight right now. Tomorrow I'd talk with some of the others. Not everyone was as cold and practical as Azazel. Michael, Sammael, Tamlel, would look at things with more flexibility. There'd be someplace to send her, where she'd be safe and I wouldn't have to think about her. Sooner or later new breath would replace hers in my body, and the connection would be broken. Wouldn't it?

I groaned, a soft sound, though if I'd screamed she would still have slept on.

It was going to be a long fucking night.

AZAZEL SAT IN THE GREAT HALL, alone in the dark. None of the Fallen knew the burden he carried. He could feel all of them—their needs, their pain, their doubts. Their secrets.

It was better that they didn't know. He wouldn't put it past some of them, Raziel in particular, to figure out a way to shield or control their thoughts, and that would put him at a disadvantage the Fallen couldn't afford. It was simply something he had to endure, a physical pain that he bore with no outward sign.

Only Sarah knew. Sarah, the Source to his Alpha, the calm voice of wisdom, the only one with whom he could ever simply let go. The only one.

The centuries, the millennia, since they had fallen faded into the mists of time. The number of wives he'd had faded as well, but he remembered every face, every name, no matter how short a time she had spent in his endless life. There was Xanthe, with the laughing eyes and ankle-length hair, who'd died when she was forty-three. Arabella, who'd lived until she was ninety-seven. Rachel, who died two days after they'd bonded.

He had loved them all, but none so much as he loved his Sarah, his heart, his beloved. She was waiting for him, calm and unquestioning, knowing what he needed. She always did.

Because of all the things he needed, he needed her the most.

She wouldn't let him get rid of Raziel's woman, even though it was the wisest thing to do. The girl wanted to leave, and he should see that she did. The Nephilim would dispose of what was left of her if she went beyond the undulating borders of Sheol. At least, he assumed so. They preyed on the Fallen and their wives, and she was neither. He didn't trust her, didn't trust her unexpected presence in a place that allowed no strangers.

He leaned back in the ornate carved chair, trying to hear the distant voice that came so seldom. The voice trapped deep in the earth, imprisoned for eternity, or so the story went. Azazel chose not to believe that story, not when he heard the voice of the first Fallen answering his most impossible questions.

Lucifer, the Bringer of Light, the most beloved of the angels, was still alive, still trapped. He could lead the forces of heaven and hell, the only one who stood a chance against the vindictive, all-powerful Uriel and the vicious creatures who served him. But as long as Lucifer's prison was hidden, as long as he was carefully guarded by Uriel's soldiers, there would be no chance to rescue him.

And without Lucifer to lead them, the Fallen were trapped in a cycle of endless pain. Doomed to watch their beloved wives age and die, never to know the joy of children, to live with the threat of the Nephilim constantly on their borders, ready to overrun their peaceful compound. To wait, knowing that Uriel would send his plagues down upon them at any provocation.

Azazel pushed back from the ancient scrolls and manuscripts, exhausted. There were hints there, perhaps even answers, but he had yet to find them. He studied them until his vision blurred, and the next day the grueling process would begin again.

There would be no answers tonight. He rose, signaling the lights to stay low, and started toward the huge expanse of rooms that had always been his.

Sarah was sitting up in bed, reading. Her silver hair lay in one thick braid over her shoulder; a pair of glasses was perched on the end of her perfect nose. Her creamy skin was smooth and delicate, and he stood and watched her, filled with the same love and desire he'd always felt.

Uriel had never been tempted as the others had been, one after the other, falling from grace. Uriel had loved no one but his God, whom he considered infallible except for the one stupid mistake of making humans.

Uriel despised people. He had no mercy for their frailties, no love for the music of their lives, the beauty of their voices, the sweetness of the love they could give. All he knew of them was hatred and despair, and he treated them accordingly.

Sarah looked at him over her brightly colored reading glasses, setting down her book. "You look exhausted."

He began to strip off his clothes. "I am. Trouble is coming and I don't know what to do about it. We can't fight Uriel—we're not ready."

"We won't know until it happens," she said in her soothing voice. "Uriel has been looking for an excuse for centuries. If the girl is the catalyst, then so be it."

Azazel rolled his shoulders, loosening the tightness there. "Raziel doesn't want her, and she doesn't belong here. I could get rid of her when he isn't looking, take her back to where Uriel charged she should go. The problem would be solved, and we could wait until we're better prepared. . . ."

Sarah took the glasses off her nose and set them beside the bed. "You're wrong, love."

"So you often tell me," he said. "You think I

shouldn't get rid of her? I have the right to send her back."

"Of course you do. You have a great many rights that you shouldn't exert. Raziel is lying to himself. He wants her. That's what frightens him."

"You think Raziel is afraid? I dare you to say that to him."

"Of course I would tell him, and you know it. He wouldn't rage at me as he would at you. The Alpha can be challenged. The Source is just that, the source of wisdom, knowledge, and sustenance. If I tell him he wants her, he'll believe it. But I think it's better if he discovers it himself."

"He doesn't want to bond again," Azazel argued. "Losing Rafaela was too hard for him. One loss too many."

"Losing me will be hard for you, love, but you'll mate again, and soon."

"Don't." He couldn't bear the idea of a time when Sarah wouldn't be there. Sarah with the rich, luscious mouth, the wonderful, flexible body, the creamy skin. The women in Sheol lived long lives, but they were merely a blink of the eye compared to the endless lives of the Fallen. He would lose her, and the thought was excruciating.

She gave him her full, sweet smile. "Come to bed, love. We don't need to think about that for a long time."

He slid in beside her, pulling her against him, pushing one leg between hers, his long fingers stroking the side of her face, her neck, the elegant collarbone. "What are you wearing?" he whispered against her skin.

She laughed, a low, sexy sound. "A nightgown, of course."

"Take it off." He was naked—he wanted her naked too.

She sat up and obliged him, pulling it over her head and tossing it on the floor. She'd pick it up in the morning, before the maid came in. She didn't like having anyone wait on her, but on this one matter he'd overruled her. She had enough demands on her, providing strength-sustaining blood for the unbonded.

She lay back down, a smile in her eyes, and slid her arms around him. She buried her face against his shoulder, and he could feel her teeth nipping lightly at his skin.

He kissed her, hard and deep, and she pulled at him, her hands restless. "Hurry," she whispered.

"No foreplay?" he teased.

"I've been thinking about you for the last two hours. That's foreplay enough."

He laughed, rolling her beneath him, pushing into her. Her back arched, and he could feel the first tremor of her orgasm tighten around him. She knew how to pull back, contain it so she wouldn't make him lose control. Their rhythms were perfectly matched, an elegant dance that culminated in a shock of pleasure.

This was faintly different. He sensed her urgency, when they usually took all the time they wanted. "Why the hurry, love?" he whispered.

She didn't answer for a moment, and he could see the shadow of an old pain in her beautiful eyes. "I'm afraid we'll run out of time," she said finally, her voice so low he could barely hear her.

"Never," he said. "Stop thinking."

Her smile was faint, lovely, one of the most erotic things about her. "Now," she whispered.

He didn't hesitate. His fangs slid down and sank into her neck, finding the sweet spot he knew so well. The blood was thick, rich in his mouth, and he felt the spasms begin to take over, felt her own helpless response as his wings unfurled. He rolled onto his side, taking her with him, his teeth never leaving the gently throbbing vein, his cock deep inside her as his wings clamped around them both, locking them together as he gave himself over to the only kind of death he'd ever know.

TEN

I OPENED MY EYES AND GROANED. I was lying sideways across a big, rumpled bed, still fully clothed—and I was alone.

I had a really annoying habit of waking up instantly, cheerfully, with no need for coffee or a hushed silence to prepare for the day. It was sheer luck that I'd survived my college years—more than one roommate had been ready to beat me to death over my tendency to prattle in the morning.

Today I could have used a little fogginess.

I had actually slept in that man's bed, though I wasn't quite sure how I'd got there. Last thing I remembered was falling asleep in the living room, and here I was stretched out on his sheets, feeling physically cozy and mentally freaked-out. I wasn't used to men carting me off to bed and then doing nothing about it. Actually, I wasn't used to men carting me off to bed at all.

Except he wasn't a man, was he? He was some kind of monster, or mythical beast, or a bizarre mix of both, but he was definitely not human. And I held the firm belief that interspecies dating was never a good idea.

I checked my neck, just to make certain, but there were no mysterious puncture wounds; and far from feeling dizzy from blood loss, I was feeling positively energetic, more than my usual morning bounce. The unthinkable had happened, the worst thing imaginable. It had been no surreal nightmare. I was dead and living with a bunch of vampires who seemed to have emerged from Old Testament Apocrypha. It was little wonder I was feeling disoriented. What I couldn't figure out was why I was cheerful.

The good thing about total disaster—at least there was nowhere to go but up. Maybe it was that simple.

Or maybe, just maybe, it had something to do with the man—damn, I couldn't stop thinking of him that way—who'd brought me here. Not that he was any too pleased to be saddled with my unwanted presence. Tough shit—it was his fault I'd ended up in this cross between Valhalla and Anne Rice territory.

The good thing was, Raziel appeared to have no interest in my far-from-irresistible charms, sexual, social, or otherwise. For all I knew, Raziel's people

were impotent. After all, no one seemed able to pro-
create.

That seemed unlikely. The heat between Azazel
and his wife had been palpable, despite the disparity
in their ages. Maybe Raziel simply wasn't interested
in women. Or, more likely, not interested in me—he
would hardly be the first who'd failed to appreciate
my particular brand of charisma.

I'd fallen asleep on the living room floor and he
must have been kind enough to carry me in to bed,
though so far kindness hadn't been a major part of
his personality. He'd left me sexually and hematolog-
ically untouched, thank God. What more proof did I
need of his lack of interest.

I had more important things to consider. I needed
a bathroom; I needed a shower. Last night I hadn't
stopped to think about the dead or undead having
actual bodily functions. All I knew was that *I* certainly
did.

I rolled out of the huge bed, landing barefoot on
the cool marble floor. The room was dim, the shades
pulled against the bright sunlight. There was a door
off to one side, and I headed for it. Eureka! A bathroom with a huge tub, a shower made for giants, thick
towels, and even a toilet. If the afterlife contained a
bathroom like this, it couldn't be that awful.

I followed the coffee aroma to a small kitchen,
bracing myself to confront Raziel, but the place was

deserted. There was coffee in a white carafe, and I filled one of the mugs, looking around me with fresh curiosity. Things didn't seem nearly so bizarre as they had yesterday—amazing what a good night's sleep would do for you.

I moved to the row of windows in the living room, looking out over the sea. It was misty, cool, the rich salt scent thick in the air. Where had Raziel gone? And did he really expect me to stay here like a good girl, awaiting my master's return?

Fat chance.

I found some white shoes that looked sort of like a delicate pair of Crocs and slipped them on, then headed out the door. I paused, staring down the endless flights of stairs, and let out a heartfelt groan.

Going down would be easier than going up, but if I did descend those forty million treacherous flights of stairs, sooner or later I would have to go back up. Why didn't they have elevators in the afterlife? Maybe most people just flew.

No, only the men could. "Sexist bastards," I said with a sniff. Maybe I could hitch a ride with one of the friendlier ones.

The stairs were endless, deserted as I descended. It wasn't until I reached the third floor that I began to run into . . . whatever they were. Fallen angels, vampires, blood-eaters, hell-transporters. Comic-book villains.

None of them looked particularly happy to see me. So it wasn't just Raziel who resented my presence. I gave each of them my cheeriest smile and a friendly greeting, and for the most part was met with cool indifference. Great. No welcome wagon here.

No sight of the Stepford wives, either, who by now were seeming pretty damned normal and friendly. Were they stuck in some kind of seraglio while the men went about their so-important business? Would I end up there?

Of course not. Seraglios were for wives and concubines, not inconvenient females nobody wanted.

I finally reached the bottom of those endless stairs, ending up in a massive hallway. It was open at one end, leading out to the churning sea, which called to me and I started toward it, something akin to joy rising in my heart, when I was brought up short by the very last person I wanted to see.

Not Raziel, who had his own dubious charms. But Azazel the Grouch, the leader of this happy band. And he was looking at me as if I carried all ten plagues of Egypt.

"What are you doing here?" he demanded.

"Looking for Raziel," I said, a complete lie. I didn't want to see him any more than he wanted to come near me, but I could think of no other excuse. The sea was calling to me, and I tried to sidle past him. "I think he might be out by the water—"

He blocked me. "He's not. Go back to your rooms and await him."

I didn't like Azazel. "I'm not one of the dutiful wives, and I'm certainly not going to hide away like someone in a harem. I'm going out to the water, and I suggest you don't try to stop me."

The moment the challenge was out of my mouth, I regretted it. I'd forgotten these weren't New York metrosexuals I was dealing with. Azazel froze, and I wondered idly if these fallen angels were capable of smiting a bitch. If so, I was in deep shit.

"Allie!" Sarah suddenly came up from behind me, tucking her arm through mine. "So nice to see you this morning. Aren't you happy to see Allie, my love?"

Azazel glowered. "No."

"Pay no attention to him, my dear," Sarah said smoothly, leading me away from him. "He's got a lot on his mind, and he tends to be bad-tempered in the morning. In the afternoon as well," she added ruefully.

"Is there ever a time when he isn't grumpy?" I asked with my usual lack of tact.

"Not often," Sarah said. "He has too many responsibilities. Now, let me find someone who will know where Raziel's gone. He's probably up in the caves—he spends most of his time there."

"I admit, he does have batlike tendencies. The black clothes."

"The wings," Sarah added cheerfully, then saw my expression. "Oh, you haven't seen his wings yet? They're quite . . . astonishing. A deep, iridescent blue. You'll love them."

"I doubt it."

Sarah smiled. "Let's find some help. I'm not allowed up there or I'd take you. Besides, with me you'd have to walk and it would take days. Come with me." She led me, blessedly, toward the open door and the sea.

I stopped for a moment, blinded by the sunlight, and let the cool salty breeze wash over me like a blessing—like a lover's caress. I opened my eyes to see Sarah watching me with a faint smile.

"You fit well here," she said.

"I hadn't realized how much I love the sea."

"It's not just that." But before I could ask her what she meant, she started walking toward two men who were standing in the bright sunlight, watching our approach.

"I still can't get over why they don't turn into piles of ashes," I muttered. "I thought vampires couldn't handle the sun."

Sarah laughed. "Vampires are a myth."

"And fallen angels who drink blood are part of reality television?"

"Reality television is a myth too, from what I hear. I would suggest you reserve judgment. Tamlel,

Sammael," she greeted them, and the two of them bowed.

Raziel was so ridiculously gorgeous he made my knees weak, and Azazel's stern beauty was impressive. These two were damned pretty as well, and for a moment I wondered if you could be gay in the afterlife.

One of them was older, with dark brown hair tied back, warmth in his eyes. The younger one was blond and cherubic, and it was probably my imagination that he looked slightly sullen. They greeted Sarah with warmth, but it was clear they were unsure about me.

"This is Allegra," Sarah said. "But you already know that. Allie, this is Tamlel, generally considered to be in charge of scribes. And the young one is Sammael."

He was looking at me with a sulky expression, and I'd always had little patience for sullen teenagers. Though this particular teenager was probably thousands of years old. "And what are you in charge of?"

There was a moment of silence, and then Sarah spoke. "In fact, he's one of the angels of death. But since the Fallen have eternal life, he hasn't had much to do since he fell. Our only connection with humans is to take them to their final home."

"One of the angels of death?" I echoed. "Like Raziel?"

"Raziel isn't a death angel."

"You could have fooled me," I grumbled, thinking back to that bus. "What's he doing now—killing someone new?"

Tamlel looked distressed. "We don't kill. We are charged with transporting—"

"Never mind." I took pity on him.

"Raziel is the angel of knowledge and mysteries," Sarah said patiently. "He keeps the secrets of the ages."

"Typical male," I muttered.

Sarah laughed, and even Tamlel smothered a grin. Sammael, however, kept a stony expression. "Will one of you take Allie up to Raziel? He shouldn't have left her alone on her first day with us."

"How long is she going to stay?" Sammael demanded in a tone just this side of rudeness. I guess if you were an angel of death, you could get away with it.

"We don't know yet. There are more important things to worry about right now. Her presence among us will be dealt with when the time is right."

That didn't sound particularly promising. I wasn't in the mood to be *dealt with*, and no one apart from Sarah seemed exactly delighted to see me, though at least Tamlel was trying, bless him.

"I'm afraid I've promised to help Michael in the weapons room," Tamlel said. "However, Sammael would be more than happy to serve." Sammael didn't look happy to do anything, but maybe that was because he looked like a teenager.

But clearly no one said no to Sarah. "Thank you, Sammael. I'll take Allie back upstairs—she'll need warmer clothes if she's to go into the caves, and I wish to talk to her. You may join us in an hour."

Sammael bowed in acquiescence, and we started back toward the house.

"I'm worried about him," she said in a low voice.

"Raziel? Or Sammael?"

She laughed. "Raziel. Sammael has always been like that. The Fallen are eternal—they tend not to change."

"Great," I said. Last night Raziel had treated me like an unwelcome interloper, when it was hardly my fault I was here. I didn't fancy spending eternity feeling out of place. But apparently it wasn't the women who were eternal, only the damned men.

I glanced at Sarah as we climbed. She looked human, normal, friendly. There were no marks whatsoever on her wrist, the wrist that had been dripping blood into Raziel's mouth.

Funny. Popular culture always seemed to suggest that vampires—excuse me, blood-eaters—were sexual, that the drinking of blood was an erotic act. In retrospect, last night's scene had seemed more like a mama bird feeding her baby. Though I doubted Raziel would enjoy being seen as a fuzzy hatchling.

"Are you certain going up to the caves is a good idea?" I said uneasily. "I don't think Raziel will be particularly happy to see me."

"Raziel gets his way far too much of the time," she said in her tranquil voice. "Jarameel is usually the one who has visions, but he's been gone for a long time, and my own are far too muddy and unclear. But I know you're here for a reason, and that reason has to do with Raziel."

There wasn't much I could say in response to that. "Okay." I let the word sit for a moment. "So what's he doing up in the caves?"

"He's doing what everyone is doing. He's looking for the First," she said.

"The first what?"

"The First of the Fallen." We rounded another landing, and I was surprised to realize we were almost at the top. It was far less torturous with Sarah by my side.

"You're looking for Lucifer? Why? What happened to him?"

She looked startled. "I forgot you were a biblical scholar."

All right, I could be embarrassed. "Hardly. I write— I wrote Old Testament mysteries. I have a certain amount of basic knowledge, but for the rest I just Googled what I needed to know."

" 'Googled'?"

I realized with sudden horror that I hadn't seen a computer anywhere in this place. Maybe this *was* hell. "Looked it up," I clarified.

"Ah, no wonder Uriel hated you," she said. "He takes history very seriously. He takes everything very seriously."

"I don't understand about Uriel. What's he got to say about things?"

"Everything. When God gave mankind free will, he left Uriel in charge. And Uriel is . . ." For a moment words failed her, and the look in her eyes was bleak. ". . . quite unforgiving. His answer to everything that even hints of evil is to destroy it. And he sees evil in everything."

We had stopped for the moment, and I considered the consequences of such an attitude. "That doesn't sound too good for the future of mankind."

"It's not good for the future of life in any form." She pushed open the door in front of us. "That's why we search for Lucifer."

The stark white apartment was just as clean and soulless as it had been when I left it. I sank down on one of the pure white sofas. "So where is Lucifer?"

She sighed. "He's in some kind of stasis, and has been for millennia, since God first passed judgment on him. He's conscious, awake, but no one can get to him. Only my husband and Raziel have been able to hear him, and the mountain caves are the only place quiet enough for Raziel to listen. As for what we want with him—the Fallen want him to lead them as they overthrow Uriel."

I blinked. Just my luck—I died, and instead of a peaceful afterlife, I got stuck in the middle of an angelic coup d'état. I pulled my legs up under me, hugging my knees, and cast a glance at a plate of blueberry muffins that was sitting on the coffee table. Before I could reach for them, Sarah went on, "Ask Raziel about it. He'll probably think I told you too much already. You know how men can be."

I was ready to make a smart-ass comment—so far Raziel had shown little inclination to tell me anything—but I stopped myself. "You called him a man. Is he?"

"A man? Oh, most definitely. When the angels fall, they take human shape along with their curses."

"Humans aren't immortal. Humans aren't cursed. They can't fly and they don't . . ." I hesitated. Once spoken, it would be too real. "They don't drink blood."

Sarah's quick laugh took the onus off it. "Don't be picky. Call them what you will—they are many things, as you already know." She moved over to the window. "They're cursed, and the curse goes deep. If you understand that, it will make things easier on you."

I stared longingly at the blueberry muffins. If I

had one, I'd be hard-pressed not to eat three, and that would use up half my calorie count for the day.

"Why don't you have a muffin?" she asked, mystified. "You've been staring at them since we arrived."

"I don't dare. The food's too damned good here—I'll end up looking like a blimp."

Sarah laughed. "That's one advantage to living here. You won't need to worry about diet. The women may not be immortal, but we still manage to live a lot longer than most humans do. It's almost impossible to kill us. In a little while your cholesterol, blood pressure, blood sugar, and anything else will be textbook perfect."

"Except that I'm not mortal, I'm dead. Aren't I?"

Sarah's forehead wrinkled. "I don't know if anyone's quite sure what you are. You're something of an original, and we have yet to discover your purpose. Even so, I think we all suffer a sea change when we come here. Those who come as wives and bonded mates become almost invulnerable. I don't think there's been a flu or a cold here in generations. We live very long lives—I was born at the beginning of the last century, I have the body of an extremely healthy sixty-something, and I expect to live at least another fifty years. It's similar for the rest of us. The good news is we can give up glasses, contact lenses, allergy meds, and diets."

"How come you know about some things and not

others, like contact lenses and Ben & Jerry's, but you don't know what Google is?" I asked, confused.

"It depends on what the newest wife brings to us. I don't believe Carrie has mentioned Google but she was very fond of ice cream."

"So am I."

"Well, you'll be pleased to know that you won't have to worry about gaining weight. You'll stay exactly the same as you are now."

"What?" I was horrified. "I'm still fifteen pounds overweight. Are you telling me I'm going to be like this throughout eternity?"

Sarah laughed and patted my hand. "Don't worry—it's a healthy fifteen pounds. And Raziel might like it."

I stared at her. "What does that have to do with anything? He didn't even stay around long enough to say good morning. Besides, I don't like him very much either."

Sarah tilted her head, surveying me with eyes that saw far too much. Or read too much into an entirely innocent situation. "He didn't say good morning?" she echoed. "Did he sleep with you last night?" The idea seemed to astonish her, which wasn't particularly flattering.

"Of course not!" I said, trying to sound horrified rather than . . . God, I was feeling almost wistful. What was wrong with me?

"But he spent the night in the same apartment?"

I hesitated, then decided to dump. If anyone was going to help me figure things out, it would be Sarah. "In the same bed, I think. But he didn't touch me. I fell asleep in here, woke up this morning in bed, alone"—I saw her mouth open to ask a question, and said firmly—"and untouched. It looked as if someone else had slept there too, and he's the logical choice since these are his rooms, but if he did he kept to his side of the bed. He didn't even bite me."

Sarah blinked for a moment, then laughed, her voice light and curiously beguiling. "He'd shag you before he'd bite you, Allie. That's the highest form of intimacy there is. It's the last thing he'd want with you."

Of course it was. Thank God, I told myself virtuously. "I'm thrilled to hear it. So he's only intimate with you?"

There was the faintest trace of color on her creamy skin. "You mean because he took my blood? Didn't the two of you talk at all? I can't believe you simply let him brood around and not answer any questions."

"We talked. We just didn't get around to the whole . . . blood thing."

"Oh," Sarah said after a moment. "Well, I don't suppose it matters—it may not affect you one way or another. Unless it makes a great difference to you, there's really no reason for us to talk about it."

It did. Everything about Raziel made a great deal of difference to me, but admitting that only made things worse. "No reason at all," I said brightly.

I looked past her toward the bank of windows overlooking the fog-shrouded Pacific Ocean. At least, I assumed it was the Pacific—for all I knew, we could be on Mars. The windows been left open, and a strong breeze tossed the sheer white curtains into the air, sending a little shiver of some unnamed emotion down my backbone. "Is everything white in this place?" I demanded, feeling cranky. Being dead would do that to a girl.

For a moment I thought I saw something just beyond the windows—the breathless shimmer of iridescent blue wings, the sun sparkling off them. I narrowed my gaze, but there was nothing out there, just a few seagulls in the distance, wheeling and cawing. *No seagulls on Mars,* I thought.

Sarah looked around as if noticing for the first time. "I suppose so. Raziel tends to see things as either black or white—never shades of gray. He'd probably really hate it if you painted anything." She grinned, suddenly looking mischievous. "Just let me know if you want some help."

The idea was irresistible, and I laughed. "Do you want to make his life a living hell?"

"No, dear. That's going to be your job."

Another odd fluttering. I rose and crossed the living room to peer out into the bright sky, the rolling mist on the ocean. There was nothing in the sky but the seagulls—I must be imagining things.

Or was I? I was stuck in the sterile aerie of a creature who could fly—why would I assume that mysterious dark wings were a figment of my imagination?

I turned my back on the windows. If Raziel was out there buzzing the building in an effort to spook me, I wasn't going to let him. Though the sight of him dive-bombing the place would have been pretty damned funny.

"Actually, I wanted to talk to you before Sammael gets here. Apart from welcoming you to Sheol," Sarah said, "I wanted to warn you about Raziel."

Oh, great. As if things weren't bad enough, now I needed to be warned about the only man I slightly, somewhat, minimally trusted. "He's an ax murderer?" I suggested cheerfully.

Sarah's responding smile was a token. "Don't be fooled by his kindness. Raziel has shut himself off from all human feeling, from caring about anyone besides the Fallen and their wives. I will speak for you at the meeting today, but if you're relying on Raziel to protect you, you're wasting your time."

I was still trying to reconcile the term *kindness* with the bad-tempered Raziel I'd been saddled with. Though more likely Raziel would consider *he'd* been saddled with *me*.

"Oh—there's a meeting?" I said, feeling doomed. "I suppose they're going to decide whether I live or die, and I'm not going to have any voice in the matter. Of course, I'm dead already, so I guess it doesn't really matter. I just don't feel like I'm dead. And I really don't want to go back to that place." I shivered. I couldn't remember much, just heat and noise and the pain of thousands of souls reaching out. . . .

"I'll speak for you. I'll do anything I can to stop them. Right now they're more worried about the Nephilim and whether Uriel will use your presence as an excuse to move against us. I just don't want you to count on Raziel. He's sworn off caring about anyone, and I'm afraid he's not going to make an exception for you." She tilted her head sideways, assessing me. "At least, I don't think so. But I'll fight for you. And sometimes they listen."

And if that didn't sound like a rock-solid guarantee, I figured it was the best I could expect. If I was going to get out of this mess, I'd have to figure it out on my own.

Sammael appeared at the door just as Sarah was leaving, and he didn't look any happier to see me than he had before.

"Are you ready?" he asked politely.

I suddenly remembered all those flights of stairs, and groaned. Once a day was enough. "I don't suppose you have an elevator hidden anywhere around here?"

"No." Sammael moved past me to push open a section of the windows that I had blithely assumed was solid wall. The wind was rising, swirling into the apartment, but in Raziel's sterile environment there was nothing loose that could be blown away. "Come with me—we'll take the shortcut."

I looked from Sammael's calm face to the wind and ocean just beyond those doors to nowhere. He was an angel, wasn't he? Albeit Sarah had said he was one of the angels of death. He wasn't going to toss me out the window, was he?

You can only die once, I thought, not knowing whether it was true or not. Taking Sammael's hand, I stepped out into a nothingness that was blindingly bright.

ELEVEN

I T SEEMED AS IF A MOMENT HAD passed, or an hour. I found myself standing on a cliff, much higher up than the house had been, and I'd never been crazy about heights. I could see out over the vast ocean, and the sun beginning to sink lower on the horizon. Pacific Ocean, then. The ground was wet beneath my feet, and there was no sign of my missing mentor. I glanced at Sammael. I couldn't remember holding on to him, soaring through those misty skies. But clearly I hadn't walked.

"Where is he?" I asked.

"In the cave. Just go straight—you'll find him."

We were three-quarters of the way up a mountain that I hadn't even realized was nearby. Its top was enshrouded in mist, as was the rocky shoreline below, and I could see the great yawning mouth of a cave closer than I would have liked. I waited for the familiar panic to set in. "I'm claustrophobic when it comes to caves," I finally admitted, glancing nervously at the rough-hewn entrance, worn smooth by centuries of scouring winds. In fact, I didn't like heights, closed-in places, places that were too open—give me a phobia and I embraced it enthusiastically.

"Not anymore," Sammael said in a colorless voice. "You should watch what you say. You'll be lucky if the Council simply decides to grant you the Grace."

"The Grace?" That sounded almost pleasant.

"Your memory would be wiped clean. I promise you, it wouldn't hurt, and you'd be perfectly happy. You'd be able to do simple tasks, perhaps even learn to read and write a few simple words."

I stared at him in absolute horror. "No," I said flatly.

"It won't be your choice." He seemed unmoved by my reaction. "Do you want me to take you to Raziel?"

"I can manage," I said, not sure that I could, but I really didn't want to hear any more of Sammael's awful possibilities. The inhabitants of Sheol seemed to have mixed feelings about me. Azazel, Sammael, and Raziel clearly thought I didn't belong, and I was happy to agree with them. Tamlel, Sarah, and the Stepford wives were welcoming, but that would probably mean nothing once they held their council meeting. "But I thank you for the offer. I think I need to figure out how to get what I need on my own, don't I?"

He barely registered my question. "I'll come back if there's a problem."

"How will you know?" I asked suspiciously. Raziel had been able to read my mind—if it turned out the whole place knew what I was thinking, then maybe I wouldn't mind getting a lobotomy.

"Sarah will know. Sarah will tell me," he said simply, as if he expected me to know something so basic.

Clearly Sarah was a force to be reckoned with. It was a good thing that she seemed to be on my side. "I'll be fine," I said firmly, and before I could add to it, Sammael had disappeared into the wind.

"Well, damn," I said out loud. I'd been hoping to see wings. If Sammael came equipped with them, I hadn't had time to notice. Which made travel convenient, but still a little bit puzzling.

I turned to look at the cave, waiting for the icy fear to set in, but I felt nothing but an entirely reasonable nervousness at the thought of bearding Raziel in his den. Sammael had told the truth—the claustrophobia had vanished. *Whoopee,* I thought with a suitable lack of enthusiasm, walking forward.

I still wasn't crazy about enclosed spaces. The wide corridor into the mountain looked as if it had been a mine shaft, if they had mine shafts in the afterlife. It narrowed a little too swiftly as I made my way down it. Normally I'd be curled up on the ground, covered with a cold sweat. The fact that I could keep moving, deeper and deeper into the mountain, was more proof of how different things were. A proof I could easily have done without.

I wasn't quite sure what I expected. The corridor took a couple of sharp turns, shutting out the daylight at the entrance, but I managed to keep going without stopping to hyperventilate. Where the hell was Raziel? I had the sudden fear that Sammael had pulled a Hansel and Gretel on me, luring me to this mountain to abandon me, thereby getting rid of a messy problem. Sarah wouldn't let him get away with that, would she?

I'd almost given up trying to find him when I turned one last corner and saw him sitting on a wooden chair in the middle of a huge stone cavern, his eyes closed.

I had planned to be a smart-ass and say something like "Yoo-hoo, imaginary creature, I'm here," but I thought better of it. He was sitting at the edge of a great yawning hole in the center of the cave, and it looked like some of the walls had collapsed inward. He was at the very edge, too close for comfort, and as I looked he seemed to sway toward the opening.

I tried to stifle my instinctive scream, but he heard me anyway and jerked, startled. He fell backward, away from the pit, and the chair went over. I could hear it splintering against the stone walls as it fell, and I shivered. He rose, focusing on me, and I tried for a cheerful smile.

As I expected, he wasn't the least bit pleased to see me. "How did you get here?" he demanded, not moving any closer.

"Sammael," I said.

He grunted. "You're wearing my clothes."

"It's better than all that white," I said. "Were you frightened by an albino when you were a child?"

"I was never a child."

Another of his flat, incontrovertible statements. At least he was talking to me. "You mean you were born this way?"

"I wasn't born." He stayed where he was, on the edge of the pit, and it made me nervous. Though I supposed if he fell, he could probably fly out of there, couldn't he? "Why are you here? I told Tam and Sammael to keep you busy. This is no place for you."

"I don't belong in this dank little cave? I can agree with that," I said. "Not that it's actually dank or little, but you get the point. Or I don't belong in Sheol at all? Because I'm willing to agree with you on that one as well, but apparently it's your fault I'm here and not back in New York dodging buses, and I really don't feel like having a bunch of men get together and decide what's going to happen to me, particularly when one of the options includes the equivalent of brain damage. And I don't like white."

He blinked at the non sequitur. "Tough," he said shortly. He started toward me, and I watched him, trying to put all the strange, disparate things I knew about him together in one package.

"Where are your wings?" I asked. If I was going to be stuck with angels, I should at least get to see some feather action.

He rolled his eyes. "Why is that always the first question? You don't need to know."

"If I stay here, do I get them?"

"You're not and never will be an angel," he said.

I was willing to put up a fight. "Oh, you never can tell. I mean, clearly I've been far from angelic so far, but I can always change my ways and become positively saintly." I gave him a hopeful beam that left him entirely unmoved.

"People don't become angels," he said in a tone that said, *Any moron knows that.*

"How about heaven? Don't people get wings there? Since I'm dead and all that, it seems like a good place to start."

His laugh wasn't flattering. "I don't think you've reached that point yet."

"Then you're stuck with me. Get used to it."

He halted directly in front of me. "For now," he said. "I wouldn't count on a lengthy stay. But for as long I have to put up with you, you can stop stealing my clothes. And you can stop talking—the sound of your voice is like fingernails on a blackboard."

"Don't be ridiculous," I said, totally unmoved. "I have a delightful voice. It's low and sexy, or so people have told me. You're just being difficult."

"I don't care how glorious your voice is, I'd appreciate hearing less of it."

I opened my mouth to protest, then shut it again. If I wanted to survive, I needed him on my side, and I was going to have to behave myself, at least a little bit. I stood perfectly still, saying nothing, waiting for him.

He tilted his head, letting his strange eyes slide down me, assessing. Odd, but it felt as palpable as a touch. "My clothes are too tight for you," he said helpfully.

"You're a man, I'm a woman. I have hips."

"Indeed," he said, and I looked at him sharply to see if there was an insult hidden behind his bland tone of voice. "I meant to have clothes provided for you."

"You did. They were all white."

"You don't like white? It's the color of rebirth, renewal."

"It's not a color at all, it's the absence of color," I said. "I may be in limbo, having to get by on your charity, but I'm not going to let everything go a dull beige."

"Limbo is a mythical construction," he said. "And white is not beige."

"Sheol is a mythical construction, and angels are part of fairy tales, and vampires are nightmares, and you don't exist," I snapped. I was getting a little tired of all this.

"Then where are you?" He wasn't expecting an answer. "What did Sammael tell you?"

"Sammael's a teenager. He barely said two words. Sarah was more forthcoming. She told me not to count on you for anything."

"Did she?"

"She said that despite your great kindnesses to me—and I have to admit I have yet to see any evidence of kindness on your part—you wouldn't speak up for me at the meeting and you'd let the others do what they want with me, and I wanted to make sure—"

"Be quiet!" It was spoken in a soft voice, soft but deadly, and I shut up.

Almost. "Are you going to let them melt my brain?"

He looked confused for a moment, before resuming his familiar exasperated expression. "Oh, the Grace. No."

It was one small syllable, but I trusted him.

"In the future, you're not to come up here," he continued, his tone cool, "and I will make certain Sarah knows where you're allowed to go and what's off-limits. There are dangerous places in Sheol, including the gates that surround us. This place is almost as dangerous."

"Have you found Lucifer?" He opened his mouth to reprimand me, and I shot back, "It's four words, for heaven's sake. Deal with it."

He looked annoyed. "Sarah's been talking too much."

"Everyone seems to talk too much to suit you. Or is it just women?" *Sexist bastard,* I thought with a peculiar lack of heat.

"No I'm not," he said.

Not what? I thought.

"You are the only female around here who seems unable to control her tongue You don't need the details of our fight with the archangel. It's none of your—"

"—business," I chimed in with him. "And Sarah didn't tell me much. Besides, I might point out that Lucifer fell because he dared ask too many questions." I shot him a wry glance. "You should have some sympathy for the curious."

"Don't get delusions of grandeur. Lucifer's questions were more important than whining about why there are so many stairs."

"And that reminds me—judging by Sammael's 'shortcut,' I shouldn't have had to walk. You have wings—you could have flown me up there in no time."

"I could have," he agreed. "But you need to know where you are, what's expected of you. There won't always be someone around to transport you. And I don't want to transport you if I can help it."

"Why not?" He probably didn't want to touch me, I thought, grumpy at the idea. He was treating me as if I had an advanced case of leprosy, which was both annoying and ever so slightly depressing. Not that I was attracted to him—he wasn't my type.

"You know why," he said shortly.

"What do you mean?"

His eyes met mine, and I had the oddest feeling I could see my own thoughts in them. Which was truly a horrible idea, because I'd had some thoughts that were decidedly warm, indecent, and embarrassing. This was hard enough without him knowing that I had feelings I was using all my excess energy trying to fight. If he could read my every thought, I was screwed.

"No, I can't always tell what you're thinking," he said by way of an answer, and my heart sank. "Some things are easy, other things are well protected inside you. It takes a lot to get to those, and I'm certainly not going to bother."

I wasn't sure if that was reassuring or insulting. At least he had no idea that I had a furtive desire to jump his—

"Stop it!" he snapped.

Shit. Okay, I could try fighting back. I batted my

eyelashes, giving him my most limpid, innocent look. "Stop what?"

He crossed the cavern so fast I wondered if he'd used magic, or whatever his abilities were called. "It will not happen, so you can stop thinking about it. I am never going to mate with you."

"*Mate* with me?" I echoed, much amused. "Why don't you just call a spade a spade? You're never going to have sex with me. Which, incidentally, is fortunate, because what makes you think *I* want to have sex with *you*?" No one likes rejection, even from someone they despise.

"There's a difference. Mating is a bond for life. *Your* life. Sex is simply fornication."

"And you don't approve of fornication."

He looked at me then, a slow, scorching look. Maybe I was wrong on the rejection part. He loomed over me, dangerously close. "I could quite easily fuck you," he said deliberately, the word strange in his faintly formal voice. "You are undeniably luscious. But I'm not going to. And you need to get it out of your mind as well. It's not just the words that distract me. It's the pictures."

Oh, crap. He could see the visuals? "I can't help it! It's like telling someone not to move. As soon as someone tells me to be still, I end up having to wiggle. Anyway, you were the one who brought up the subject in the first place."

He opened his mouth to argue, then closed it. "I have things to do," he said finally. "I don't want to transport you."

I looked around the cavernous room. "You'll have to put up with it," I said. "Otherwise there's no way down and I'm stuck here."

"You tempt me," he said, and his stark, beautiful voice danced down my backbone. I really was much too susceptible to him. "But someone would come to find you." He moved past me, heading toward the corridor that led to the outside world. As outside as Sheol might be. He paused, looking back at me. "Are you coming?"

I would have loved to tell him no, but there was a chill to the place, and I didn't want to wait there alone until someone came to rescue me. I was managing pretty damned well, given the situation, but I was *his* responsibility and I was not about to let him abandon me.

I raced after him, catching up as we reached the mouth of the cave and the misty daylight. "What next?" I said. "Do I climb on your back, or do you carry me in your arms, or—"

"You stop talking," he said.

I almost tripped over the white rug that covered part of the white marble floor. We were back in his sterile apartment, and he was in the kitchen. My legs felt a little wobbly, and I sank down on the sofa and put my head between my legs to keep from passing out. Then I looked up. "You could give me some warning next time," I said irritably.

"There won't be a next time if I can help it." He leaned against the counter, looking at a plate of doughnuts someone had left. "Aren't you going to eat these? I suppose Sarah told you you can't gain weight."

I bristled slightly that he would even mention my weight in such an offhand manner, but hey, that was permission enough. I got to my feet and moved into the small kitchen.

And it *was* small. Too small to hold both of us, really, but he wasn't shifting away and I wanted those magic doughnuts.

It was a novel experience, having a beautiful man tell me to eat fattening foods, the stuff of daydreams. *"No, dear, at one hundred and eighty pounds, you're too thin. You need to put on some weight."* Be still, my heart. Oh, he was hardly the first beautiful man I'd been around. I was shallow that way—I liked men who were pretty and just a little stupid, and I'd always preferred them on the beefy side. I had the unhappy suspicion that Raziel was a little too smart for my peace of mind. But I was beginning to see the appeal of lean, powerful elegance.

Most of my boyfriends had wanted me to go on a diet, get down to a size six or eight from the comfortable size twelve I'd worn since college. We'd go out to dinner, I would dutifully order a side salad with a spritz of lemon juice or vinegar, and then the moment I was home alone I'd plow through the Ben & Jerry's. Super Fudge Chunk had marked the end of many a dull date.

"So I'm still going to be hungry and eat, use the bathroom, sleep, bathe, and never gain weight. Sounds delightful. Do I get to have sex with anyone if *you* don't want me?"

He stared at me, momentarily speechless. "No," he said finally. "Absolutely not. It's forbidden."

"But you said you could happily—"

"I said you and I won't have sex," he interrupted before I could drop the F-bomb as he had.

"Why would you want to?" I said, managing to sound bored with the idea.

"I *don't* want to," he snapped. "*You* asked *me* if we would have sex."

"You misunderstood. Deliberately," I added, just to annoy him. In this strange, otherworldly place, annoying him was one of the only things that made me feel alive. "I do understand why you'd want to, but I really don't think it's a good idea. You being my mentor and all."

This was working even better than I'd expected. He was ready to explode with frustration. Not the right kind of frustration, unfortunately. Indeed, it was too bad that I was taunting him, but I couldn't resist. He really was freaking gorgeous. It was probably unwise—I needed him on my side.

"No," he said repressively.

I shrugged, taking another doughnut. "Do we get sick? Will I start feeling bloated if I eat a fourth doughnut?"

"Yes," he said.

I put the doughnut down. "Well, at least you'll outlive me. Cheer up. You can dance at my funeral."

"I won't know you when you die. Assuming we figure out what to do with you, we probably won't see each other again."

This wasn't very comforting news, but I wasn't giving up the battle. "Once they decide, how long will it take to get rid of me?"

He just looked at me, his expression saying it couldn't be soon enough.

Oddly enough, I wasn't sure I wanted to leave, even if they could give me back some semblance of a normal life with mental acuity intact. Yes, I enjoyed picking on him, and the white had to go. But despite my arguments, I . . . kind of liked it here. Liked the sound of the ocean beyond the open windows, the taste of salt on my lips. I'd always wanted to live by the sea. I was getting my wish a little earlier than expected, and it wasn't technically living, but it was close enough.

I liked the bed I'd slept in, I liked Sarah, and I most definitely liked to look at Raziel, even if he was frustrating, annoying, and all the other negative adjectives I could think of. And if he could read my mind, tough shit.

In fact, I was living my dream. I'd spent most of my adult life sifting through arcane literature and Bible criticism to come up with my far-fetched mysteries, and I was well acquainted with the totally bizarre fantasies of Enoch, with his tales of the Nephilim and the Fallen.

Except it turned out Enoch wasn't the acid freak I'd always thought he was. All of this was real.

The kitchen was too small for both of us, but for him to leave he'd have to brush past me, and I knew he really didn't want to touch me. It was lovely to think that it was unshakable lust keeping him away, but I knew it was more likely annoyance—I'd done my best to make him want to strangle me.

"No," he said, "I don't want to strangle you. I just want you to go away."

Grrrr. "How long are you going to be reading my mind?" I demanded, thoroughly annoyed.

"As long as I need to."

"Well, that time is now over. Turn off the switch, or whatever it is you do. Stay the fuck out of my brain. Don't read my mind, don't cloud my thoughts, don't wipe out my memory. Keep your distance." I didn't bother trying to keep the snarl out of my voice. I'd had enough of this crap.

He was looking dangerously close to be being amused. His gloriously striated eyes glinted for a moment, but I seriously doubted that Raziel possessed even a tiny trace of a sense of humor in his cold, still body. Sure enough, the expression vanished so quickly I was sure I'd imagined it.

"Or what?" he said.

Asshole. He knew I didn't have much to fight back with. Little did he know that I'd always been wickedly inventive. Maybe that was why I'd been sent to hell.

Hands sliding down my body, beautiful hands, his mouth following, on my breast, sucking—

"Stop it!" he said with complete horror, pushing away from me as if burned by the sultry image in my brain.

I smiled sweetly. "I've got a hell of an imagination, Raziel," I said, calling him by name for the first time. "Stay out of my head or prepare to be thoroughly embarrassed."

Taking the plate of doughnuts, I sauntered back out into the living room.

CHAPTER

TWELVE

SHE WAS A WITCH. SHE SHOULD have been humble and weepy and afraid of me. Instead she was the complete opposite, and the quick vision of her sex fantasy was having the expected effect on my body. Azazel was right—I'd been celibate too long.

I stayed in the kitchen, not moving. I'd thought I at least had my body under control. In truth, it was no wonder I was hard, with that brief fantasy she'd indulged in. I had no idea whether she really found it appealing or whether it was just part of the game she was playing.

No, it was real. As I'd seen the thought, I'd felt her own fevered reaction, as intense as mine despite the brevity of the image. If that had simply been an intellectual exercise, it wouldn't have been so . . . disturbing.

I had to get rid of her, and fast. I needed her out of my rooms, out of my world. There was no way in hell I was going to let them invoke the Grace of forgetting, but apart from that anything would be an improvement. Sarah was always looking for someone to mother—Allie Watson was the very thing. I could pass her over, then go out on my own and not have to think about her anymore. It might take a day or two to get her out of my system, but I could do it. I could turn myself off. As long as she wasn't living in my apartment and taunting me.

I was getting closer to Lucifer's burial ground. I could sit and listen and hear him deep in the earth, feel his call vibrate through my body, and I was close, so close. I didn't need to get distracted by a woman with a mouth that wouldn't stop moving and erotic images invading my mind.

Why the hell had Sammael brought her up to the cave in the first place? He knew better than anybody that place should be off-limits, particularly to an interloper like Allie Watson. It was the closest we'd come to Lucifer, the Light, and to have her bumbling around with her incessant questions was close to blasphemy.

Not that I believed in blasphemy. That was part of why I was here, wasn't it? Because I, like the others, refused to follow the rules, to kill without question, to wipe out generations and scourge the land. I had looked on a human woman and fallen in love, and for that I was forever cursed.

Surely there was something wrong with an ethos that equated love with death. It was so long ago I wasn't sure I could remember what we'd been thinking, could barely remember her. But I couldn't forget the emotion, the passion that had driven me, the certainty that choosing life, choosing human love, was the right thing to do. It had been worth it, worth everything, and I had never regretted it.

I could regret the vulnerability, the need that had driven me to such a desperate act, but it no longer mattered. I had done what I had done, and I wouldn't wish it changed. But it would never happen again.

Uriel knew how to use vulnerabilities. He knew how to torture, even with the rules that kept him from wiping us out. I wasn't going to let him use me again.

So perhaps there were times when I wished I could still feel that innocent, powerful love. Hundreds upon hundreds upon hundreds of years, millennia, piling up, and I'd never been able to recapture that pure, essential passion that had made me destroy everything.

But I still would have done it. Chosen to fall. We'd been taught that the humans were like cattle—you trained them, destroyed them if they disobeyed, never answered their questions, and, most of all, never looked upon them with lust.

We'd been sent to earth with our appointed tasks. Azazel had been sent to teach the people metalwork; his job had been to train and to pass on the magic. The first twenty each had jobs, and we'd done well enough at first. But the longer we remained on earth, the more human we became. The hungers started, hunger for food, for life, for sex. And we started thinking that we could make this benighted world a better place. We could bring our wisdom and power, we could experience love and dedication. We would intermarry and our children would grow strong and there would be no more wars and God would smile.

God didn't smile. There were no children—the curse was swift and vicious. We were damned for eternity. Because of love.

No wonder the woman wandering around my rooms annoyed me. It wasn't just her prattle—she was right, it was a pleasant voice. But after all these years I had no use for humankind, for women in particular. And this woman, of all women. A moment of unexpected sentimentality, and I'd complicated my existence and that of the Fallen. No woman was worth it.

Still, it was my choice, my mistake, and my only option was to fix it, even if I wanted to pass her off. There had to be someplace we could send her where she wouldn't cause trouble. And then we could deal with Uriel's wrath.

I was the keeper of secrets, the lord of magic. Within

me resided all the wisdom of the ages, and I had been sent to earth to give that knowledge to its hapless inhabitants. So how could I be so fucking stupid?

I glanced down, adjusted myself, and followed her into the living room. She was sprawled on one sofa, barefoot. My clothes fit her too damned well—I was going to have to see about something loose that covered up all the curves but was colorful enough to keep her happy.

God, why did I have to start worrying about keeping a woman happy? Especially a woman like Allie Watson.

Her long, thick brown hair was much better than the short bleached cut she'd had when I found her. Her face was prettier without makeup. She shifted, turning to look at me without getting up.

I walked over to one end of the sofa. "Where do you want to live?"

She'd been looking both annoyed and slightly downcast, but at this she brightened. "I've got a choice where I go?"

I didn't think so, but I was grasping at straws. The one thing I knew, it couldn't be hell. It was nothing personal. I hadn't come this far to let Uriel win. "Maybe," I said, not exactly a lie. "I imagine it depends on your talents, where you can make yourself useful. What can you do?"

She appeared to consider this for a moment. "I

can write. My style is slightly sarcastic, but I'm sharp and literate."

"We have no use for writing."

"So I'm in hell after all," she said glumly. "No books?"

"What would we read? We've lived millennia."

"What about your wives?"

"I have no wives."

"I don't mean you specifically, I mean all the women here. Sarah and the others. Don't they want to read? Or do you guys give them such a fulfilling life, trapped here in the mist, that they don't need any kind of escape?"

"If they wanted to escape, they wouldn't be here," I said in the voice I used to shut down arguments.

I should have known it wouldn't do any good. She didn't seem to realize that was what my voice signified. "I'm not talking about physical escape," she argued. "Just those times when you want to curl up in bed and read about crazy make-believe worlds. About pirates and aliens and vampires . . ." Her voice trailed off beneath my steady gaze.

"What else can you do?"

She sighed. "Not much. I'm useless at Excel. I type fast, but I gather you don't have computers here." For a moment she looked horrified as she understood everything that meant. "No Internet," she said in a voice of doom. "How am I going to live?"

"You're not alive."

"Thanks for reminding me," she said grimly. "So clearly you don't need Excel. Let's see—I'm a demon at trivia, particularly when it comes to old movies. I'm actually quite a wonderful cook. I kill plants, so I'd be no good in a garden. Maybe you could find me some commune-type thing? Without the Kool-Aid."

I remembered Jonestown far too well. "You don't need the Kool-Aid, you're already dead," I said.

"Lovely," she said sarcastically. "So do I get married? Have kids? For God's sake, at least have sex again?"

"Again?" It always managed to startle me, the way women of the current times simply gave their bodies when and where they wished. Two thousand years ago they would have been stoned to death. A hundred years ago they would have been outcasts. The human women who came to Sheol had been the same over the ages. They had never known anyone but their bonded mates. Azazel had seen Sarah when she was a child and known she was going to be his, and he'd watched over her, keeping her safe, until she was old enough to be his bride. The same was true for all the others.

She was looking at me, clearly annoyed. "Yes, again," she said. "Women have sex, you know. They find a man, or a woman if they prefer, and if they're attractive and there's no reason not to, they have sex. Are you totally unconnected with modern reality?"

"I know people have indiscriminate sex," I said irritably, feeling foolish. I didn't like the idea of her with another man. I wasn't about to consider why; I just didn't. "And I should have known you'd be one of them."

"Yes, I'm the Whore of Babylon."

"Not even close," I drawled.

"Oh, Jesus," she said. "Are you always so literal?"

"What other choice is there?"

She was fuming. This was good—I was annoying her as much as she annoyed me. I could keep this up for a while without any difficulty. We struck sparks off each other.

I decided to sum things up. "All right, we've decided you can cook, which might be a valuable skill elsewhere. Anything else?"

She looked at me as if considering something, and I had no intention of trying to divine what. That brief glimpse of her sex fantasies had been disturbing enough. And then she smiled, a slow, wicked smile. "You don't want to know," she said in a lazy, totally sensuous drawl.

This was a waste of time. In a short while the Council would convene, and they would decide what would happen to her. I could argue, but in the end there wasn't much I could do to save her. I knew what their decision would be.

It shouldn't bother me. But it did. And the sooner I got away from her, the easier it would be.

"You're right," I said. And I ran.

THIRTEEN

I WAS ALONE AGAIN IN THE STARK white apartment. The relief mingled with anxiety—it was easier being alone. I knew I'd basically driven him away; all I had to do was mention sex and he ran like a terrified virgin. Though if anyone was a virgin around here, it was me.

No, not literally. I'd had tons of lovers. Well, four, but you couldn't really count Charlie, who had performance issues, and the one-night stand with what's-his-name was more the result of too many cosmopolitans and a fit of self-pity. It hadn't been a pretty sight.

Still, two relatively decent relationships hardly made me a virgin. But compared to Raziel's thousands of years of sex and marriage, I most assuredly came up short. So how dared he have that "You've had *sex*" attitude? Typical of this patriarchal place, but I had no intention of putting up with it.

At least sex was a weapon I could use when I was feeling far too defenseless. I could get rid of Raziel simply by envisioning having sex with him, and he wouldn't linger to see the truth behind the erotic fantasy, see just how pathetic a lover I really was. Not that it mattered—I was getting the feeling that I was looking on an eternity of celibacy, just like Raziel. Except in my case, it wouldn't be by choice.

Who would I have here if I could have anyone? That was a no-brainer. Azazel was nasty, and I'd learned to avoid self-destructive relationships. Sammael was too young, even if he was millennia older than I was. I just got a wrong feeling from him. There was Tamlel, who seemed quite sweet, but I didn't want him either. If I was forced to have sex with anybody I'd met so far, I'd choose Raziel. Like it or not, I felt bonded to him, even if it only went one way. He was my man, the only connection with my old world, and I was holding on for dear life.

That bond was going to break, of course. It was temporary, just long enough to get me through to the other side. Hey, maybe I'd get to go to heaven after all, despite what he'd said, a sunny, happy place with angels who actually played harps. I could live among the clouds, visit my dead relatives, and look down on the poor foolish mortals with compassion.

Though an eternity of that could get old pretty fast. This was no trip to Hollywood, but the alternatives weren't that appealing. As long as I could keep Raziel out of my brain, I'd be able to figure out a way to deal with all this. Or a way to get out of it. There was always some kind of loophole. These things weren't written in stone.

Well, come to think of it, they probably were, literally, somewhere. And my efforts to keep Raziel out of my brain had only resulted in his abandoning me, which wasn't particularly helpful. I was probably going to need him if I wanted to get out of here, and making him crazy might not be the smartest thing to do. He might get pissed off enough to agree to the Grace, which was more like a curse. If he was really motivated, he might be able to return me to the one place he said he couldn't. Home.

Oh, I wasn't picky. It didn't have to be the same life, the same job, the same face. I could go back as anyone. I just wanted, needed, to go back.

On the other hand, my only defense was thinking about having sex with Raziel, and I found it . . . distracting. Disturbing. Arousing. Okay, I had to admit it. He was inspiring some wickedly lustful thoughts, whether he was around or not. I could spend a perfectly delightful afternoon doing absolutely nothing but indulging in sex fantasies about my beautiful, angry kidnapper and enjoy myself tremendously.

Unfortunately, that might leave me a bit too vulnerable, and I couldn't afford to let him see that. If he saw weakness, he'd exploit it without hesitation.

At least I was alone, with no one watching me. I didn't have to make conversation, be perky, put on a cheery face. All I had to do was try to make sense of what had happened to me. I didn't need to be distracted by a blood-sucking angel with the face of a . . . well, of an angel and the personality of a puff adder. Whom I somehow, inexplicably, longed for.

There, I'd admitted it. The 12-step groups were right—admitting it was the first and hardest part of owning a problem. Raziel was most definitely a problem, as far as I was concerned.

He didn't like me. I shouldn't find that particularly distressing. Yes, I was counting on him to protect me when my case was brought before the tribunal or whatever the hell it was, and he'd promised he wouldn't let them Grace me. Still, he'd made it clear that he thought women should be seen and not heard. Fat chance of that. I'd never been the silent, docile type and even the fear of God, or Uriel, wasn't going to get me started now.

If it weren't for Sarah, I'd be feeling completely defeated. I liked her, even if her husband seemed like an even bigger asshole than Raziel. Azazel was tall, dark, and grumpy, his body radiating a kind of bleak disapproval that made Raziel seem warm and fuzzy in comparison. Even Sammael hadn't been a barrel of laughs. I didn't know the names of the others, except Tamlel, of course, though I'd seen several of them. There had been at least a dozen men in the room where I'd seen Raziel at Sarah's wrist. Would Sarah and Raziel and maybe Tamlel be enough to sway them?

Suddenly I could see that strange scene all over again, the odd, unearthly light, the chanting, the smell of incense and something more elemental: the coppery scent of blood. I shuddered, feeling warm and slightly faint. I would have given a lot not to have walked in on that. Knowing about it would have been difficult enough; seeing it gave me a strange, edgy feeling. Like I'd watched someone having sex, or accidentally witnessed something slightly perverse but . . . arousing.

Slightly perverse? He was drinking the blood of his friend's wife. No wonder I was left with an unsettled feeling every time I thought of it. It felt almost as if someone had touched me.

I wouldn't make that mistake again. No flinging open doors—I'd knock first and wait for someone to open them. What these . . . these people did in the privacy of their own rooms was fine with me. I just wanted to get the hell away from here.

Though not literally. Being a reasonable, twenty-first-century woman, I had never believed in hell. It seemed to me that there was enough horrific punishment meted out on earth to satisfy the most vengeful god, and why should the universe duplicate efforts? Hell was warfare, children who died before their parents, drug addiction, poverty, violence. It always seemed to me that if someone screwed up big-time, it was simpler just to send them back for another go-round.

Then again, I'd never believed that people who suffered had brought it on themselves, so that sort of shot a hole in my cosmic theory of justice. Nevertheless, some fiery pit with a chortling devil holding a pitchfork had seemed more of a twisted Disney fantasy than anything else.

Apparently I was wrong.

Though no one had said anything about Satan. Come to think of it, some of the biblical propaganda posited that the first fallen angel, Lucifer, was Satan, king of hell. Which didn't really jibe with what was going on here.

I was curious, but truth be told, it wasn't just intellectual curiosity that made me determined to stay right here.

Raziel had something to do with it.

Okay, he was way too gorgeous, and gorgeous men made me feel like a troll. I could make an exception. Whether I liked it or not, I felt drawn to him, tied to him, turned on by him; and while I was putting out a lot of energy fighting it, I was losing the battle. It didn't matter—he was more than capable of resisting me, and I wasn't going to make a fool of myself. It wasn't the first time I'd suffered the adolescent pangs of unrequited, er, lust.

The sun was already setting, sinking into the dark green ocean, the golden color streaking toward me with greedy fingers. I looked down, and I could see Raziel walking on the beach, with Azazel and some of the others beside him. They were deep in conversation, and from such a distance I could barely see their expressions, much less hear what they were saying. But whatever it was, it wasn't good.

Of course there were no women walking and talking. No women angels. It really annoyed me—the patriarchal control extended millennia, apparently.

I turned away. Apparently the only way to make baby fallen angels was to have female angels in the first place, and someone had neglected to create them.

I was starving. How had he gotten that food up here last night? Was this some kind of fairy-tale world, where all I had to do was wish to make it happen? I closed my eyes and tried to visualize a quart of Ben & Jerry's, then opened them again. Nothing on the coffee table in front of me, but on a whim I slid off the sofa and went to the freezer, looking inside to see . . . absolutely nothing. Crap.

Maybe it needed Raziel's magic touch.

I started moving around the apartment, restless, trying to keep my mind off my stomach. One bedroom—his, with the king-size bed in the middle of it. Looking at it made me start thinking about points south of my stomach, and I quickly elevated my mind to purer matters. Someone had made the bed, so maybe the place came with maid service, which was a good thing. I wasn't about to start picking up after him, though chances were he was neater than I was. Most people were.

One closet, and not much in the way of clothing. I'd already rummaged through and borrowed the stuff most likely to fit me. The rest would be impossibly tight on my far-from-coltish figure, assuming I could even get the clothes on. Besides, the black was almost as depressing as the white.

I guess had to give up on the idea of ever being lithe or willowy. I was going to spend eternity being just this side of voluptuous, and I didn't like it.

On the other hand, I'd never get fat, so that was something.

I wandered into the kitchen. The sun was flame red now, reflecting off the windows in front of me, and only a small sliver was left above the horizon. Once it dropped, everything would be dark, and I leaned against the counter, watching. If the sun rose and set here, surely this must be the real world, and I must be alive. Otherwise it made no sense. Why bother with all the trappings of normal life when reality was so far removed?

The last shimmer of red dipped beneath the foamy surface, and I didn't move, almost in a meditative state as I watched the water churn and splash, the air cool and damp against my face. I licked my lips and could taste salt, and I found myself smiling. My mother had told me to lick my lips when we went to the seashore— it was the souls of the dead babies giving me a welcome kiss, trying to drag me down with them.

Hildegarde Watson had never been a bundle of laughs. Why she thought dead babies would end up in the ocean had never made sense, but I never tried to reason with my mother. It was always a losing proposition.

But damn, the old lady would be tickled pink to know that her blasphemous daughter was consorting with angels. Sleeping with one, in fact, though it wasn't quite the kind of "sleeping with" that I tended to think of. And it was safer not to let my mind go in that direction, not when it came to Raziel.

Actually, it was much more likely to be Neptune or Poseidon who was going around kissing me with salt-chapped lips. The gods of Mount Olympus were always a lot more entertaining than the Judeo-Christian God, who tended to be obsessed with punishment and sin. Not that Hildegarde believed in any god but her own angry, moralistic one who'd somehow morphed out of a gentle, loving Jesus.

I really should have hedged my bets, since it was

my mother's gloomy god who'd turned out to be the one with the power. Though it seemed he was even pre-Judeo-Christian. I wondered what Hildegarde would think of that. She'd flip.

I should try harder to get the hell out of here, and I probably would if I knew where to go. I was on borrowed time with Raziel—sooner or later he was going to sneak into my brain and see the doleful daydreams I was trying to fight, see the unbidden, lustful feelings that were stronger than anything I'd ever felt in my life. And that would be humiliating. If I couldn't control my—my crush, then I needed to escape. I just needed to know where.

I was so hungry I could eat his pristine white sofa. Someone had cleared away my dishes from the night before, so I couldn't scavenge for leftovers. The doughnuts were long gone, and I was bereft.

I flopped down on the sofa, putting a hand over my eyes as I moaned piteously. Ben & Jerry's, I thought longingly. Super Fudge Chunk or Cherry Garcia, to start with. If I hadn't already embraced the motto "Life is uncertain, eat dessert first," the last twenty-four hours or so would have convinced me. But Raziel's refrigerator had been as stark and barren as this apartment. No help there.

After that, lasagna, thick and gooey, with gobs of garlic bread and cheese, accompanied by a nice cabernet. At this rate, I'd settle for a can of Ensure.

I moaned again, turning over on my stomach and hiding my head against the cushions. The thought of food filled me with such longing I almost thought I could smell it. Lasagna, which I'd assiduously avoided during my dieting years. In retrospect, that seemed to be my entire freaking adult life.

"Allie." Sarah's soft voice penetrated my misery.

I flipped over, rattled, to find Sarah standing in the living room beside a younger woman holding a tray. "I didn't hear you come in," I said, feeling embarrassed. Apparently Sarah didn't hold with knocking.

Sarah's faint smile might have been an apology or it might not. "This is Carrie. She's Sammael's wife, and she's one of our newest residents. I thought you two might like to talk."

I looked at the newcomer. Carrie was another tall one, with long blond hair, a sweet smile, and a shadow in her perfect blue eyes. Clearly the Fallen chose Aryan Amazons to marry, which let me out. Not that I wanted to be in the running anyway, I reminded myself. I even managed a welcoming smile. "That would be great. That wouldn't be dinner, would it?" I looked pointedly at the tray, my spirits rising.

"I hope you like lasagna," Sarah said cheerfully. "I'll go put the ice cream in the freezer."

I recognized the Ben & Jerry's packaging—who wouldn't?—and I didn't bother to ask what flavors. I knew.

Carrie set down the tray and sat opposite me, pulling the covers off the plates. "No garlic bread," she said with a faint smile. "It interferes with the blood flow."

A stray shiver danced down my backbone. I looked carefully at the young woman, probably five years younger than I was, but there were no marks on her neck or wrists. Then again, there had been no marks on Sarah's wrist just after Raziel had fed from her. I squirmed, still bothered by the thought. Though far more bothered by the notion of Raziel at Sarah's thin, blue-veined wrist than of anyone else feeding from her.

"What blood?" I asked, helping myself to the lasagna, too hungry to be squeamish. I didn't really want to know, but I was trying to be polite.

"The blood I give Sammael," she said simply. "Garlic affects clotting time."

This sounded perfectly reasonable, if you didn't consider what they were doing with the blood in the first place and how they were getting it. I forcibly swept it out of my mind. "Do you want some of this?" I gestured toward the overburdened plate. They seemed to bring me twice as much as I wanted. At this rate I'd get—no, I wouldn't.

"I'll wait and eat with Sammael. He prefers it that way. Right now he and the other Fallen are looking at the defenses before the meeting, making certain there's no way the Nephilim can break through. There have been rumors that they're going to try."

"There are always rumors," Sarah said softly, coming in from the kitchen. "It's better not to pay any attention to them. The men can walk around and mutter things and feel important, but in the end the Nephilim will either break in or not, and I don't think there's any way we can affect that."

"And the Nephilim are the flesh-eaters?" I asked, suddenly taking a good look at my bright red pasta. I set my plate down again.

Sarah nodded. "There are no words to describe them. A living nightmare. They've never been able to pierce the walls of Sheol, but that's no guarantee they won't." She fell silent for a moment, as if she were looking at something in the distance, something unbearable. And then she rallied, serene as ever. "In the meantime all we can do is live our lives. They've been a threat since the beginning of time—worrying gets us nowhere."

The lasagna was no longer sitting very well on my stomach, but I knew that the ice cream would take care of my nausea. There was nothing in this world, or whatever world I was in, that ice cream couldn't fix. I headed for the fridge, pausing to look out the windows at the men on the wide expanse of beach. "When would they be likely to attack?" I asked, staring at them. At him.

"After dark. The Nephilim cannot go out in daylight—it burns their flesh. They sleep during the day; then the hunger rouses them and they go in search of whatever they can find. And apparently they have found Sheol."

"Found it?"

"Sheol is guarded by the mists. They were lifted when you were brought in, and we're afraid that was enough to alert the monsters."

"You mean, I'm to blame for letting the crazies in?" I turned away from the beach.

"Of course not," Sarah said in her soothing voice. "They're not in, and they won't get in. They can storm the gates and threaten, but they cannot come in unless someone invites them. And no one would invite their own death."

Suddenly the air felt cold, almost clammy, and there was a feeling of foreboding that I couldn't shake. So much for a cheerful afterlife. "What about the Fallen? They can go out in the daylight. Do they have to be invited into a place before they can enter?"

She shook her head. "That's only for the unclean."

"And vampires aren't unclean?"

"We don't use that term," Carrie spoke up. "They're blood-eaters."

"It has too many negative connotations," Sarah explained. "The roles of the Fallen and the Nephilim have gotten mixed up over the years, and people have made them the stuff of nightmares. Only the Nephilim are the monsters."

"Who created them? Your just and loving God?"

Sarah ignored my sarcasm. "God sent new angels after the Fallen, to destroy them. To make certain they weren't tempted, he made it impossible for them to feel. They fell anyway, and were driven mad, and he cursed them as well, made them flesh-eaters and abominations. After that, he stopped trying."

"But they can't get in, right? The Nephilim, I mean. And even if they did, they'd probably have a hard time getting to the top floor of this place, wouldn't they?" I wasn't usually such a wuss, but I had a horror of cannibalism. Jeffrey Dahmer made me physically ill. I always figured I'd been eaten in a previous lifetime, though the way things were going, maybe that was part of my future and not my past.

"If they get in, everyone will die," Sarah said. "There will be no place to hide, not even up here." She must have seen my expression, for she quickly came up with a slight, dismissive laugh that was almost believable. Almost. "But you're right, they're not going to get in. The Fallen are worried because they've reached our borders, when they never have before. They still won't be able to break through the final barrier."

She sounded very certain. And I didn't believe it for a minute. I needed ice cream.

It was Cherry Garcia *and* Super Fudge Chunk, which cheered me up, at least partially. I grabbed one container and a spoon and went over to sit cross-legged on the pristine sofa next to Carrie's silent figure. I was half-tempted to spill some, just to add some color to the place. I gestured with the round container. "Either of you want any? There are more spoons. Sharing Ben & Jerry's is a very bonding experience."

Sarah laughed. "We're already bonded, Allie. The ice cream is unnecessary. You enjoy it." She took the seat opposite me. "How are you and Raziel getting along?"

"He hates me," I said cheerfully. If I couldn't have him, I could at least enjoy annoying him.

"Oh, no!" Sarah said. "Raziel doesn't hate anyone. At least—"

"Trust me, he hates me. I'm not too fond of him either." It wasn't exactly a lie. "He thinks I'm a pain in the ass."

"Surely not," Sarah said.

"Surely yes. And explain to me about the hive mind."

"The what?"

"How does Raziel know what I'm thinking when I'm with him? How did you know I wanted lasagna and Ben & Jerry's? Does anyone have any secrets, any privacy, in this place?" I knew I was sounding querulous but I couldn't stop myself.

"Secrets usually cause trouble," Sarah murmured. "But there is privacy. While most of us can discern what other people are thinking if we listen carefully, it's more polite not to. We can pick up on your basic needs, if you want food, or would like to go for a walk, or want company. The more important things will only be accessible to Raziel. And I'm afraid he doesn't have to be in your company. He knows what goes on in your mind even when he's elsewhere."

"Great," I said. "No wonder he doesn't like me. My thoughts have been less than charitable." And less than pure. So he knew absolutely everything. If he wanted. He was also capable of turning off the one-way radio. I allowed myself a brief flash of how I'd looked in the racy underwear Jason had bought me in the hopes of rekindling our love affair. I'd really looked quite luscious, but it had been too little, too late.

At least it might help to keep Raziel out of my mind.

Carrie suddenly stiffened. "We need to go," she said, rising in one fluid motion, more graceful than I'd ever managed.

Sarah nodded, her serene expression replaced with a worried frown, and the dank, anxious feeling that had been slithering around inside me hit with full force.

I was on my feet before I realized it. "Is it time for the meeting?"

Sarah nodded. "Just stay put. If there's a problem, Raziel will come for you."

"Fat chance," I started to say, but they were already gone, abandoning me in the sterile apartment as darkness closed down around me.

FOURTEEN

I MANAGED TO STAY PUT FOR APPROX-imately fifteen minutes. Patience had never been one of my particular virtues. Consider-ing that I spent the time pacing from the window in the kitchen to the living room and back, sitting down and jumping up again, I would have considered five minutes to be quite remarkable. Fifteen was a world record, as far as I was concerned.

But if the Nephilim were coming, I was damned if I was going to stay in these rooms like a sitting duck, waiting to be someone's dessert. I headed for the door, steeling myself for the endless flights of stairs. At least it was downhill, and if I didn't end up as stew meat I'd make Raziel fly me back up. The thought sent little prickles down my spine.

The door was locked.

The knob turned—it wasn't a simple matter of

picking a lock. Not that I'd ever picked a lock, but I'd watched enough caper movies that I figured I could probably handle it if I had a bobby pin. Did they even make bobby pins anymore? Probably not in Sheol.

No, the door was sealed, as if there were no separation between the thick walls and the door at all.

I wasted far too much time pounding on it, kicking it, cursing Raziel, since I knew he, not Sarah, was to blame for this particular heinousness. I didn't waste any time calling for help—no one would pay any attention, even if they heard me. For a very brief moment I considered sitting back down on the sofa and coming up with the most scorchingly torrid sexual fantasy my imagination could create, and I had one hell of an imagination, especially with Raziel for inspiration. But that was a double-edged sword. The more I fantasized, the more vulnerable I felt. The longer I was around him, the more I was drawn to him. And that was far too dangerous.

Maybe they were still arguing over what to do with me. Maybe if the Nephilim breached the walls, my future would be moot.

I wasn't about to give up without a fight. I looked over at the windows. Sammael had pushed out a section when he'd taken me up to the mountain—surely there must be some kind of emergency exit from the top floor of this place? I wasn't sure just how vulnerable the Fallen were, but their wives were certainly mortal.

I moved along the bank of glass, pushing gently, but nothing seemed to shift. I leaned out one window, peering into the darkening night, and shivered, even though the night was warm. In the distance I thought I could hear the muffled sounds of animals, strange growls and strangled screams. The Nephilim, still outside the gates of Sheol. But for how long?

There was a narrow balcony directly below the windows, no more than a yard deep, with a low wall beyond it, the only barrier between the house and a free fall to the ground far below. The lower floors of the building were cantilevered out—surely there was a way to climb down if I was careful. I'd always been relatively sure-footed, at least before I'd taken a header in front of a city bus. I pushed the window open, swung one leg over the sill, and climbed out into the night air.

The sounds in the darkness were louder, the animal howls and cries of the lost souls filling the night, and I almost changed my mind. But the ocean breeze came through, calming my nervousness, and I concentrated on that, trying to shut the other noise out of my mind. I moved down to one end of the narrow balcony, peering over the edge.

It didn't look promising. I could try sliding down the smooth expanse of what might be concrete and hope I landed on the balcony one flight down, but that would get me down only one floor, and there were multiple flights below that.

I found the perfect spot and climbed onto the ledge atop the retaining wall, then sat, staring up into the inky sky, watching as the stars came out, breathing in the night air and the tang of the ocean as a slow, decisive calm began to fill me. Nothing would get to me. No creature was going to rip me into pieces. At least, not now. I was safe here. I had absolutely no idea how I knew it, but I did. This was where I belonged.

Raziel would see to it. If nothing else, I could trust him. Nothing would happen to me. He was down there arguing my case, and he had Sarah for backup. I knew he would keep me safe.

I leaned back, lying down on the ledge to stare at the sky overhead. I wasn't used to counting on someone else to look after me—I treasured being self-sufficient, needing nothing and no one. My crazy-ass mother had brought me up practically isolated from a normal environment, awash in her extremist religion that was a combination of fundamentalist Christianity and survivalism, seasoned with an odd touch of anti-Semitism. Odd, because my mother had been born Hildegarde Steinberg, of devoutly Orthodox Jewish parents. I never knew who my father was, though she'd insisted they'd been married. I always figured she'd bitten his head off after mating.

It was little wonder I had always considered myself an atheist. I had firmly consigned gods, angels, and demons to the ranks of mythology.

Wrong. I could imagine who was having the last laugh now. Trust me to have found an afterlife ruled by vampires instead of cherubic babies with bare bottoms and tiny harps. I suppose it was better than no afterlife at all, but the Elysian fields would have been preferable.

The animal howls were fading—the walls of Sheol must have held, at least for now. Raziel was on his way back—I seemed to know that as well. Was his annoying mind-fuck a two-way street? Or was it some kind of cosmic GPS? He was coming back to me, and I felt my skin heat beneath the clothing. His clothing. I should take it off.

I did nothing, lying there on the ledge. I kicked off one loose shoe, letting it drop onto the balcony, then the other. It slipped and went over the edge, and I could hear it, bouncing, hitting against things as it fell, it fell—

I automatically sat up, trying to reach for it even though it was too late, and at the last minute I sat back before I went over as well. I lay back on the ledge, trembling slightly.

I closed my eyes, concentrating on the sound of the surf. For a moment I could feel his hands on me, on my breasts, and my body lifted instinctively, then sank back, wiping the image from my mind. Where had that come from?

Two-edged sword, I reminded myself. Was it possible it had come from him? No, it couldn't be. And I was much better off thinking about Super Fudge Chunk.

Wasn't there a song about love being better than ice cream, better than chocolate? Did that go for sex as well? And, damn, why was I suddenly plagued with the one-track mind of a horny adolescent boy?

So, I wouldn't think about ice cream. And I most definitely wouldn't think about sex. Even though I could almost feel his hands on me, feel my nipples harden in the warm night air, feel him—

Shit, I thought, jerking in protest.

And immediately fell over the edge.

I KNEW THE MOMENT I walked into the council chamber that things were going to take a very ugly turn. Azazel stood at the head of the table, wearing an expression that said there was no negotiating, and the others, most of them, looked equally grim. Only Sarah and Tamlel looked concerned, and that wasn't enough to keep the rest from disposing of the unfortunate female in the most logical way possible.

I didn't want to call her by name. For some reason, if I called her by name it would make the damnable tenuous bond between us even stronger. Allegra.

Allie. A thorn in my side, a pain in my ass. But I wasn't going to let them get to her.

"We will discuss things in order of importance," Azazel said. "Starting with the Nephilim. They are at our gate. For thousands of years we've kept Sheol hidden from them, and suddenly they have found us. They are gathering there—I do not know their number, but all it would take would be a moment of inattention, a slip, and they would overrun us."

"We can fight," Michael said. "I don't know why you assume they would have the upper hand. I say let them in, and we'll get rid of them once and for all."

"Assuming we managed to prevail." Azazel's voice was stern. "And assuming our numbers are not too greatly diminished, we still have the problem of other Nephilim. They roam throughout the world in search of the Fallen, and if these know of us, then others will follow. It will be battle after battle, death and carnage."

"So?" Michael said.

"Not all of us are warriors, Michael."

"We need to be. We are at war, with Uriel and his legion, with the Nephilim who roam and devour at his behest. This won't be over until the Nephilim are wiped from the face of this earth."

"And then what do we do? Uriel will send someone else, sooner or later, and I sense it might be sooner." He turned his cold gaze on me. "What do you know of the girl?"

I tensed. "I was sent to take her. I was about to pass her over to the next life when I saw the flames and pulled her back. I don't know why—instinct. She had done nothing to merit eternal damnation."

"And that's your place to judge?" Azazel said.

I'd known Azazel too long to react. "No. But we shouldn't follow blindly when our instincts say it's wrong. That is why we fell in the first place—because we questioned. We failed to follow orders but followed our hearts instead. It's bad enough when we have to face Uriel's merciless wrath. If we judge each other, then we are doomed. She didn't deserve eternal damnation. She'd done nothing."

"She fornicated outside of marriage. She mocked the covenants. That would be enough for Uriel to condemn her."

"But not enough for us." Sarah's voice broke through, calm and assured. As the Source she had a voice on the Council, one she seldom used. Tonight was different. "Do we aspire to Uriel's level of perfection? Have we ever considered mindless punishment a reasoned response?"

Azazel's glance softened for a moment, but he said nothing.

"There's another possibility we need to discuss." This was Sammael, usually silent during these meetings, and I looked at him in surprise. I had always been one of Sammael's closest friends, a mentor of sorts. He hadn't been among the first of the Fallen, despite folklore, but followed soon after, and his adjustment had been more difficult. Eternal damnation was never easy, but Sammael had once been an idealist. Until Uriel had done with him.

"Yes?" Azazel's eyes narrowed.

"Her presence here might not be accidental."

For a moment I was speechless. "You think I betrayed the Fallen—"

"No, my brother," he said. "I think Uriel might have tricked you. Who is to say she's not a demon, sent into our midst to betray us to the Nephilim and to Uriel himself? How did the Nephilim suddenly arrive at our gates, when we have remained hidden for thousands upon thousands of years? We have never had a stranger come among us. You, Raziel, have never before stopped to consider who a traveler was or where he or she was heading. You've never believed it to be your concern, and the rest of us have felt the same. There are too many to deliver—we can't stop to pass our own judgment. But something made you stop." He looked at me, his brown eyes earnest and troubled. "I think she may have cast a spell on you."

I laughed. "Now you're saying she's a witch? I believe we left all that behind many hundreds of years ago."

"I'm saying she's a demon. Sent by Uriel to infiltrate and destroy us. You cannot deny he has demons at his command."

"No," I said slowly. Uriel ruled over both angels and demons, using them for whatever task he deemed necessary. Once long ago, in a moment of weakness, he'd explained himself: that it was far better for him to rule the demons and dark spirits of the world than let them fall into the hands of the Evil One.

The Evil One he believed to be Lucifer.

We knew there was no source of evil. No Satan, no Iblis, no Prince of Darkness. Evil came from within, just as love and beauty did. Evil was the price humans paid for being alive.

It was a price that had never entered the hallowed confines of Sheol. Unless Sammael was right, and Allie Watson was one of Uriel's servants.

It would explain a great deal. The attraction I felt to her was irrational, when I had sworn to mate with no human. I liked soft, sweet women, not females who talked back and questioned my decisions and dared to enter my consciousness, as only a bonded mate should do. If she'd been sent by Uriel, then we had only one choice.

Azazel had turned to me. "Does this seem likely? You know her best. Has she been sent to open the gates of Sheol and bring us all to ruin?"

"No," Sarah said before I could speak. "Absolutely not. She has a reason to be here, one I don't yet understand, but there is no evil—"

"I was speaking with Raziel," Azazel said in a cold voice, and Sarah's mouth snapped shut. I could almost be amused—he was in for trouble tonight—but I was in no mood to laugh.

"It's possible," I said reluctantly. "It would explain a number of anomalies."

"I think we have no choice, then," Azazel said. "Either she was properly judged and sentenced to hell, or she is here to destroy us. She needs to be returned to the eternal fires."

He was right. For her to have been sent there in the first place, there had to be a reason, even if I hadn't been able to discover it. And if she was a traitor, a demon in our midst, then hell was where she belonged.

"You don't have to be the one to take her," Azazel added with a trace of compassion. "One of the others can go."

I said nothing, refusing to accept their ruling. They couldn't do this. I wouldn't let them.

"You're idiots, all of you," Sarah snapped, finally having had enough. "Do you no longer trust your Source? Do you think I have no knowledge of what is to be and what is right? None of you count divination among your gifts, but I have seen things."

"What?" Azazel said sharply.

But Sarah shook her head. "That is not for you to know. Not yet. You may either ignore my counsel and destroy a woman because you think she might be a witch, just like the wicked ones of old. Or you can give her time. Give Raziel time to discover why she's here." She turned to look at me. "Are you certain she's not your mate? That would explain everything."

It would indeed. It would also be a lie. I had known the women I loved from the first time I saw them. There had been a recognition, a knowledge, a peace that was far removed from the anger I felt around Allegra. Allie.

But I wasn't going to condemn her to death, not without being certain.

So I lied.

"There is a strong bond between us," I said, with at least a bit of truth. "And an attraction."

"Then go to her, Raziel," Sarah said. "Look into her eyes. You would know a demon if you looked deep enough. Touch her. A demon cannot make love; they can only steal your essence. It's a simple test."

A simple test. Put my hands on Allie Watson and see if she turns into a monster. I would kill her then, if she did. Demons were easy enough to kill as long as you recognized them. Their throats were delicate, easily crushed. All I had to do was taste her. . . .

I wouldn't do that. I was ready to prove she wasn't

a demon, but I was far from willing to perform the one act that would bind us irrevocably.

"I'll give you this night, Raziel," Azazel said. "But no one is to let her move around the compound without a guard. We cannot afford to take any risks. If she's human, we need to discover if she was sent by Uriel. If she's a demon . . . kill her. Do you understand?"

"I believe I've never been particularly slow," I said, keeping my anger in check. "If you think I'd have any hesitation about destroying a demon, then you don't know me very well."

"In the meantime, no one is to disturb them unless Raziel calls for help," Azazel warned the others.

"And what if she's simply an ordinary human woman, unfairly judged by Uriel, who has thrown herself on our mercy?" Sarah demanded.

"We can't afford to have mercy when Uriel shows none. Whether he's behind this woman's presence here or not, we can't let down our guard."

I looked at Azazel's stony face. He was right, of course. I knew it, Sarah knew it. I pushed back from the table, letting no expression cross my face. "I will let you know," I said, and left the room.

I stopped four flights up, finally alone in the dimly lit stairwell. I leaned back against the wall, closing my eyes. I didn't want to touch her. She was everything I wanted to keep away from—I didn't want her mouth or her body, I didn't want her soul or her heart. It would have been so easy to get rid of her. To say nothing. Even Sarah had been helpless to stop the inexorable judgment.

I could see her, practically feel her beneath my hands, her breasts, the sweet taste of her skin. It burned inside me. At least my own thoughts and fantasies were shielded from her inquisitive mind. It was the only thing that made the hunger bearable.

I shoved away from the wall, furious with myself. Who the hell did I think I was? I had never shied from a task before, and this was simple enough. Touch her, look into her eyes, and I would know. If the answer was the wrong one, I would snuff out her already dubious existence. I put my hand on the railing and closed my eyes, listening for her.

And then I flew.

FIFTEEN

I WAS GOING TO FALL, I KNEW IT. MY hands were numb and slippery with sweat, and even though I'd managed to gain a tiny bit of purchase on the masonry with my bare foot, it wasn't enough to hold me. It was a long way down. *How many times can a woman die?* I thought wildly. This time there wouldn't be any coming back from it—if you died in heaven, or whatever the hell this place was, then you must be really dead.

Maybe Raziel could get out of trouble by scooping up my dead body and dropping it into that hole in the middle of nowhere. Would I perk up once I was roasting in hell, or was I going to be lucky enough for a big fat nowhere?

I didn't want to die. Not again. I didn't want an endless night, silence, nothingness. I wanted whatever I could grab at, food, sex, music, laughter. But my fingers were slipping, my foot lost what small hold it had, and I felt myself let go, falling backward into the darkness, the brightness of the stars overhead the last thing I was going to see.

And then something moved in front of them, the dark iridescent blue of death, I thought dreamily, when death should have been black, and I smiled. It wasn't pain after all; it felt as if I were being cradled in someone's arms. If this was death, then I shouldn't have been afraid of it. It felt safe, warm, as if I were exactly where I belonged and—

Bright light slammed into my eyes, and I let out a howl as I put up my arm to cover them as someone dumped me on my back. Maybe I was going to end up in hell after all, I thought grumpily, refusing to move my arm. If I didn't look, maybe it would all go away.

But curiosity had always been a character defect, and the sound of his footsteps was enough to make me move my arm and look. I was back in the apartment, on one of the pristine sofas, and Raziel was just slamming the window shut before turning to look at me, furious. As usual.

"How big an idiot are you?"

I ignored him, sitting up and looking around me with a blazing smile. "I'm not dead," I announced.

"That depends on your definition," he said, moving to the door. So he was going to abandon me as quickly as he'd saved me. I couldn't complain—it was better than being smashed to bits on the terrace below.

But he wasn't going anywhere. He simply locked the door. I was going to point out that it was already hermetically sealed, but figured he knew what he was doing. He waved his hand and the lights dimmed, and I wondered whether it was cosmic power or some kind of motion sensor. A celestial Clapper. "What did you think you were doing?"

Well, at least he was talking to me. "I just wanted some fresh air," I said hopefully. "Someone locked me in, and I don't like being shut up. I'm claustrophobic."

"No you're not. Not anymore. You were looking for a way to get downstairs, weren't you? So you could see what was going on." Ah, he knew me too well. Already. "Curiosity is not a trait we value in Sheol. You're lucky I came in time."

"Yeah, what about that?" I said in a calm voice. "I thought you knew what I was thinking. I was sending you every distress signal I could come up with. Why didn't you come?"

"If I had to spend all my time in your convoluted mind, I'd immolate myself," he said. "I'd prefer to keep away, but I was coming up here anyway and I thought I'd find out whether you were asleep or not."

"Hardly asleep. I haven't had dinner yet."

It was too dark to see if he rolled his eyes, but I had the definite impression that he'd done the angelic equivalent of it. "You don't need to eat as often here."

"It's not a question of need, it's a question of want. I eat for the same reason I read. Not for nourishment, but for sensual pleasure," I said brightly. And then regretted it. Mentioning sensual pleasure opened up a subject that was far too sensitive, as far as I was concerned. I didn't want him wandering around inside my mind, reading my irrational and badly banked desires.

He was holding himself very still, looking at me, and there was something in the air, a tension that slid beneath my skin. I could feel my heart beating, not the terrified flutter of minutes ago as I'd faced death, but a slow, relentless thudding that seemed almost audible. *Damn,* I thought.

He made a gesture, and the lights in the kitchen dimmed. The room filled with shadows, making me even more nervous. "You know, a gas fireplace would be nice in here," I said in a conversational tone, trying to lessen the tension that rippled beneath the surface. "It would make it cozy."

I half-expected him to wave his arm and a magic fireplace to appear, and then I shook myself. He wasn't a genie, granting my three wishes. Though I wasn't sure exactly what he was, at least as far as I was concerned.

"Since even a match could end up destroying me, I don't find fireplaces cozy at all. You'll have to do without one."

I'd forgotten. "Good point," I said brightly, trying not to look at him. I'd always had a healthy interest in sex, in men, but more often than not I found better things to do. I had better orgasms on my own, something that would doubtless shock the slightly prudish Raziel, and I'd often found boyfriends not worth the trouble. So why did I suddenly have to become obsessed with someone?

"I'm not prudish."

"Shit!" I shrieked as if I'd been pinched. I could feel the color flood my face. How could I have forgotten? His ability to hear my thoughts was almost the worst thing about this entire experience.

"Worse than dying?"

"Stop it!" I snapped, thoroughly flustered.

"How are your hands? Are you hurt?"

I looked down at them. My fingers were red, cramped, and I pushed off from the couch. "Fine," I said. "I'll just run some water over them." I wanted to get away from his far-too-observant eyes.

"You don't need to."

He was standing between me and the kitchen, effectively blocking the way. "I think that's my decision," I said, trying to circumvent him.

He was too big to get around. Before I could guess

his intention he'd taken both my hands in his, and his touch zinged through my arms like an electric shock. I jumped back, tripping over my own bare feet in my effort to get away from him.

He caught my elbow as I fell, righting me, then releasing me immediately. "You're very clumsy, aren't you?" he observed.

It didn't do any good to guard my tongue—he already knew what I was thinking. "You make me nervous."

"Why?"

"Let me count the ways," I said. "You're a guardian angel who tried to toss me into the flames of hell; you're a vampire; you think I'm a pain in the butt; and if it weren't for you, I'd be alive and living in New York City, minding my own business."

For a moment he said nothing. Then he spoke. "First of all, I'm not a guardian angel, not yours or anyone's. Guardian angels don't exist—they're just folklore."

"Sure they are. Like vampires."

He ignored that. "Second, you are most definitely a pain in the butt. You've disrupted my life as badly as I've disrupted yours—"

"I doubt that," I broke in dryly.

"Let me finish. If it were not for me, you'd be in hell right now. You were scheduled to die, and nothing can contravene that. Normally you would have simply ended up in the dark place. Most people don't have escorts, only the ones Uriel deems necessary. I have no idea why he thought you were so important—at first glance, you seem ordinary enough."

"Thanks so much," I said.

"But he had something in mind. You must have offended him with your books. Uriel is easily offended."

"I'm harmless," I protested, fully believing it.

"I doubt that. As for my being a blood-eater, that is no concern of yours. It has nothing to do with what is between us."

His words gave me an uncomfortable jolt. "What's between us? There's nothing between us."

"Of course there is." He moved away from me then, and I found I could breathe normally again. Or at least more normally. Apparently I'd been holding my breath, though I wasn't quite sure why.

I could see him quite well through the thick shadows. The light from the bedroom pooled at the entrance to the main room, and I could see the glitter of his strange eyes, the expression of weariness across the elegant lines of his face. He pushed his hair away from his face, as if pushing something unacceptable away from him. And then he lifted his head to look at me.

And I knew what was coming next, as clearly as if I'd thought of it myself.

"No," I said flatly.

A faint smile curved his mouth. "No, what? I didn't ask you anything."

"Just no," I said, refusing to show how nervous he made me. I moved, suddenly busy. "Do you have extra sheets, maybe a pillow? I can make up the couch for the night until we find someplace else for me to sleep. I certainly don't want to drive you out of your bedroom, though you were very kind to have brought me in there last night. At least, I assume it was you— maybe Sarah was responsible, which is very like her. She's quite kind, and I'm sorry I ever suggested she was—"

"Be quiet, Allie," he said.

It was the first time he'd used my name. Not my full name, but the more familiar nickname. I froze, my words vanishing, as if he'd shut them off with a wave of his hand as he had the lights.

He approached me slowly, and a part of me wanted to run. Not that there was any place to go except straight off the balcony. He'd locked the front door. Why?

He stopped directly in front of me, too close for me to escape, crowding me and yet not touching me. "Look at me," he said in a low, soothing voice.

"I am."

He shook his head and made another gesture, and overhead lights I hadn't known existed blazed on.

They should have been blinding, but I was already in some kind of daze. "Open your eyes and look at me," he said again, and his soft voice had steel beneath it.

So I did. Looked up into his gloriously striated eyes, almost like those of a cat. Looked up and felt him invade me, as surely as if he had me underneath him, skin to skin. He was inside me, an act of complete possession, and I tried to say something, to protest, but all that came out was a soft, defensive mew of pain. He didn't retreat, and I felt staked, like a butterfly with a giant pin through my heart. I could feel my body lift, rise slightly, and I knew I was no longer touching the floor. I tried to push him out, but he was much too strong to fight. All I could do was remain there, suspended, as he scoured my body, and I felt a scream inside my chest, my heart, desperate to escape.

And then, as quickly as it had happened, it was over, and he released me. The bright lights vanished, my feet touched the floor, and I collapsed, nerveless.

He caught me as I fell, and I wanted to scream at him, to hit him, but I couldn't summon the energy. He set me down on the sofa with unexpected gentleness. "Lie down," he murmured. "It will pass in a moment."

I had no choice. I lay back, trying to catch my

breath, trying to fight the sharp pain between my breasts, as if he'd caught my heart in his fist and squeezed it. I closed my eyes, and felt everything begin to fade. I had long enough to wonder if I was dying all over again, if Raziel had done something to end me. And then darkness came down.

CHAPTER

SIXTEEN

I SAT BACK ON THE SOFA ACROSS from her, watching her. Even in the shadowy light she was color against the soothing white, the richness of her thick brown hair, the warm tones of her skin, the black silk of the clothes she'd taken from me. She was heat, she was fire, deadly to me, and yet somehow irresistible.

She was no demon. I was as sure of that as I could possibly be, short of taking her blood. She was human, and vulnerable despite her attempts to shock me. She was vulnerable, and the best thing I could do was leave her alone.

I couldn't. Not after the Grace of Knowing. Looking so deeply into her had been an act of intimacy from which there was no coming back. There was a bond between us that I didn't want, but it existed anyway, and it was purely sexual. An animal need that I wasn't going to fight anymore. I was going to fuck her. I could imagine Uriel howling, and I thought the word again. *Fuck.* I was going to take her bed and wear myself out with her, and when she was climaxing I would look into her eyes and know the last bit of her, the place where even a demon couldn't hide. I would fuck her and make her come and know her.

And if she was a demon, I would kill her.

She stirred. She was going to be angry with me for what I'd done to her, and I didn't blame her. It was an invasion, one she'd accepted. One of many she'd accept.

I could scoop her up and carry her into the bedroom, have her clothes off before she realized what I was doing. It would simplify matters. But just as she had allowed me to look inside her, she would have to allow me to be inside her. And if she had any remaining defenses, they would shatter as she did.

She moved, then lay still. "You son of a bitch," she said quietly.

"I'm not the son of anything. How do you feel?"

"Like I've been violated."

"That's about right."

She sat bolt upright and glared at me, ready for battle. "And I don't suppose you feel any remorse."

"Why should I? I needed to see if you were a demon."

She looked at me blankly for a moment. "A

demon? Do they even exist? Hell, of course they do. Angels and demons and vampires and cannibals. What other treats do you have in store? Shape-shifters? Werewolves?"

I didn't move. I was hard, and had been since I'd gone into her, my body desperate to follow. And I knew, even as I'd pulled back, that I'd left enough behind that her defenses would be down.

I needed them that way. More than anything on this earth or the next, I wanted to be able to walk away from her. To leave my rooms, report to Azazel that she was an innocent, and leave her disposal up to them.

But I was afraid *disposal* would be the operative word. And even in such a short time, we'd come too far for me to let them take her. Too far for me to turn my back on her.

If Uriel had sent her to infiltrate us, then he would have sent her well armed. The Grace of knowing was powerful, but underestimating Uriel was always a mistake. I was sure she was innocent, caught by a series of coincidences. But I couldn't afford to be wrong.

She was still glaring at me, her eyes shuttered. I had seen all she would let me see. If I wanted to be certain, to protect Sheol as it needed to be protected, then I had no choice.

I was prepared for resistance. I had kept out of her

head as much as I could, but there was no mistaking that she felt the same bond I felt. The same intense, sexual need that I was an expert at denying, had been denying since the moment she had come into my world, thanks to those terrible shoes that had caused her death. I'd been counting on that resistance, along with my own, but that was out the window. The Grace of knowing was not enough.

I rose, and reached my hand out to her. "No," she said.

I waited. I could do anything I wanted with her. I could force her, then wipe the memory from her brain. I could simply take her blood, just enough to read her, not enough to make me sick. Blood from anyone but the Source or my bonded mate was dangerous, even in small amounts, but it was a risk I had to take.

"Come with me, Allie," I said. And I made her move, because I could. "Come."

And she rose.

I DIDN'T WANT TO MOVE. It didn't matter. He pulled me up and stood over me. I hated tall men— they made me feel weak and inconsequential. I was still wearing his clothes, his black jacket, his black T-shirt, his black silk trousers. He took the lapels of the jacket and pushed it off my shoulders, down my arms. I stood still, knowing I ought to argue, protest, anything but stand there and let him slide the jacket off me and toss it behind him onto the sofa.

He reached for the hem of my T-shirt, and I wanted to back away, but my feet were rooted to the floor. I tried to stem my panic. This was the fulfillment of a fantasy that obsessed half the teenage girls in the world. It didn't matter. Having sex with a fallen-angel-slash-vampire was a really bad idea.

"Please don't," I said, trying to sound calm and sure of myself. If he did this, I'd have nothing with which to fight him. If he did this, it would matter too much, and I wouldn't be able to break away. If he did this, it would break my heart.

He pulled my T-shirt up, and I unwillingly lifted my arms to let him peel it off, so that I was standing there in nothing but his loose pants low on my hips. I felt conspicuous, vulnerable, and it took all my self-control to just stand there and look at him.

"I should point out," he said with surprising gentleness, "that my favorite period of time was the Renaissance."

With all those voluptuous beauties. He was probably lying, but I gave him points for trying. I still didn't move.

"I'm not going to hurt you," he said. He was leaning down, his mouth so close I could feel the warmth of his breath on my face. "I wouldn't do this to you if it wasn't necessary."

I'd been ready for his kiss, but at this my eyes flew open. "What do you mean, 'necessary'?"

I was silenced, not by one of his slight gestures, but by his mouth on mine as he pulled me into his arms.

It was no sweet kiss of seduction, no chaste, heavenly kiss. It was full and openmouthed and carnal, and I stood frozen in shock as he put one arm around my waist, pulling me against his hard body, and the other had caught my chin, his long fingers cradling my face.

I'd been kissed before, of course. But never like this, with an almost cosmic sense of urgency and longing. I could feel my nipples harden against the solid warmth of his chest, and I could feel the heat between my legs, the clutch of longing in my belly. Who the hell was I trying to fool? I was turned on every time he was in the room.

He dragged his mouth away. "Stop thinking," he said a little breathlessly, and if it were anyone else, any other circumstances, I'd have thought he was turned on.

In fact, I could feel his cock against my belly, a hard ridge of flesh. Must be some angel trick, I thought dizzily, to be able to perform on command, even if he was doing it for obscure reasons that had nothing to do with desire—

"Stop thinking," he said again, his voice hot. "I

want you. All right? I don't want to—you're nothing but trouble. I wish I could just walk away from you. But I can't."

"I'm not getting into that bed with you," I said, one last attempt to preserve my self-control.

"If you say so."

There was no escape. Particularly because I didn't want to escape. I turned my back to him, but he simply pulled me against him, his arm around my waist, and carried me into the bedroom.

After the dimness in the living room the lights were blindingly bright, and I shut my eyes. I was pressed against him, his strength and heat spreading through me, and I wanted to sink back into him, letting my body flow into his, and I knew I was past protesting. Who was I fooling? I wanted this so badly my heart was pounding, my hands shaking, and I knew I was already wet. Ready for him.

He must have felt it. "Yes," he said, a low murmur of approval as he set me on my feet, my back still turned to him. His hands were on me, pushing the silk trousers and my underwear down with one movement so that they pooled around my ankles. He lifted me out of them and turned me so that I faced him, naked, totally vulnerable.

He looked at me, and the heat in his strange eyes was palpable, burning away the last of my doubts. And the last of his. I could feel his reserve melt away in the heat between us, and his breath was coming sharp and fast. "Were you sent here to torment me?" he whispered, sliding his arm around my waist, pulling me against him. "Did he know exactly what I needed, what I couldn't fight?"

He? Who? But before I could ask the question, he kissed me again, and I was lost, needing to get closer to him, needing his skin beneath my fingers. His tongue was in my mouth, and I welcomed it, reaching between us and pulling his shirt apart so I could touch his skin, his hot, smooth skin. His heart was racing, and I wanted to put my mouth against it, wanted to taste his flat nipples, wanted my mouth all over him.

Before I realized what he was going to do he slid his arm under me, lifting me. I twined my fingers through his thick hair, kissing him back, using my tongue, hearing my own quiet moan of surrender as surely as he unbuttoned his jeans. And then I could feel him against my sex, hard and heavy, and I knew it was going to hurt. He was too big, and he hadn't even touched me there, and I was the kind of woman who required a lot of foreplay, and if he was going to try this he was going to have trouble and it was going to—

He slid into me, smoothly, no pulling, no resistance, and reaction spiked through my body. I was sleek and wet and welcoming, and I shivered in primal delight. The more I had of him the more I needed, and the heat of his skin against my breasts was unbearably arousing. I was burning with need, shaking with it. He started to pull out, and I clutched at him, suddenly terrified he would leave me.

But he was already pushing back into me, deeper than the first thrust, slick and sure, deeper, thicker, harder, and when he pulled back I let out a cry, desperate.

This time he slammed into me, all the way in, pushing me hard up against the wall, and my body suddenly shattered. I let out a muffled scream, burying it against his shoulder, against the smell of clean cotton and warm skin, and another wave hit me, and then another, until I was sure I couldn't take any more.

If anything he seemed to grow bigger still inside me, and he pulled away from the wall, supporting me in his arms, and he was so strong it seemed effortless. He was moving faster now, filling me so deeply I thought I could taste him, and I convulsed in helpless pleasure at the thought. He gave in, pushing deep inside me, and I felt the hot pulse as he climaxed, my body milking him with answering contractions, and as the final wave washed over me I lost myself, as everything dissolved around us.

It was darkness, shimmering, shattering darkness, iridescent blue folding down around us, tightly, as soft as feathers wrapping around my back, sealing me into a cocoon of such infinite delight that I felt a stray climax sweep over me before everything vanished and there was nothing but pure, healing warmth.

I had no idea how long that blessed, velvet darkness lasted. I must have fallen asleep, because I opened my eyes to find that I was lying in the middle of his bed, naked, a sheet wrapped around me, and Raziel was nowhere to be seen. Of course. What man stayed around long after the fact?

I tried to turn over, then groaned in sudden discomfort. It had definitely been too long since I'd had sex, I thought dimly.

It must be the middle of the night. I managed to sit up, wincing slightly at the discomfort between my legs. I still felt the faint lingering of postcoital bliss, that heavenly warm feeling that washed over me, when I knew I shouldn't be quite so happy. Something was wrong, something was off, yet I couldn't remember what. I still felt as if I were floating, so pleasured that I probably could have climaxed again just thinking about it.

I'd told him not the bed, and he'd taken me at my word. Up against the wall. I hadn't ever done that before—my erstwhile lovers weren't what you'd call adventurous. That was good as well—the up-against-the-wall part. Everything was good, except for that nagging worry.

I needed to put it in perspective. It was sex, for God's sake, no big whoop.

Though in truth it certainly *had* been a big whoop. This was a far cry from the pleasant little shimmers that Jason had been able to coax from me at his most creative. A far cry from the fast, efficient orgasms I'd managed on my own. This was like nothing I'd ever experienced.

I was wet, dripping between my legs, and I realized with a shock that he hadn't used a condom. Well, why should he? There were no pregnancies in Sheol, and presumably no sex-borne illnesses. God, this was the first time I'd ever had sex without a condom.

That was it. That explained the whole multiple-orgasm, best-I-ever-had, oh-my-God-I'm-going-to-die reaction. Sex must be impressively better without a condom. It was the lack of a thin rubber sheath getting in the way. Nothing at all to do with Raziel, thank God.

I heard the shower stop, and for a moment I panicked, looking around me for escape. I hadn't even realized the water was running—otherwise I would have been up and out of there. It was too late, and in truth, there was nowhere I could go. If I were a good virginal Victorian heroine, I could fling myself from the ramparts, though I would have to do so stark naked, somewhat ruining the effect.

But I was neither virginal nor a heroine. It had

been fast and erotic and inexplicably wonderful. And for some reason I expected it was something he wasn't going to want to repeat.

He walked out of the bathroom, and he was naked. Totally and comfortably naked. He had something in his hand, not that I was looking at his hand, and he tossed it to me.

I reached out and caught it automatically. It was a warm, wet washcloth, presumably to clean myself off. I didn't move, holding it in my hand, slightly dazed.

He was exquisitely beautiful, even more so without clothes. I'd always found naked men to be sort of silly, with their drooping parts bouncing as they walked. Raziel wasn't silly. He was magnificent, with white-gold skin stretched over a lithe, strong frame, and his sex didn't bounce. I jerked my face away, refusing to think about it.

I felt the bed sink beneath his weight, and I turned and looked at him, startled. He was looking at me with a troubled expression, one I couldn't read. He took the washcloth out of my hand and pressed me back against the bed, his hand gentle. I clutched the sheet that covered me, but he pulled it away effortlessly, and I let it go rather than get into an undignified tug of war I was bound to lose.

"Open your legs," he said, putting one hand on my thigh.

I considered ignoring him. I didn't want to face

him, didn't want to talk to him after that hot, urgent coupling that undoubtedly meant far more to me than it had to him. I closed my eyes, letting him pull my legs apart, and the wet warmth of the washcloth made me shudder in unexpected reaction. Those were his hands, washing me with an unlikely tenderness, and for some reason I wanted to cry.

I lay perfectly still beneath as he took care of me, my eyes closed, just wishing he'd go away and leave me. He was going to, sooner or later, and he might as well get it over with.

"I'm not going away," he said.

"Stop reading my mind!" I cried, my voice catching on a sob. I didn't tend to become emotional after sex, but this was an anomaly on every front.

He cursed under his breath. And then he simply moved over me, between my legs, and before I realized what he was doing he'd pushed inside me again, fully hard, and I let out a little yelp of shock as I shifted to accommodate him.

He held very still, and I opened my eyes to look at him, to see the expression on his face. He was staring down at me, his long fingers cupping my face, his gaze intent.

"Don't move," he whispered. He made a small gesture, and the lights dimmed, covering us with shadows. His head dropped, his mouth against my neck, his breath on my skin. "Am I hurting you?"

I tried to find my voice. It felt as if I were sinking into a dark place of pleasure and forgetfulness. The feel of him inside me was like nothing I'd ever known before, and now that the first, fevered rush was over I could let my body experience it fully. It felt like a blessing, a benediction, a powerful act of claiming that still somehow eluded me. I shook my head, unable to speak, and I knew he smiled against my skin.

"Good," he said softly. He kissed my shoulder, and I could feel his tongue, his teeth, lightly graze the base of my neck, and I suddenly went into overdrive. My body reacted instinctively, tightening around him, and I could feel his smile again. "No," he whispered. "You don't want that."

I wanted to tell him yes, I absolutely did want that, but my voice had disappeared. Just as well—I would probably have begged him.

"You don't have to beg," he said. "Just hold still and let me do this." He slid his hands beneath my butt, pulling me up close against him, and I wrapped my legs around him. The faint ache disappeared in a second, almost before I felt it, and the shift of position brought him in deeper still, and I reacted once again with that instinctive tightening.

He lifted his head to look down at me, and I stared up into his strange eyes, mesmerized. I no longer wanted to hide, to look away. He was invading my soul again, just as he had earlier, only this time he was invading my body at the same time, and I wanted more.

"There's a limit to what you can take, Allie," he whispered in my ear, reading me again. "I don't want to hurt you." And he began to move, a slow, sweet slide, and I found I could make noise after all, a deep, longing moan, as I slid my arms around his back and held him close, feeling his muscles bunch and release against my hands, wanting the feel of him, the taste of him, all around me.

The slow, steady rhythm of it was shattering. All I had to do was hold on to him as he moved, and each time he filled me I felt a dancing shimmer of delight wash over my body. There was something devastating about the measured, steady ease of it, no rush to completion, no rules, no judgment, just the thick slide of him inside me, touching places I hadn't known existed, building toward a climax so powerful I wasn't sure I could survive.

It would be a good death. He pulled me tighter against him, going deeper, and I cried out as the first climax hit me.

We were both covered with sweat, sliding against each other, and I bit his shoulder, tasting him, tasting the salt sweat of him, and I wanted faster, harder, but he wouldn't be rushed, thrusting into me at a steady rate that was going to make me scream, I knew it, he needed to stop, I couldn't bear any more, I needed him to go faster, harder, I needed more, and I clawed at his back in desperation, reaching for a completion like I'd never known.

He reached behind him and took my arms, slamming them down on the mattress as he rose up, pumping into me. The second climax hit me, and then I couldn't stop. I needed nothing more than the steady movement of him inside me to bring me to a place I hadn't believed existed, and I threw myself out into the stars as his hands pressed down on mine and the iridescent darkness closed around us once more.

I could feel him inside me, coming, and I arched back, wanting his mouth on me, wanting his teeth on me. *Please,* I thought, and I felt his mouth against my neck and the first sharp bite of his teeth.

And I was complete.

CHAPTER

SEVENTEEN

I COULD TASTE HER BLOOD ON MY tongue. I touched my mouth, drew my fingers away, and saw the blood on them. I brought my hand back and licked it, the richness of her blood pulsing through me. It had been nothing. The slightest puncture. No veins, not the pulsing artery at the base of her neck that was only allowed for bonded mates. This was barely more than a scrape of my teeth against her soft skin. And it was intoxicating.

I had left her asleep in the middle of the big bed, a small figure wrapped in a down blanket. She looked exhausted, as well she might. I had done my level best to wear her out, and she'd sleep for a long time.

I could see the mark on her neck, the place where I'd bitten her. At least some tiny portion of sanity had remained and I'd managed to pull back. There was a love mark where I'd sucked at her, and the tooth marks were already fading. It had been dangerously close, though. We were already too tied to each other, with breath and now with semen. If I took any more of her blood, there would be no way out.

It had been enough to give me the answers I needed. Uriel could cloud a great many things. He had the harsh powers of a Supreme Being, without the mercy or compassion or any interest in them. But even Uriel couldn't keep a veil up when she reached her completion and lay cocooned in my wings. And there was no way her blood would be so pure, so rich, so nurturing, if Uriel had touched it. It would have been as bitter as acid.

I should have stopped with the one time. No one in Sheol could deny her right to be here from this point onward. I had claimed her, tasted her. No one else could touch her now. She was my responsibility, nothing more, I reminded myself. Little wonder that I'd lost myself in the sweet welcome of her body. I'd been celibate too long.

But with my mouth on her neck, breaking through the frail barrier of her flesh, I had almost made an irrevocable mistake. At least I'd managed to pull away before I'd poisoned myself. She'd been reaching for it, not knowing what she sought. Arching her neck against my mouth, offering herself, but it was my fault, my responsibility. And after that first light taste, I was consumed with need.

It was a need I could control. I washed and dressed, then headed out onto the narrow balcony. I could sense where she'd been sitting, and it jarred me. It was a long terrace—she could have chosen any number of places. Why had she sat in the same spot where I usually stayed, looking out over the ocean, my wings outspread to the night air?

I didn't think she'd noticed my wings wrapped around her. She'd been too caught up in her climax to realize when my wings unfurled and surrounded us tightly, a protective hood.

It doesn't always happen. It hadn't with any of the women I'd used over the last decade or so to relieve my needs. It should have surprised me that it happened this time, but it didn't. Nothing about Allie Watson surprised me anymore.

My body was still humming with satisfaction and rekindled desire. I could have stayed in that bed, but the closer to her I got, the greater my hunger.

It would be so much easier if I could send her somewhere else to sleep, but that would cause too much gossip. With luck I'd be able to convince the Council that she was no threat, and I could keep my distance, keep the ties between us from growing any stronger. I'd been very careful not to touch her more than strictly necessary in a vain attempt to keep the act impersonal. If I could just shut off this sudden raging need for her, I'd be fine.

Her sleeping mind was a blank to me, and her waking mind was fading with each sex act. If she'd known that, she probably would have jumped me earlier. Between bonded mates, the mental link lessened and evened out between the two. It was easy enough to read human sex partners, but after multiple couplings that ability lessened, probably from lack of use. The women I'd slept with were straightforward and simple to read, just as Allie had been in the beginning. I'd known perfectly well that she wanted me, or at least thought she did. But I'd also known she was uncertain about something as simple and logical as sex, despite her experience. And that she didn't like her body, which amazed me, since I thought she was close to perfection. Her body had distracted me from the very beginning, the sheer lushness of her curves, the delicious softness of her thighs, the high, round butt. I'd done very well not thinking about it, skittering out of her mind whenever she allowed herself to fantasize.

I'd been too caught up in my own reactions during sex to see hers, beyond her blind pleasure. For me the sex had been disastrous—so much worse than I'd expected, because I'd been shaken by it, so overwhelmed by the power of it that I'd had to repeat it immediately. The wiser thing to do would have been to walk away from her. Instead I'd thought I'd tend to her, be gentle and distant, and within moments I'd been inside her again, lost in her.

With luck, she'd be disappointed. I'd heard and seen her fantasies—no one could live up to that. With luck, my ability to read her would have faded enough that I wouldn't see anything that might . . . precipitate something. Touching her again would be very unwise.

Now, if only my cursed body understood that.

IT WAS EARLY AFTERNOON WHEN I finally awoke, alone. I knew he wasn't in the apartment, though I wasn't sure how. I could drag myself out of bed and into the shower without running into him. It was a small blessing, but I'd take it.

I wasn't sure what I'd say to him. How to react. I knew instinctively that this wasn't the start of a love affair. If I went up to him, touched him as a lover would, I could just imagine his reaction, and I shuddered. I would have to do my best to read him. If he was suddenly affectionate . . . the thought was seductive in ways far more dangerous than simple sex. Not that sex was simple, in particular sex with Raziel. Sex with an angel. Sex with a vampire. The best sex of my life, afterlife included.

But that wasn't the way it was going to be. As sure as I knew he was gone, I knew he was going to act as if last night had never happened. And I could damned well do the same.

I was going to have to be careful, though. He could

read my thoughts, see my fantasies, and he'd never believe my lies. Really, that was as close a definition of hell as any. A place where you couldn't fool your lover.

Your lover. He wasn't my lover. He was the man who'd taken me to bed last night for reasons I hadn't quite understood. It had been necessary, he'd said. For an act of duty rather than desire, he'd managed pretty damned well, I thought, letting the shower pound down on my body. But why had he done it a second time?

I wrapped myself in one of the huge bath towels, white terry cloth, of course, and went to the closet, resigning myself to white cult couture. Instead my eyes were met with an explosion of colors, rose and green and aqua and pale yellow. For the first time, my heart lightened. Sarah had come through. And how Raziel would hate it. It was enough to cheer me up.

I pulled out a swirling dress of rainbow colors. The neckline was too low, exposing my abundant charms, and I almost chickened out. But I pulled it on anyway, heading back into the bathroom to check it out.

It fit perfectly. I stared at my face in the mirror, shocked. I looked like me, and yet like a stranger. My thick brown hair curled around my face, my eyes were huge, my lips . . . I had to admit it, they were swollen from his mouth.

But that wasn't the only place his mouth had been. I saw the mark on the side of my neck. Not the distinct puncture marks from vampire movies, but a scrape, made by something sharp. His teeth? He'd tasted me, I realized, but he hadn't fed.

He'd had sex with me, but we hadn't made love. And I was suddenly depressed.

As far as I could tell there were no clocks in Sheol, but I surmised it was somewhere around midday, both by the level of the sun in the misty sky and by the growling of my stomach, which was impressive. I climbed out one of the windows and went out onto the parapet. The damp sea air caught my hair and tossed it back, and I breathed in deeply. Suddenly looking at the ocean wasn't enough—I needed to be down there, walking barefoot in the grass, wading in the gentle surf. I was tired of being a pariah.

The apartment's front door opened easily, to my relief. I passed people on the stairs this time, but the hostility I'd felt from them seemed to have disappeared. No one glared at me—they even managed a friendly smile here and there—but clearly I was the least of their worries. Something was going on, and my self-centered mopiness faded as a real sense of anxiety began to intrude.

I made it all the way down the endless flights of stairs, though I knew that was the easy part. I half-expected one of the angelic gatekeepers to stop me as I went toward the door, but no one seemed to have any time for me, an absolute blessing.

I stepped outside onto the thick green grass and quickly kicked off the sandals I'd found. The wind was blowing in from the sea, and I let the damp air sweep over me, closing my eyes in pleasure. My skin would taste of salt, I thought. His skin would taste of salt. And that familiar/unfamiliar heat surged between my legs. Where he had been.

I walked over the grass, then the layer of small stones, then onto the sand, leaving wet footprints as I moved toward the retreating waves. It was odd that I'd never learned to swim, when I loved water so much. I think I'd always been slightly afraid of it, certain that I'd drowned once in a past life. How strange to think that in truth it had been in an afterlife, while trying to save a fallen angel.

I looked around me. The grounds spread off to the right, and for a moment I stared. It almost looked as if there were a shimmer at the distant edge, like a heat mirage, but the weather was temperate and there was no bright sun. I started toward it, walking in the sand, half-expecting it to move. Would I be able to touch it? Put my hand through it? Could I walk through it, to the other side and the real world that Raziel insisted no longer existed for me?

I would be a fool not to try.

I thought it might coalesce as I got closer, but it didn't. I was close enough to feel it, and I stopped short, staring at it. It was some kind of *Star Trek*-ian energy field. It pulsed, almost as if it were alive, and I reached out my hand to touch it—

"Move away from the wall, Allie," Sarah said, her tone sharp, and I jumped back, startled.

"Is that what it is?" I said disingenuously. What else could it possibly be? But for some reason I didn't want Sarah to know I was thinking about running away.

"That's what it is," she said, her usually warm blue eyes flat. "What were you doing?"

I shrugged. "I was curious."

She surveyed me for a long moment. "You're lying," she said eventually. "And I don't know why. Raziel told us he lay with you, that he used the Grace of Knowing and even tasted your blood, and that there was no darkness within you, so it must be true."

"He told you?" I said in a strangled voice. "All of you?"

"All of us. Otherwise you'd be back where he was told to leave you. Most of the Council wanted you gone anyway—only Raziel and I fought for you."

"Raziel fought for me? Why?"

A small smile curved Sarah's mouth. "You'll have to ask him. I know you have a reason to be here in Sheol, but I see things others don't. Maybe Raziel was simply being stubborn. Maybe It was something more. But you need to come away from the wall. The others won't be as open-minded. They still think

Raziel might be blinded by . . ." She let the words trail off, and her smile widened.

"By what?"

She threaded her arm through mine. "Never mind. Let's just get away from here. It will be getting dark soon, and the Nephilim are near."

I shivered, suddenly cold, remembering those howls during the long night when I'd watched over Raziel's body. Time seemed suspended, moving oddly. It seemed so long ago that I'd curled up next to him, and it was only three days.

I'd heard those unearthly screams last night as well. Before Raziel gave me something else to think about.

By the time we reached the grass, I'd almost managed to shake off my feelings of dread. Until I looked into Sarah's eyes. "What's wrong? Where is everyone?"

She looked at me for a long moment, considering. "They're going to break through. Everyone knows it, we just don't know when. Someone has led them to the gate, and someone will let them in."

"Not me!" I said in horror.

"No, not you. Though the others suspected you. And still would, if they saw you lingering down there. But someone inside *is* going to open the gates, and the Nephilim will overrun us."

"Why? Why now?"

She shrugged. "Who knows how Uriel's mind works? He's wanted to destroy us for millennia, and he is very patient. We believe he finally has found a way in."

"Through the Nephilim?"

"And the traitor."

I looked out to the churning sea, breathing in the fresh salt spray. "So we're all going to die," I said in a flat voice.

"Not all of us. You have got something—"

"Raziel's looking for me," I broke in, startled.

She looked just as surprised. "Where?"

I looked around. There was no one in sight. The lawn and beach in front of the house were deserted in the waning light. "I'm sorry. I must have imagined it. What were you saying?"

Sarah shook her head. "It doesn't matter. You'll find out soon enough."

"Don't do that—I'll die of curiosity!" I protested. And then I heard him. His voice, calling me. "He's sounding really pissed off," I said regretfully. "I'd better go to him."

"How do you know this?"

I hadn't even considered it. I shrugged. "I have no idea. I just know."

A slow smile curved Sarah's mouth. "How lovely," she said in a soft voice. "Then you'd better go back. The two of you will have a lot to talk about."

"I doubt it. I don't think he's going to want to talk to me at all. Couldn't you come with me?

Sarah shook her head. "We'll talk later. Just don't let him bully you. Raziel can be very strong-minded."

"I don't really want to be left alone with him," I said, feeling desperate.

"Why?"

"He's either going to want to talk about it, which will be excruciatingly uncomfortable, or he'll pretend it never happened, which will be even worse. If you're with me, then it will be a moot point."

"Sheol isn't that different from the world," Sarah said. "Men never want to talk about things."

"That's what I figured. But still—"

"You'll be perfectly safe ignoring the entire situation until you decide not to ignore it any longer," Sarah said smoothly. "Go on now."

I had started walking up the slope when her voice trailed after me: "By the way, that's a very pretty dress on you."

I turned back, mortified. "And I never said thank you! It's gorgeous, and so are all the others that I found in the closet. Thank you so much, Sarah!"

Her eyes twinkled. "I haven't had time to get you new clothes, Allie. Raziel must have seen to it."

I stared down at my dress. "Impossible," I said flatly.

"If you say so. You'd better hurry. You probably don't want to keep him waiting."

I didn't give a damn if he was kept waiting, I told myself as I double-timed it up the stairs. I had no idea which way he was coming, only that he was near, and sprinted toward the apartment.

I didn't bother wondering how I knew. Presumably just part of the magic juju of this place. I made it to the apartment ahead of him, gasping for breath as I slammed the door behind me. I grabbed a loose sweater to pull around the less-than-generous top. Why did dresses in Sheol have décolleté? I wondered. Wouldn't a nun's habit be more fitting?

Apparently not. This place, unlike the celibate, puritanical afterlife I'd always envisioned, was practically seething with sex. I raced into the bathroom, shoved rough fingers through my hair, and headed back out to the living room, taking a flying leap and landing on the sofa seconds before the front door opened.

"Where were you?" he demanded.

"I went for a walk. With Sarah," I added. "I didn't realize I was supposed to be a prisoner in here."

"You're not. Not anymore. But it would still be better if you went out with someone else. Someone told me you were at the gates, alone. Why?"

I saw no point in lying, particularly since he was able to read my thoughts whenever he wanted to. "I was thinking of leaving."

"That would have been a grave mistake. The Nephilim are out there. You wouldn't have survived five seconds once the sun went down."

"Maybe I could have gotten past them—"

"Don't you realize there's no going back?" he demanded. "That life is over. Gone."

Frustration filled me. "And what do I replace it with?"

"If Uriel has his way, absolutely nothing."

"You think the Nephilim are coming as well?" I shivered, pulling the sweater more closely around me.

"Sarah told you that, did she? We all know it. We just don't know when. But it seems as if your arrival was some sort of signal. One last piece of disobedience on the part of the Fallen."

"You mean it's *my* fault?" I said, horrified. "I'm the reason everyone is going to die?"

"If it's anyone's fault, it's mine, for pulling you back. But the truth is of little matter. Uriel would find a way sooner or later, and the presence of the Nephilim at our gates means it will be sooner."

I digested this. I'd died once in the last three days. If it happened again, at least I'd have some experience.

I was watching him as he sat on the coach opposite me, wary. "Would you answer a question?"

"It depends on the question."

"Why did we have sex last night? You said it was

necessary. Sarah said it had something to do with finding out whether I was evil or not. Why don't you tell me the truth."

"Sarah's right," he said. "But you don't need to worry. It won't—"

"Happen again," I jumped in. "You needn't bother to explain—I already knew what you were going to say."

He looked disturbed at the idea. "You did?"

"Isn't it obvious? You needed to find out if I was evil, and for some reason having sex with me was the only way to do it. That seems far-fetched, but I'll accept it. But we've done it, it's over, I passed inspection, so there's no need to repeat it, right?"

"Right."

"So why did we do it twice?" I said it to make him uncomfortable, not because I expected a real answer.

He didn't look the slightest bit uncomfortable. He leaned back on the sofa, watching me, his eyelids drooping lazily as if he weren't paying much attention. But he was, I knew it instinctively. I was beginning to understand a lot about him on a purely instinctive level.

"Just to remove any doubts," he said deliberately. "A quick fuck up against a wall might not have given me quite enough information. Which is why I had to . . . taste you. Blood never lies. People do. Bodies do. Blood, never."

I squirmed. "What kind of angel uses words like *quick fuck*?"

He cocked an eyebrow. "Fallen ones." He tilted his head, observing me like I was a scientific specimen he was about to stick a pin through, and I remembered that feeling from the night before as he searched inside me. "In truth, it might be better if everyone thinks we're in the midst of a torrid sexual affair. The Fallen don't like anomalies, and if you can act as if your only interest is being in bed with me, it should make everyone less nervous."

Not much of a stretch, I reflected, then tried to slam down the thought.

Too late. "That's good," he drawled. "It's what everyone will expect—anything else would be a red flag."

"You're supposed to be that good?" I mocked him, trying for distance.

"It's the nature of the beast," he replied "Bondings are never casual. Intense, consuming, occasionally dangerous, but never casual. You can spend most of your time up here, if you prefer not to have me touching you. It would probably be safer."

He was hoping I'd choose that option—it didn't take a psychic or someone with angelic superpowers to figure that out. He wanted—needed—distance from me even more than he had before. I just couldn't figure out why.

"There's no need to overthink things, Allie," he said. "We simply have to keep things quiet until Uriel forgets about you."

"The archangel Uriel is forgetful?" I said doubtfully.

"No. But we can hope." *And if he doesn't forget, I'll take Allie away from this place, somewhere Uriel can't get to her without sending his avenging angels, and one small human female won't be worth the effort. He won't forget, but there will be other things demanding his attention— such as punishing mc for disobedience.*

I stared at him. "No."

"No what?" he said, rising and heading for the kitchen, secure in the belief that the conversation had ended.

"You're not going to sacrifice yourself for me, you're not going to stash me where Uriel can't find me, and this conversation has not ended." And with a mixture of dawning horror and delight, I knew I'd read his mind.

CHAPTER

EIGHTEEN

THE FIRST FLOOR WAS DESERTED when Sarah made her way up from the kitchens. Everyone was too tense to eat, the kitchen staff were in disarray, and it was up to her to keep things running smoothly. The long hike made her a little breathless, and she waited for a moment to regain her composure. If Azazel realized she was having trouble breathing he would overreact, and the Fallen couldn't afford to have that happen right now.

With everything else he was calm, measured, unemotional, able to make the hard decisions without flinching. He would have condemned Allie to Uriel's hell, and he would have been the one to take her, if necessary. He wouldn't have thought twice about it.

But if he knew Sarah was getting weaker, it would distract him, and right now Sheol needed his undivided attention.

The Nephilim were at their gates. She could hear their howls and moans in the night, the hideous, bone-chilling sounds as they attacked the impenetrable door. Impenetrable for now, but sooner or later they would get through. Someone was a traitor, the Nephilim horde would be shown a way to break through the barriers, and there would be a blood-bath.

She knew it. Azazel knew it. She wondered how many of the Fallen were aware of what awaited them. Quite possibly most of them.

Her breathing had steadied now. She checked her pulse—it was slow and even. People lived longer, healthier lives in Sheol. But they couldn't live forever, and her life was drawing to a close. Sooner than it should have in this sacred place, but she accepted it. Azazel, however, would not.

She pushed away from the long sideboard in the front hall and went to her husband. He was down by the water—her knowledge was instinctive and sure. She knew him so well, knew how he'd fight to keep her. But in the end there was nothing he could do. She would have to leave, and he would go on.

He didn't turn when she joined him on the moon-lit beach. He was sitting on the grass, and she sat beside him, leaning against him as he put his arm around her waist. She pressed her face against his shoulder, breathing in the familiar smell of him. Her blood kept him alive—their joining was so complete they seldom had need for words.

But tonight she felt like talking. "I've been talking with Allie."

He settled her more comfortably against him. "He really did bed her, didn't he?"

"Most thoroughly. Though there was only the slightest scratch on her neck, and it hadn't healed. But he would have taken enough to be certain—Allie is not your traitor."

"I know," he said, not sounding happy about it. "And how is she?"

"That poor creature," Sarah said with a laugh.

"She'll manage," Azazel said with his customary lack of sentiment.

"I'm talking about Raziel. He doesn't realize what he's gotten himself into. She knew where he was."

That was enough to make Azazel sit up straight and look down at her. "Are you certain? Maybe she just guessed."

Sarah shook her head. "She knew. It won't be long before she can read his thoughts just as he reads hers. And he's not going to like it."

Azazel managed a dry laugh. "He'll hate it. So you're telling me this woman really is his bonded mate? And she can already hear him? That's extraordinary."

"So it appears. No wonder he hauled her back

from the pit Uriel had consigned her to. Clearly it wasn't an accident. What bothers me is why Uriel set it up. It couldn't have been a coincidence that Raziel was supposed to dispose of his bonded mate."

"Why should it surprise you? If Uriel can deprive us of our bonded mates, it weakens us. He can't kill us, can't send his legion of soldiers against us without sufficient reason. All he can do is torture us. As long as Raziel has no mate, he will remain at less than full strength. That's the way Uriel wants us, if he can't have us dead. Too bad for him it backfired."

Sarah smiled. "Raziel's still fighting it."

"That's his problem, not ours. He needs to claim her and feed, but he's a stubborn bastard. He's going to have to figure this out on his own. I just hope it doesn't take him too long. We need him at full strength, the sooner the better." He looked out toward the ocean, his blue eyes wintry. "What about the woman?"

"Oh, I think she knows, deep inside. She may have always known. She's probably going to fight it as well."

Azazel sighed. "Just what we need. Soap operas in Sheol."

A bestial scream rent the night air, and Sarah shivered. "The Nephilim are coming closer," she said in a low voice.

"Yes."

"They're going to get in, sooner or later."

"Probably sooner," he said in his pragmatic voice.

She managed a shaky laugh. "Couldn't you at least lie to me, tell me everything will be all right?"

He looked down at her, reaching up to brush her moonlit silver hair away from her face with a tender hand. "Now, what good would that do me? I don't shield my thoughts. Unlike you," he added.

"You really don't want to know some of the things that go on in my tortured mind," she said lightly. If he knew what was going to happen, he would try to do something to stop it, and there were things that couldn't be changed. Her death was one of those things, whether she liked it or not.

He rose, pulling her up into his arms, against his hard, strong body. Once her body had almost equaled his, lithe and young and beautiful. Now she was old, and he still looked at her, touched her, like she were twenty.

"Let's go swimming," he said as another howl echoed in the distance. He reached up to push her loose robes off her body.

She let him, and a moment later he was naked as well, and they ran into the surf, holding hands, diving under the cold salt water as the bright moon shone down. She swam out, secure in the knowledge that he could get to her at a moment's notice, and once past the breaking swells she rolled over to float on her back, letting her hair drift around her. Ophelia, she thought. He had to be able to let her go.

He came up beside her, and she kissed his mouth, cold and wet and salty, and wrapped her body around his, floating, peaceful. There weren't many moments like this left to them, and she was greedy, she wanted everything she could get.

He smiled against her mouth. "Shall we go back to our rooms? Or is Raziel's soap opera going to demand your services again tonight?"

"You're the only one who gets my services tonight," she murmured, letting him pull her in toward the distant shore.

They were back in their bedroom, the doors open to the night air, when she heard the screams of the Nephilim once more.

"Close the windows, love," she said softly, sliding between the cool sheets.

He did as she asked, not questioning, and then came to bed.

"WHAT DID YOU SAY?" I stared at the woman with horror. I'd been having a hard time not thinking about taking her to bed, but her blithe announcement had driven that straight out of my mind.

"I knew what you were thinking," she said smugly. "Is that because we had sex? Earlier I knew you were coming here long before you showed up. I realized that was odd because of Sarah's reaction, and now I can sort of pick up your thoughts."

"Can you indeed?" I said calmly, wondering if I could get away with throwing her off the balcony and telling everyone she'd slipped. No, I couldn't, but it was a nice thought.

One she didn't pick up on, fortunately. So her ability to read me wasn't that well developed. Yet.

Shit. Under normal circumstances, there was only one reason a woman would be able to read me— because she was my bonded mate. But for me there would be no bonded mates ever again. This was just an anomaly.

"Not now, of course," she said, frowning. "Just the occasional thought sort of drifting through my brain. Are you doing that?"

"Letting you read my thoughts? No," I said, controlling my instinctive shudder. I couldn't let her know how she affected me. "This is a fluke— by tomorrow, it should have passed. Don't worry about it."

"I'm not worried about it. I like it. It gives me something to fight back with," she said.

Interesting. "Why do you need to fight me?" I asked her.

That stumped her for a moment, and I tried to touch her mind. A mistake. She wanted me, I could feel it quite clearly. It was almost a physical touch, even though she was trying hard to suppress it. That was what she needed to fight.

"I feel powerless here," she said finally.

"You *are* powerless here." I moved over to the bank of windows that faced the sea. They were open, the sheer white curtains fluttering inward on the strong wind. I could hear the soothing sound of the ocean as it beat against the sandy shore. It almost—almost—drowned out the screams from the world beyond. I glanced back at the woman sitting curled up, a stain of color against the pristine white of the sofa. I had an easier time resisting her when she was dressed in white. Why had I ordered those clothes for her? The colors assaulted my eyes, assaulted my senses. They drew me. "What else did Sarah want?"

"To welcome me into the fold of Sheol sex slaves."

She was trying to annoy me, as usual, and succeeding, as usual. "No one is a sex slave around here."

"The women don't seem to have much else to do. Fuck and let you drink their blood. I'm assuming that only goes one way."

I tried to keep my face blank. "Of course."

"Then why don't you take my blood?"

I turned away from her. She'd have a harder time reading the truth if she couldn't see my face. "I took enough to make certain you were innocent. That was all I needed or wanted. The Fallen can feed only from a bonded mate or the Source, and you're neither."

"Then what am I? Besides a nuisance," she added, immediately reading my mind.

It unnerved me, but I was determined not to show any reaction. "I don't know."

She rose, saying nothing, and the dress swirled around her bare ankles as she moved past me into the kitchen. Her skirts brushed against my legs like the caress of a warm breeze, and without thinking I reached for her.

But she had already moved past, and she didn't even notice, thank God. She turned, as if aware she'd missed something, but by then I was leaning negligently against the counter, concentrating on the almost imperceptible pattern of the white Carrara marble.

She'd pulled out a glass bottle of milk when a louder scream split the night, and she dropped it. If I hadn't been so attuned to her, I wouldn't have been able to catch it in time and set it on the counter.

"What the hell was that?" she asked in a harsh voice.

"The Nephilim. They're getting closer."

She turned pale. "They can't get in, can they?"

"Presumably not. There are all sorts of wards and guards placed on the borders. The only way they could get inside is if someone let them in, and whoever did that would die as well."

"What if someone would rather die than spend eternity trapped here?" she demanded, rattled.

"You won't be here an eternity. I'll find some way to get you out."

"God, I hope so. I don't want to live to be one hundred and twenty without falling in love," she said, and I winced. "But I wasn't talking about me. What if someone else has a death wish?" She shivered, and I wanted to warm her, calm her. I stayed right where I was.

"There is no one else. The Fallen chose this life. Their mates have chosen the Fallen. No one's going to sneak out to the walls and let the monsters in." I could lie about my reaction to her. Lying about the danger we were in was beyond me. "The truth is, I don't know," I said. "They're beating against the walls, frustrated because they can't break in. There's no way they can break through the walls that guard this place, no way that anyone can. It's inviolate."

She didn't believe me. I didn't need to pick up specific words to know that she was filled with distrust. If I knew how to reassure her, I would have. I didn't even know how to reassure myself.

"I don't think the milk's going to do it," she said.

"I beg your pardon?"

"I thought some warm milk was going to calm my nerves, but I don't think it'll work as long as that caterwauling is going on. I don't suppose this place comes equipped with whiskey? No, I forgot—whiskey isn't white."

"There's vodka," I said.

"Of course there is." She opened the refrigerator to put the milk back, then emerged with a chilled bottle of Stoli. "You really need to let a little color into your life, Raziel."

I looked at her in the brightly hued dress I'd given her. Everything about her was vibrant, colorful, disrupting the calm emptiness of my world. She poured two glasses, neat, and pushed one toward me across the marble counter.

It wasn't a good idea. Keeping my hands off her was requiring every ounce of concentration I had. Even half an ounce of alcohol might be enough to weaken my resolve.

Then again, getting her drunk would be an excellent idea. I found drunken women completely unappealing. And if she passed out, I wouldn't be tempted to put my hands on either side of her head and draw her face up to mine, to kiss her. . . .

She'd already picked up her glass and drained it, giving a delicate little shudder. "I don't really like vodka," she said in a small voice. She looked pointedly at my untouched glass. "Clearly, neither do you."

I said nothing. She wanted me to put my arms around her. I knew it, and wished I didn't. The noise of the Nephilim was growing louder, the howls and screams, the roars and grunts deeply disturbing. I knew the horror that lay beneath that sound. I thought I could smell them on the night air, the foul stench of old blood and rotting flesh, but it had to be my imagination. I tried to concentrate on them, but her thoughts pushed them away. She wanted my arms around her; she wanted to press her head against my chest. She wanted my mouth, she wanted my body, and she wasn't going to tell me.

She didn't need to tell me. There was a crash outside, followed by a louder roar, and she jumped nervously. "If you don't like vodka, why do you even have it?" she said, clearly trying to distract herself.

"I like vodka. I just think it might be better if I didn't let alcohol impair my judgment in case something happens."

If anything her face turned whiter. "You think they're going to break through?"

I had to laugh. "No. Worse than that."

"Worse than flesh-devouring cannibals?"

"Is there any other kind of cannibal?" I pointed out.

"What's worse than the Nephilim?" she said irritably, some of her panic fading.

"Sleeping with you."

Shit. And I meant to not even mention it. She stared at me for a long moment, then tried to push past me. "Enough is enough," she snapped. "If you prefer the Nephilim to me, you can damned well go climb over the fence and fuck them."

I caught her, of course. My arm snaked around her waist and I spun her around, pushing her back against the wall, trapping her there with my body pressed against hers. "I didn't say I preferred them," I whispered in her ear, closing my eyes to inhale the addictive scent of her. "As far as I'm concerned, though, you're worse trouble." I kissed the side of her neck, tasting her skin, breathing in the smell of her blood as it rushed through her veins. So easy just to make one small piercing, just take a taste. I moved my mouth behind her ear, fighting it.

She was holding herself very still. "W-w-why?" she stammered.

"I can kill the Nephilim," I whispered. "I can fight them. But I have too hard a time fighting you."

She turned her face up to mine, and her hands reached up to touch me. "Then don't fight," she said in a tone of such practicality that I wanted to laugh. "At least I won't rip out your heart."

"I wouldn't be so sure," I said. And like a fool, I kissed her.

CHAPTER

NINETEEN

I KNEW PERFECTLY WELL THAT I WAS an idiot to do this, but right then nothing could have stopped me. His body was pressed up tight against me, and the heat and strength of it calmed my panic—but brought out a whole new raft of fear. His mouth was hot, wet, carnal, as he kissed me, his slow deliberation at odds with the crazed rush of lust that had overwhelmed us last night. He slanted his mouth across mine, tasting, biting, giving me a chance to kiss him back, his tongue a shocking intruder that somehow felt right. In my somewhat limited experience, men didn't really like to kiss; they simply did it to get to the part they did like.

Raziel clearly enjoyed kissing—he was too good at it not to enjoy it. He was in no hurry to push me into bed, no hurry to do anything more than kiss me.

He lifted his head, and his strange, beautiful eyes with their striated irises stared down at me for a long, breathless moment. "What are you doing?" I whispered.

"Kissing you. If you haven't figured that out yet, I must not be doing a very good job of it. I must need practice." And he kissed me again, a deep, hungry kiss that stole my breath and stole my heart.

"I mean *why* are you kissing me?" I said when he moved his mouth along my jawline and I felt it tingle all the way down to . . . I wasn't sure where. "You just told me you'd rather face the Nephilim—"

"Shut up, Allie," he said pleasantly. "I'm trying to distract both of us." He slid the dress straps down my shoulders, down my arms, exposing my breasts to the cool night air, and I heard his murmur of approval. "No bra," he said. "Maybe I'm going to like your new clothes."

He moved his mouth down the side of my neck, lingering for a moment at the base of my throat, to the place where he'd left his mark, and I reflexively rose toward him, wanting his mouth there, wanting . . .

But he moved on, and I stifled my cry of despair. And then forgot all about it as he leaned down and put his lips on my bared breast, sucking the nipple into his mouth. I caught his shoulders, digging my fingers into them as I arched up, offering myself to him. I could feel the sharpness of his teeth against me, and I knew a moment's fear that he would draw blood from my breast, but his hand covered my other breast, soothing, stimulating, so that my nipple became a hardened button to match the one in his mouth, and I knew he wouldn't hurt me, not there, not anywhere, he told me, and I felt his consciousness enter my mind, a deliberate invasion as intimate and arousing as his tongue and his cock.

His eyes were black with desire now, and he pushed the fabric of the dress down to my hips, baring my torso, nuzzling beneath the swell of my breast; and then his hands were on my thighs, drawing the dress slowly upward, and I was feeling rushed, greedy, desperate for him, wanting him inside me, wanting him now, and I raised my hips, mindlessly searching.

He wants this, I thought dazedly, reveling in the certainty of his need. He wanted me. He wanted nothing more than to bury himself in my body, to soak in the forgetfulness of lust and desire and completion, to lose himself, and to bring me with him on a journey of such transcending desire that the very thought frightened me, and I tried to pull away. I hadn't had time for second thoughts during our frantic couplings. Now I could be calm, detached, dismissive as I needed to be, except that I needed him even more than I needed calm, and his hands were running up my bare legs now, his fingers inside the lace-trimmed edge of my panties, touching me, and I let out a muffled yelp of reaction, followed by a moan of pure pleasure as he began pulling the panties down my legs.

And then he jumped away, so quickly I almost fell. The blackness was gone from his eyes and at the moment they were like granite, and I wondered what the hell had happened. And then I heard the screams.

Different from the distant howls and shrieks of the Nephilim, safely beyond the borders of Sheol. These were closer, the guttural howls echoing through the five floors of the building. These were here.

"Stay here," he ordered tersely. "Find someplace to hide. If worse comes to worst, go out on the balcony and be prepared to jump."

I stared in astonishment at the angel who'd just told me to commit suicide. "What . . . ?"

"They're here." His voice was flat, grim. "The walls have fallen."

I froze, the numb, mindless horror washing over me. "The Nephilim?"

He was almost at the door, but he stopped, wheeled around, and came back to me, catching my arms in a painful grip. "You can't let them near you, Allie. No matter what. Hide if you think you've got a chance. This is a long way to climb, and their bloodlust will send them after the nearest targets. But if they reach this floor . . ." He took a deep breath. "Jump. You don't want to see or hear what they're capable of, you don't want to risk getting caught by them. Promise me, Allie." His fingers tightened. "Promise me you'll jump."

I had never backed off from a challenge, never taken the easy way out in my entire, too-short life. I looked up into Raziel's face and could sense the horror he was seeing, the horror he was letting me catch only a glimpse of. A glimpse was enough. I nodded. "If I must," I said.

To my astonishment, he kissed me again, a brief, fast kiss, almost a kiss good-bye. And he was gone.

There was no place to hide. The bed was too low to the floor, and when I burrowed into the closet, the screams from below still echoed, even when I covered my head with my arms and tried to drown them out. I struggled back into the bedroom. I didn't know if the screams were getting louder or the Nephilim were getting closer. I'd promised him, and I might have a thousand and one characters flaws, but I never broke a promise. I pushed open the window and climbed onto the balcony. And then froze.

The sand was black in the moonlight, and it took me a moment to realize it was blood. There were bodies everywhere, or what was left of them. Headless torsos, arms and legs that had been ripped free, gnawed on, and then discarded. And the stench that was carried upward on the night breeze was the stuff of nightmares. Blood, old blood, and decaying flesh. The stink of the monsters that crawled below, searching for fresh meat.

I climbed onto the ledge, peering over, and had my first shadowy sight of one of them. It was unnaturally tall, covered with some kind of matted filth, though whether it was hair or clothes or skins of some kind I couldn't be sure. Its mouth was open in a roar, and I thought I could see two sets of teeth, broken and bloody. It had someone in its hands, a woman with long blond hair and black-streaked clothes.

She was still alive. The creature was clawing at her, ripping her open so that her guts spilled out onto the sand, but her arms were still moving, her feet were twitching, and I screamed at it to stop, but my voice was carried away by the crash of the surf, lost amidst the screams and howls.

For a moment I stood paralyzed. The woman was finally still, her eyes wide in death, and the creature turned, moving in an odd, disjointed shuffle, heading inside. I couldn't even count the number of bodies on the beach—they were ripped in too many pieces. And I knew then I couldn't join them on the beach, doing a graceful swan dive to my death. What if I didn't die right away? What if I lay there while the Nephilim found me, tore me apart while I still lived?

And how could I hide in my room when I could do

something? That poor woman down there—if someone had been able to distract the creature, she might have been able to crawl to safety. But there was no one alive on the beach.

I didn't hesitate, didn't allow myself to fear. By the time I reached the third-floor landing I'd decided I was crazy, but I didn't let it slow me down. *Destiny* was a stupid word, a word for heroines, and I was no heroine. All I knew was that I could do something to help, and I had to try.

The bodies started on the second floor, women of the Fallen who'd tried to escape, but were clawed and hacked and gnawed on by the monsters who'd somehow invaded the vale of Sheol. The stench was overpowering. Way in the past, when I'd started writing, I'd done research on crime scenes, had heard about the smell of week-old bodies that clung to the skin and hair of the police and couldn't ever be eradicated from their clothes. It was that kind of smell that washed over me now, one of decayed flesh and maggots and rotting bones. Of old meat and ancient blood and shit and death.

The first floor was a battleground. I could see five of the Nephilim, tall and ungainly, easily recognizable. I took in the scene quickly: Azazel was fighting fiercely, blood streaming from a head wound and mixing with his long black hair. Tamlel was down, probably dead, as was Sammael, and I realized with belated horror that it had been Carrie out on the sand, fighting to the end with the monster who was devouring her.

The noise, the smoke, the blood, were too much. I couldn't see the other women, couldn't find Raziel in the melee. The Nephilim who fought Azazel went down, and a moment later its head went flying, the rest of it collapsing into a useless pile of bones as Azazel turned to face the next attacker.

And then I saw Sarah behind him. She held a sword in her hand, and her face was calm, set, as Azazel defended her. There were others protecting her as well, Fallen whose names I didn't know. I saw Raziel by the door then, cutting down the horde as they poured into the building, wielding a sword of biblical proportions. The noise was deafening: the screams of the dying, the clash of metal, the unearthly howls of the Nephilim as they set upon their prey. A blade slashed, and I felt blood and bile spray me, hot and stinking of death. The Nephilim were everywhere, and I watched in horror as the madness surrounded me.

Something grabbed my ankle and I screamed, looking down to see one of the women lying on the stairs, grasping at me for help. Poor thing, she was well past help of any kind, but I sank down, pulling her ravaged body into my arms, trying to stanch the endless flow of blood. "You'll be all right," I murmured, rocking her, trying to hold her broken body together. She was going to die, but at least I could comfort her. "They're going to stop them. Just hold on."

To my amazement, the woman reached up and touched my face with one bloody hand, and she smiled at me, peace in her fading eyes. A moment later, she was dead. Blessedly so, given the horror of her wounds. I let the woman go, setting her down gently on the stairs, and looked up.

I could try to run. Back up the endless, blood-soaked flights of stairs, through the torn pieces of what had once been living flesh. Or I could face the bastards.

One of the Fallen lay across the bottom of the stairs, his torso ripped almost in half. One arm was gone, but the other still held a sword, fighting to the end.

I stepped down and took the sword in my shaking hand, then turned to look for Raziel.

One of the Nephilim must have spied me on the stairs. It turned away from the men defending Sarah, advancing on me with its hideous disjointed shuffle.

It was too late to run, even if I wanted to. The thing had seen me, caught my scent; and when one of the Fallen attacked it, the creature simply tossed him away, and the body flew across the room, landing on a table that collapsed beneath him.

I wanted to scream for Raziel, but I kept my mouth shut, gripping the sword tightly in my hand. If I was going to die, then I was going to die fighting, and I wouldn't distract Raziel from his defense of the portal. Maybe death wouldn't hurt, I thought, still backing up, the screams of the dying belying my vain hope. It hadn't hurt the first time. It didn't matter. I was supposed to be here, I'd been drawn down here, and if I was going to be torn apart, then so be it.

The Nephilim rose up over me, so close I could see the maggots living in its skin, and the smell of blood and death was enough to make me gag. If I was lucky, it would rip off my head—it would be quick, rather than having my stomach and intestines clawed out—and I wondered if I could get away, run far enough up the stairs to jump, as I'd promised Raziel. Maybe that was what I was supposed to do, land on a Nephilim or two and crush them.

The creature had a hideous open hole for a mouth, and the double sets of teeth were jagged, sharklike, made for tearing flesh, and I wasn't going to scream, I wasn't, even when it reached me. Its hands were deformed, more like pincers, razored and bloody, and I slashed at it, blindly, severing one of them. It didn't react, coming closer, and its remaining claw made a horrible clacking sound. I clutched the sword, prepared to fight to the death.

And then the hideous head disappeared, simply

vanished, and I stared in shock. The monster collapsed in a welter of bones in front of me, and Raziel
stood behind it, a bloody sword in his hand, the
sword he'd used to decapitate the creature.

I almost didn't recognize him. He was covered
with blood, his eyes dark and glazed, and I half-
expected him to yell at me. But he simply turned
around, keeping his station at the foot of the stairs,
protecting me as Azazel protected Sarah.

Some of the Nephilim carried swords, knives,
spears—primitive weapons. Others simply relied on
their claws and teeth and superhuman strength. They
fell beneath the fierce onslaught of the Fallen, making
no sound as they went. Their howls had been screams
of hunger, and that had been assuaged by the torn
bodies that littered the hall. They died in silence.

We were going to survive, I realized with sudden
shock. I'd come downstairs prepared to die, certain I
was going to, and now everything had shifted. Only
one Nephilim was left standing, a thick pole in his
claws, out of reach of Azazel's blazing sword, and I
felt the pull of Sarah's gaze from across the carnage.

I turned to look, and Sarah gave me a sweet, loving
smile—almost a benediction—a second before the
heavy pole pierced her chest, slamming her against
the wooden door behind her and impaling her there.

I heard Azazel's scream from a distance. I scrambled past Raziel as if he didn't exist, climbing over

corpses and twitching victims, pushing past Azazel himself to reach Sarah's side.

Someone had wrenched the pole free, and Sarah slid to the floor, her eyes glazing as I caught her, lowering her carefully. That sweet smile still clung to her mouth, even though her blue eyes were filled with tears. "I'm . . . so glad . . . you're here," she managed to gasp. "You'll help . . . Raziel."

There was nothing around to use for a bandage, so I simply mashed together an armful of my full skirts and held it against Sarah's ruined chest. "It's going to be all right," I said desperately, refusing to admit it wasn't. "Hold on."

I'd said the same thing to the girl on the stairs, the girl who'd died in my arms. Just as Sarah was going to.

"Try to help Azazel," Sarah whispered, trying to gather her ebbing strength. "He's going to be in trouble. Raziel can help him. You can help Raziel. Promise."

"I will," I said helplessly. "But you're not going to die."

"Yes, I am," she whispered. "I've known it for quite a while. You must . . . stop the one who betrayed us. You must . . ." Her voice faded, but her eyes sharpened, grew warm with love.

Someone picked me up and forcibly hauled me away from Sarah—Azazel, who handed me off to

Raziel and sank down beside his wife. When I resisted, just for a moment, Raziel simply used force, putting an arm around my waist and carrying me out of the building, which was knee-deep in bodies and blood.

He dumped me on the beach, not even bothering to tell me to stay put. "I'm going to seal the wall," he said. "Azazel and Sarah need to be alone to say good-bye."

I sank down in the grass just above the sand and put my face in my arms. The tall, oddly shaped bodies of the Nephilim littered the beach, and the smell in the night air was thick and poisonous. I tried to muffle the stench, but all I could smell was Sarah's blood that had soaked into my dress. Her life's blood, draining away.

My own blood as well. I hadn't even realized that I'd been hurt. There was a rip down my arm, a shallow slice from shoulder to wrist, made by a talon of that hideous creature. It had begun to throb, and I ought to find something to stanch the flow. I could use my skirt, already soaked with Sarah's blood, but I didn't touch it. There was already too much blood everywhere.

I looked around me, dazed, when I saw Tamlel lying at the edge of the water. He must have staggered down there and then collapsed.

I managed to pull myself to my feet, picking my way carefully through the carnage toward him. He was lying facedown in the surf, and his body had been scored by the claws of the Nephilim. I remembered how they'd taken Raziel into the ocean to heal him. Perhaps Tamlel had sought the same healing power.

"Help . . . me . . ." he gasped.

I knelt beside him. "Do you need to go into the water?" He was already soaking wet, and still he was dying.

He managed to shake his head. "I need . . . my wife is dead. She was one of the first. I need Sarah."

I froze. "Let me get some bandages. Is there a doctor here? Your wounds will heal."

He shook his head again. "Lost too much blood. Need the Source. Find . . ."

I couldn't tell him. There must be some other answer, some other way to help him, but he wasn't listening. "I'll go find her," I said simply, rising. The water couldn't hurt, and there must be someone back on the littered battlefield that had once been the grand hallway, someone who could help.

By then the moans of the dying had faded into background noise. I moved like an automaton, past tears, past grief, past horror. I'd made it to the open door when someone grabbed my skirt, pulling at me, and I stared down at another of the Fallen, one whose name I didn't even know.

"Help me," he choked.

"I'll try to find someone," I said patiently, looking back toward Tamlel where he lay in the surf.

"No." His grip was strong on my dress. "Save me."

My heart was breaking for him, for them all. "There's nothing I can do," I cried. "I can't help you."

Still he clung to me, and without thinking I sank to my knees beside him, feeling the tears start in my eyes, and I dashed them away angrily. Tears wouldn't help. Tamlel was so close to death nothing would help him. This one was almost as bad, and all I could do was hold him, as I'd held the woman on the stairs, until he was gone.

He closed his eyes, all color draining from his face as he began to shudder, and I brushed his hair away from his bruised, bloody face. The blood from my arm, my own blood, smeared his lips, and I quickly tried to wipe it away; his eyes flew open, and he somehow managed to catch my wrist with sudden, unexpected strength, twisting it painfully as he tried to bring it to his mouth.

"It won't help," I started to say. It had to be the blood of his bonded mate or the Source, and Sarah was dead or dying. And then I stopped fighting. If he thought it would help, if it eased his passing, then I wouldn't deny him. I let him bring my torn flesh to his mouth, felt his mouth clamp onto me, and I pulled him into my lap, holding him as he drank from me.

Slowly the shudders stopped, and he lay very still. The fierce sucking on my flesh stopped, his hold loosened, and my arm fell away, free. He was dead, I thought, brushing the hair away from his face again. He looked so young, so innocent, even though he had to be thousands of years old, and I wanted to lean forward and kiss his forehead as a last benediction.

So much for touching gestures. His eyes flew open, and they were no longer dull and listless. His breathing had become regular, and his color was back. Whether it was supposed to work or not, my blood had given him enough strength to hang on.

I eased him down carefully on the grass. "I'll be right back. I need to see to someone." Tamlel was no longer moving. The tide was receding, leaving him beached on the wet sand, and I knew it was too late. And I knew I had to try.

I ran back down to the shore, tripping over the carnage, falling to the sand beside him. He still breathed, but his eyes were closed, and I knew that he was very close to death.

I put my bloody arm against his lips, but he didn't react, and I cursed my foolishness. It had been a fluke—there was no way my blood could save anyone. I didn't belong here—the poor creature at the front entrance was simply in better shape than I'd thought, and my weak, *wrong* blood had been enough to stabilize him.

Tamlel's skin was icy cold now as death began to move over him, and I knelt beside him, hopeless, crying, the useless blood dripping down my arm. And then, at the last minute, I pried his mouth open and held my arm over it, letting the blood drip onto his tongue, twisting the cut to make it bleed more, oblivious to the pain.

His mouth fastened on my wrist, and I felt the sharp pierce of his teeth in my skin, opening my vein so that I bled more freely. The other man hadn't bitten me, but Tamlel was holding me, sucking at me, his hands clutching my arm so tightly that it was numb.

I was growing dizzy, and I wondered if it was blood loss or the horror of the night. It didn't matter—dizziness was preferable to the reality that surrounded me, to the death and horror that had turned an idyllic escape into a charnel house. I closed my eyes, growing weaker, when I heard a roar of such blind fury that I knew that all the Nephilim hadn't been defeated, that I would be torn limb from limb. Something grabbed me, jerking me away from Tamlel, and I went flying through the night air, landing breathless on the bloody sand, prepared for the death I had managed to avoid.

I looked up, expecting to see the huge, unwieldy shape of a Nephilim. But it was no monster silhouetted against the moonlight. He was covered in blood, it matted his hair and covered his skin, but I knew those eyes, Raziel's eyes, blazing in fury as he turned on Tamlel, his fangs bared in attack.

"No!" I screamed, certain he was about to tear his friend limb from limb. A moment later the rage drained from his body, and he turned to me, sinking to his knees beside me in the sand, pulling me into his arms. The smell of death and sweat and blood covered him, and I sank against him in weak relief.

"I'm sorry," he gasped. "I don't know . . . did I hurt you?"

I was past speaking. I could only shake my head against his chest, trying to get closer to him.

Something folded around me, soft as feathers, dark as the night as everything went black.

TWENTY

IF IT HADN'T BEEN FOR THE FOUL stench, I might have slept forever. It was a gray day, somehow different from the gentle mist that usually enshrouded Sheol. I lay in bed, unmoving. The light that came in through the windows was murky, filtered, and the bed beneath my poor, aching, bruised body was much too comfortable to leave. I rolled over reluctantly. The last thing I could remember, I'd been flying through the air, dragged away from Tamlel by a furious monster, and in that brief flash I'd been convinced I was going to die. Until I looked up and saw Raziel.

I couldn't remember much more. Someone had managed to drag my ass upstairs and cleaned me up. I hadn't slept alone—somehow I knew that. I was stark naked, and the blood and filth had been washed from my body by some ghostly handmaiden. Raziel had tended to me, despite his own wounds. Raziel had carried me upstairs and seen to me.

Had I dreamed it all? I looked at my arm, searching for tooth marks. The wound was still there, a long scratch from my biceps down to my wrist, but it had already closed up, healing, and there was no sign that two of the Fallen had fed on me.

Just as Sarah's wrist had healed instantly when she'd fed Raziel. But I couldn't think about Sarah.

I pushed back in the bed. I hadn't meant for it to happen last night and I couldn't believe it had done them any good. My blood had been nothing more than a pacifier. An empty breast for a starving infant, bringing momentary comfort but no sustenance. But at least it had eased them, and for that I could spare a few pints of blood. Until Raziel had appeared with a roar of rage, pulling me away from Tamlel, about to kill his old friend. Had the battle temporarily stripped his sanity from him? Why would he want to hurt Tamlel?

My scream had stopped him. And his arms around me, his mouth against my temple, had been safety, protection, love.

No, not that. He wasn't going to love anyone ever again.

That horrible smell, mixed with oily smoke, was enough to make me throw up. I climbed out of bed slowly, my body aching, and grabbed the robe that hung on the back of the bathroom door. It was an ancient kimono, the heavy silk oddly reassuring as it draped over my naked body, and I walked barefoot into the living room, half afraid I'd find Raziel there, half afraid I wouldn't.

He wasn't there—the place was deserted. I headed over to the open windows and looked out, hoping to see a tall, familiar figure on the beach.

The bodies were gone, but the sand looked black with the spilled blood. I could see smoke off to the right, and without thinking I climbed out onto the balcony to get a better look, wincing as my knee cramped up. There was a huge bonfire, tended by three of the women. I couldn't recognize any of them—they looked as battered as I was feeling—but they kept a close watch on the flames, and it took me a moment to realize what was causing the horrific stench. It was a funeral pyre for rotting flesh. They were burning the bodies of the Nephilim.

The Fallen couldn't do it. Fire was poison to them—a stray spark and they might die. It was up to the humans to deal with the fire. Up to us to clean up the mess. But Sarah was gone.

The bloodstained beach in front of the house was deserted. The mist was light, covering everything like a depressed fog, but there was no sign of life. Who had survived? What were they going to do now?

I climbed back inside and went to the closet and

then froze, looking at the colorful clothes. The dress I'd worn yesterday was nowhere to be seen. The dress that Raziel had almost managed to pull off me, the dress I'd used to try to stanch Sarah's blood as it poured from her body.

Sarah was dead. There was no get-out-of-jail-free card, no way for Sarah to become immortal like her husband. If there were, Azazel wouldn't be so grim, and Raziel would still be happily married to bride number forty-seven or whoever. And I'd be roasting in hell.

Today wasn't a day for colors, it was a day of mourning. I considered Raziel's black clothes, then went with a loose white skirt and a tunic, looking like a cult member once more. I ran a brush through my tangled hair and took one last look at my reflection in the mirror. I looked pale, as if I'd lost a lot of blood, and I wondered just how much Tamlel had taken from me. Had he even survived?

There wasn't a thing I could do about how I looked—I was probably a lot healthier than most of the other survivors. Which damned well better include Raziel. No, I wasn't even going to consider any alternative. I closed my eyes for a moment, trying to reach into his mind.

I met with the mental equivalent of a door slamming shut, and I laughed with overwhelming relief, a relief I didn't want to examine too closely. He was alive, and still bad-tempered.

There was blood on the stairs. Someone had made an effort to clean it up, but the smears were still visible, and I was glad I'd decided to put on the white sandals instead of going barefoot. The thought of walking on dried blood held a tinge of horror. I'd as soon force my feet into those damned stilettos that had brought a swift end to my promising life.

I didn't know whether my exhaustion was physical or emotional. I had to stop at each landing to catch my breath, and it gave me plenty of time to observe the battle stains that marred most of the surfaces. Blood on the rugs, gouges in the walls.

The dratted dizziness lingered. Had giving my blood to Tamlel and the other Fallen done this to me? Raziel had told me the wrong blood was dangerous—the horror of last night was making my memory far from clear, but Tamlel couldn't have taken that much blood, could he? There were no marks on my arm apart from the long scratch, and no reason why giving my blood should have helped them or hurt me. At least, not according to Raziel.

But I was feeling like I'd just donated blood and forgotten to take a cookie. Did they give blood transfusions here? Because I had the unpleasant suspicion that I could do with one.

The massive entry hall looked very different in the murky light of day. The bodies were gone. So was most of the furniture, which had been smashed during the battle. The smell of death lingered, the wretched stench of the Nephilim, the smell of decay. I shivered, peering out the open door, but the beach was still deserted. The blood on the sand had dried to a dark rust. It would take a heavy rain to wash it away.

I looked over at the funeral pyre. I had no desire to get closer—the smell upwind was bad enough. I looked closer at the fire, at the burning limbs and the spit of roasting fat, and I shuddered, feeling faintly nauseated. Was Sarah part of that mountain of flames? Were the others? Surely not.

I turned and walked back into the house. There was no one in the public rooms, and I had the sudden uneasy suspicion that the surviving Fallen might have left, abandoning this place and the few women who'd survived.

And then I thought of the Council room, where the Fallen gathered. Where Raziel had fed from Sarah's wrist, forever changing the way I looked at things. They were there, I knew it.

The doors to the grand meeting room were shut. There were gouges in the heavy wood, and one handle had been smashed. I'd run away from here once in shock and horror. This time I was here to stay.

I pushed open the door and stepped inside, and a sudden rush of emotion hit me. I wasn't going to cry, I told myself, no matter what. The men sitting at the table stared at me like I was an annoying interloper, but I had no intention of going anywhere. I kept my expression calm and smooth. *Help me, Sarah,* I said silently. *Don't let these bullies unnerve me.*

Azazel sat at the head of the table, his face drawn with grief and fury. He stared at me with such hatred that I was momentarily shocked. He'd never liked me, that much had been obvious, but now he looked as if he'd like to kill me, and I couldn't figure out why. I'd never done anything to him.

"Sit."

It was Raziel's voice, and the relief that washed over me almost made me dizzy. Just great: I'd fall at his feet in a maidenly faint. Schooling my expression, I turned to look at him. Like all the others, he looked like hell, like he'd been in a battle that he'd barely won. But he was alive and in one piece, though he appeared almost as angry as Azazel. Did they think I'd let the Nephilim in? What had I done to make them so angry with me?

Whether I liked it or not Raziel was my closest ally. I started toward him, but he stopped me with a word. "No," he said. "Sit on the side. In Sarah's seat."

I froze. "I can't."

"Sarah is dead," Azazel said in a savage voice. "Do as your mate tells you."

"But he's not—"

"Sit." Raziel's voice was low and deadly. I went and sat.

There were only a handful left. But Tamlel was sitting beside Azazel, trying to look encouraging, and the other man, the first one I'd given blood to, was sitting nearby. So near death, and they'd somehow managed to survive, which was astonishing.

There were no other women in the room. I missed Sarah's comforting presence, missed her so badly that I wanted to cry. I sat and said nothing.

Azazel continued as if my arrival didn't mean diddly, which I suppose was true. "Someone opened the gate," he said. "We all know it. And until we find out who did, and why, we aren't safe."

"It wasn't me," I said promptly.

Azazel glared at me, and Raziel snarled, "No one thinks it was. Be quiet for now. Your turn will come."

Hardly reassuring, I thought, sitting back in the hard chair that had held Sarah for so many years. Both Raziel and Azazel were furious with me, and it was only logical that they were pissed about the blood. I had a hundred excuses. My arm had been slashed by one of the Nephilim, and the men were down—what was the harm in trying to help? And it certainly hadn't been my idea in the first place. The wounded man had simply latched onto my bleeding arm like a starving kitten. He'd been too out of it to realize what he was doing—it was no one's fault.

Going back to Tamlel had been a different matter, but Tamlel was looking so calm that I was sure he'd speak up for me. After all, he was the one who'd latched on and used his teeth like some giant lamprey eel. He owed me support, considering the way Raziel was glowering at me.

"How do you think you'll discover who let them in?" Sammael said in a flat voice, and I started. I'd thought he was one of the dead, but somehow he'd managed to survive. "It's a waste of time. They probably ate whoever opened it, or else he or she was killed in the battle. I don't know that you'll ever be able to find out who did it. We should be putting our energy into rebuilding, not into useless quests for an irrelevant truth."

"I know you are grieving the loss of your wife, Sammael," Azazel said in a cold tone. "And the rebuilding process will start as soon as the boat is finished. In the meantime, the truth is never irrelevant. We will find who did this. Who was responsible for the deaths of seven of our brothers, and nineteen of our women. The Nephilim followed orders very well—they knew that to destroy our women would destroy us."

"We are not destroyed," Tamlel said quietly. "We mourn. But we are not destroyed."

"Whoever let them in is still alive," Azazel said. "I know it in my heart. We will find the traitor."

"And then what?" Raziel said, refusing to look at

me. "No matter how much you want to tear him limb from limb, we don't kill. Not our own."

Azazel set his jaw, not denying Raziel's charge. "He will be banished. Forced to wander the earth. One who has committed such a crime will never find a bonded mate, and he will be allowed nowhere near the Source. So he will eventually weaken and die. There will be no revenge, no rejoicing. Simple justice."

The Source? Sarah was dead. Someone must have been lined up to take her place, a kind of Source-in-waiting. That woman must have followed in my footsteps last night and saved the ones I'd tried to help.

But as much as I would have loved to believe that fairy-tale nonsense, I had the horrible feeling that that wasn't the case at all. I had a really awful suspicion about what was coming, and I didn't want to hear it.

Azazel turned his black, furious gaze on me, and I had the distinct impression he would have reached out his big strong hands and strangled me on the spot if he didn't have an audience. He hadn't liked me, not from the moment I'd arrived in this place, and that dislike had grown to monumental proportions.

"Why did you attempt to feed Tamlel?" he demanded. "You have little knowledge of our ways, of the laws that govern us. In your ham-handed attempt to help, you could have killed him."

"He looks just fine to me," I said.

No thanks to you, he probably wanted to say. "Answer my question." His voice was icy.

I looked toward Raziel, but there was no help from that quarter. He looked almost as angry as Azazel. "I certainly didn't plan to do anything," I said apologetically. "I came downstairs to see if I could help—"

"Even though I ordered you to remain where you were." Raziel's voice was low and deadly.

Damn, was it some kind of crime to disobey one's supposed lord and master? If so, I was in deep shit, and would continue to be as long as I had to put up with Raziel's high-handed ways.

If he could ignore me, then I could just as easily ignore him. "I came downstairs," I said again, my voice overriding Raziel's, "to see if there was anything I could do. I saw Sarah—" My voice caught for a moment, and I deliberately kept my gaze from Azazel. "I saw Sarah wounded, and Raziel took me outside. When I went to get help because I saw Tamlel lying there, one of the wounded grabbed my skirt, begging me to help him. There was nothing I could do, but I knelt and held him, hoping to either comfort him until medical help arrived or at least be there with him as he died." I glanced over at the young man, and he nodded.

"That was me," he said. "I'd been trying to get to Sarah when one of the Nephilim came up behind me. I managed to kill it, but he'd slashed me pretty badly, and I couldn't make it."

"Gadrael," Azazel recognized him. "And you are well?"

"Quite well, my lord."

Azazel turned his cold, empty blue eyes back to me. "Go on. You were cradling Gadrael and you suddenly decided your blood could help him?"

"No. I was trying to comfort him. But I had a long scratch on my arm. As I held him, my arm brushed against his mouth and he instinctively began to suck at it. He was barely conscious and he had no idea who I was—he just recognized the smell of blood."

"I see. But he didn't pierce you, just drank from your wound. What happened next?"

This was the trickier part. I'd been entirely innocent the first time around. The second had been sheer hubris on my part, and I couldn't blame them for being pissed. "Well, Gadrael was looking better. And I knew Tamlel was dying, and I didn't think help would get to him in time, and I thought that maybe since the wrong blood seemed to help Gadrael, then maybe it would help Tamlel, at least long enough for help to come. So I went back to him and . . . offered him my arm."

"It never occurred to you that your blood might have helped Gadrael because you might be his bonded mate?" Azazel said.

The low growl was startling, and I looked back across the table at Raziel. He looked positively . . .

feral. I'd heard that growl before. Last night, just before he'd grabbed me and flung me away from Tamlel.

"No," I said, looking away.

"With Tamlel," Azazel continued his inquisition, "Did he too lick at your blood, respond to the offer of blood from your wound?"

"No. He was unconscious. Much closer to death than Gadrael." Another growl from Raziel.

"Explain."

Shit, I thought. But really, what was so terrible about what I had done? It was a crisis situation and I had reacted instinctively, and they should be spending their time figuring out who let the Nephilim in instead of harassing me. I sighed, knowing Azazel wasn't going to stop until he got his answers. "When Tamlel didn't react to my arm pressed against his lips, I . . . I opened his mouth, then twisted my wound to make it bleed more freely, so that drops of blood fell in his mouth. It was enough to bring him back, at least partially, and he held on to my arm and, er . . . drank." I did my best to look ingenuous, but I doubted Azazel was fooled. Any more than Raziel was.

"And he used his teeth, did he not? Pierced your vein?"

"Yes."

"And you let him continue, almost to the point of death, before Raziel found you and stopped him?"

I glanced at Raziel. I'd never seen him looking so angry. "I suppose so," I said reluctantly. "I wasn't thinking clearly. I never thought Tamlel would actually bite me—after all, Gadrael hadn't. And then I assumed he'd stop when he had enough." I glanced at Tamlel, who was looking stoic. Was he in the same kind of trouble I was?

"So we have two possibilities here," Azazel said in his cold, emotionless voice after a long moment. "The most likely is that Gadrael was less grievously wounded than you thought. Don't interrupt," he added as he saw me start to protest. "With him, the taste of blood, even the wrong blood, was enough to bring him back. You are here only as a partner for Raziel, you have no bonding to him, and while it is unusual, it seems likely that you are Tamlel's mate and neither of you realized it."

"No," said Raziel in a low, savage voice.

Ignoring Raziel, I glanced at Tamlel. He seemed sweet, charming, but I didn't want to be his mate. I didn't want to kiss him, fuck him, fight with him. . . . I glanced back at Raziel, who looked ready to explode. Raziel was a different matter. I couldn't begin to know what I wanted, needed, from him, not now, when I was too weary to think clearly. I only knew that I needed him.

Damn it. And he'd probably read that revealing thought, smashing what few defenses I had left.

"Then there's the other option, which seems unlikely."

The silence in the room was so thick it was practically choking, and Azazel seemed in no mood to elaborate. I was beginning to get annoyed. I knew what was coming.

"Are you going to go on, or are we all going to sit here in uncomfortable silence?" I snapped.

"We've already discussed the possibility," Azazel said forbiddingly. "We're just considering it."

Why in the world had lovely, sweet Sarah married such a hard-ass? I leaned forward. "But you forgot to include me in this discussion, which seems to concern me the most. I know your patriarchal bullshit style makes you forget that women have brains and opinions, but since this is about me, then you can just spit it out."

"The only other alternative is that for some reason, by some cosmic joke or bizarre twist of fate, you are the new Source. Which doesn't make sense. The Source must be the bonded mate of one of the Fallen, and you haven't had the bonding ceremony. Don't think you've fooled me with your charade—I know perfectly well it was all an act. Besides, there has always been a long period of mourning before a new Source became apparent. Therefore it's impossible for you to be the Source."

"Impossible," I agreed, my stomach churning. I'd

known this was coming. I'd just hoped I was wrong. "But if I were? That doesn't mean I have to be *your* bonded mate, does it?"

If anything, Azazel looked more revolted by the thought than I was. "Hardly. The Source can belong to anyone."

"'Belong'?" My voice was dangerous. Once again I was being discussed as if I were a commodity, and I was getting past the point of being the Good Girl.

"If you are the Source, then it's always possible your connection to Raziel is deeper than either of you want or realize."

All the humor had left Raziel's face. It was nothing compared to how I felt. He might be the most gorgeous male who had ever put his hands on me, but he was arrogant, brooding, manipulative, and lying, and worst of all, while he might have wanted me, he certainly didn't love me. And damn it, I wanted love. True love, gushing, romantic, oh-my-darling love. Something Raziel was never going to give again, and certainly not to me.

The only defense I had was to push him away first. "So how do we find out?" I said in a practical voice. They looked startled. Clearly they'd been so caught up in horror over the possibility that I might somehow have a role in their little boys' club that they hadn't even thought about that. "What would happen if someone drank from me and I wasn't the Source? Would he die?"

"Possibly," Azazel said slowly. "At the very least he would become sick, run a fever, possibly throw up. We can't tell with Tamlel or Gadrael because their bodies were already compromised by the wounds they had received."

"Then we need a volunteer," I said brightly. "It's the only way we can be certain."

Raziel rose, pushing back his chair, but Azazel fixed him with a look. "You know it can't be you. If she's your bonded mate, you'd be able to drink from her and you know it. I assume you haven't done so as yet."

"None of your damned business," Raziel snapped.

"It's all of our business," the leader replied. "Sammael, you may try."

Sammael was sitting near me, and I immediately held out my arm, more curious about Raziel's reaction than anything else. I could feel the tension and rage washing over him, a mindless, animal response. He hadn't resumed his seat; he was just standing there, vibrating with something I wasn't sure I wanted to interpret.

Sammael didn't look any too happy about the idea, but he took hold of my arm as if it were an ear of corn, and his incisors elongated. I watched with fascination, wondering what set off that reaction. Was it blood flow, like an erection? Did old vampires have trouble getting it up, or down, or whatever?

Sammael set his mouth against my wrist, and I felt

the twin pinpricks, just a quick, sharp pain. And then nothing at all as he fed at my wrist.

"Enough!" Raziel snapped, and Sammael pulled his mouth away quickly. "She has already lost too much blood from Tamlel's carelessness."

Azazel was focusing on Sammael. "Well? Are you feeling ill?"

Slowly Sammael shook his head. "She is the Source," he said quietly.

"Shit." Raziel's muttered expletive expressed it for all of them, me included.

Dead silence. I considered whining, "But I don't want to be the Source," then thought better of it. I kept quiet, letting it sink in.

After a moment Azazel spoke, and his low, angry voice was defeated. "Very well. As blood-eaters we know that blood doesn't lie. You'll have to discover who your mate truly is—"

"She's mine," Raziel said fiercely, throwing himself back down into his chair. "No one else's."

"Well, we'll leave you time to discover whether that, indeed, is true. In the meantime, the woman will have to be instructed in the duties of the Source, the proper diet and training, and she—"

"Hell, no," I said. I'd had enough of this patriarchal crap.

Once more the silence was deafening. "What did you say?" Azazel demanded dangerously.

"I said hell, no. If you think I'm going to be Raziel's sex slave and your personal blood bank, you have another thing coming. This is your problem—figure it out yourself."

My magnificent exit was marred slightly when the flowing sleeve of my tunic caught on the door handle, but I yanked it free as dramatically as I could and strode from the room.

Once out of sight, I wanted to pump my fist in triumph. Assholes, all of them. I wasn't about to let anyone push me around, particularly not Azazel and Raziel. They could find someone else to be their goddamn Source, preferably someone more like Sarah, with her serene smile and calm nature.

At the thought of her I wanted to cry, but I dashed the tears away. I needed fresh air and the smell of the ocean to clear my head of all that testosterone. If any of them made the mistake of trying to follow me, I would simply head over to the fire and grab a burning branch or something. I could even build a ring of fire around me if I felt the need. It would serve them right and probably make them crazy with frustration. I found I could manage a sour grin.

As I moved out into the sunlight I felt someone behind me, someone tall, and I knew who it was. I turned, ready to lash out at him.

Raziel looked as furious as I felt, which only made things escalate. "What's your problem?" I demanded hotly. "It's not like they're expecting *you* to be a cross between a whore and a bloodmobile. If you think I'm going to sit quietly by while men suck at my wrist, you're dead wrong. If you'll pardon the expression."

"I don't think that." His low voice was surprising.

"You don't?"

"No one is touching you but me," he said.

TWENTY-ONE

SHE WAS LOOKING SHELL-SHOCKED, and I couldn't blame her. She'd witnessed the kind of carnage unthinkable for someone of her world, she'd watched people she cared about die, she'd lost too much blood because of Tamlel's carelessness, and to complete the disaster, the worst possible scenario had come to pass. She wasn't just bound to me—she was bound to all of us.

It wasn't as if I hadn't had plenty of warning. I had simply refused to recognize it. She was reading me, more and more. I had a will of iron, yet I hadn't been able to keep away from her. I had known, deep in my heart, and I could deny it no longer. She was my bonded mate. I would watch her grow old and die, and just to twist the knife further, I would have to watch the others feed from her narrow, blue-veined wrist, and there wouldn't be a thing I could do about it, even as my atavistic blood roared in response.

And I had hurt her. When I'd returned from sealing the wall, I'd found her down by the edge of the water, sitting back on her knees, Tamlel's head in her lap while he drank from her. She was pale and dizzy from blood loss, and rage had swept over me, a killing rage that had only just abated. I'd ripped her away from Tamlel, too blind with jealous fury to realize what I was doing.

I'm not sure what I would have done to Tamlel if I hadn't heard her quiet moan. I spun around in the blood-soaked sand to see her lying against a rock, and guilt and panic swept away the rage. The healers were too busy with the dying to help her—all I could do was bring her back to my rooms and tend to her as best I could, washing the blood and gore from her, letting my hands soothe and heal her. We all had healing power, some more than others, and it was always stronger with our mates. I should have known, when I'd held her hands and healed them, that she was mine.

I *had* known. I had just refused to face it.

I still didn't want to. Uriel must have known she was my mate. Her sins were too slight to deserve either an escort or a sentence to the flames. Uriel had assumed I would follow orders and throw her over the precipice, denying the Fallen their next Source.

So that when his traitor let the Nephilim in, there'd be no one for the survivors.

I didn't know how much she was reading from me. We were too new—her sense of me would deepen, and then the natural boundaries would develop. Whatever she could hear from me, she didn't like it.

She backed away when I tried to touch her, shaking her head. "You hate me," she said flatly.

I controlled my flare of irritation. Of course she thought so—my anger was so powerful it would swamp any other feeling. "No I don't," I said, trying to sound reasonable and failing.

"I'm not doing this." She was close to tears, which surprised me. Throughout the last few days, no matter what she'd had to deal with, I'd never seen her cry, something I was profoundly grateful for. I hated it when women cried.

"Yes," I said. "You are." And before she could avoid me, I scooped her up under her arms from behind and soared upward, deliberately keeping her mind open, not shutting it down as I had the last time I flew with her.

I heard her gasp over the sound of the wind as it rushed past us. I crossed my arms over her chest, holding her against me, and I could feel her heart racing. She was warm against me, despite the cool air, and after a moment I felt her stiffness relax so that she flowed against me, sweetly, like a reed in the water, and her skirts covered my legs as we climbed higher.

I'd only meant to take her as far as our apartment on the top floor, but the moment I felt her joy I changed my mind. I soared over the huge old house, turning right to avoid the oily smoke of the funeral pyre, heading deeper into the virgin forests with their dark trees, past sparkling water. I rose above the mist, where the sun was bright overhead, warming me, and I let that warmth flow to her, sending tendrils of heat throughout her before she could be chilled by the atmosphere. We went up, way up, over the peak of the mountain, and out of instinct I called for Lucifer's faint voice. Uriel's plans had worked well—the fierceness of the Nephilim attack had kept us all too busy to search for the one man who could save us. I called, but there was no faint whisper. For once all I could hear was Allie's longing, singing to me, her body dancing with mine even as her mind still fought it.

We banked, passing a startled flock of Canada geese, and I felt her laugh against me, felt the sheer joy that suffused her, just as it suffused me when I flew, and my arms tightened imperceptibly, holding her even closer, somehow wanting to absorb her into my bones.

My wings spread out around us as I headed back toward the house. Allie was relaxed now, warm and soft and yielding against me, and I knew the unexpected flight had been a wise idea. Not that she wouldn't be ready to fight me all over again, the moment we set down. But at least for now she had accepted my strength, accepted my touch. She would again.

I landed on the narrow ledge lightly enough, planning to hold on to her until my wings had folded in, but standing still on the terrace felt too good, and instead I put my face against her neck, breathing in the sweet smell of her, until she panicked and jumped away, turning to stare up at me with an expression of shock.

Which wasn't surprising. My wings were particularly impressive—an iridescent cobalt blue veined with black, they were emblematic of one rule of the Fallen. The longer we'd lived, the more ornate were our wings. The newly fallen had pure-white wings. Lucifer, the First, had wings of pure black. I was somewhere in between.

I let them fold back into place, hoping this would be enough to calm her, but she still stared at me. Her unexpected tears had dried, thank God, and she was ready for battle. I could still feel the lingering trace of her pleasure at our flight, and I stifled a grin. No one had ever enjoyed flying in my arms before, and it was almost as heady an experience for me.

"All right," she said. "What are we going to do about this mess?"

She'd decided to be reasonable. I could sense it, sense her struggling for her usual pragmatism. No problem was ever so big that it couldn't be solved, she was thinking. There had to be a way around this.

"There isn't," I said. "We're talking about forces beyond your comprehension. Things that can't be reasoned with."

She didn't snap at me for reading her. "In other words, we're trapped."

"Yes."

"And you don't like it?"

I could feel the too-familiar rage simmer inside me. I had never had to share my mate, ever, throughout the endless years of eternity. Only Azazel had wed the Source, and I could remember only too well the difficulties during times of transition. Difficulties I'd attributed to grief and the usual problems in a new relationship. Now I wondered.

"You don't need to answer," she said glumly. "I can feel it." She was misreading me again, mistaking my anger at sharing her for a rebellion against her as my wife. I looked at her, and a stray memory surfaced.

"Where did you grow up?" I demanded, more intent on answers than on soothing her wounded pride. I could take care of that quite effectively when I got her into bed.

"I'm not going to bed with you."

I laughed, which startled her. She expected that her ability to read me would be annoying, but by now it was just the opposite. It was proof that whether I liked it or not, she was mine, just as I was hers. "You grew up in Rhode Island, didn't you?" I said, ignoring her protest.

"You already know everything about me, including the number of men I've slept with and whether I enjoyed it or not," she said bitterly.

"I never paid attention to your childhood," I said. I remembered her. She'd been seven years old, sitting alone outside a small house near Providence. Her long brown hair had been in braids, her mouth set in a thin line, and I could see the tracks of her tears as they'd run down her dirty face. She was using a stick to dig in the dirt, ignoring an angry voice that came from the house. I'd stopped to look at her, and she'd seen me, and for a moment her eyes widened in wonder and her pout disappeared.

I knew why. Children saw us differently. They knew we were no threat to them, and when they looked they knew who we were, instinctively.

Allie Watson had looked at me and smiled, her misery momentarily vanishing.

I should have known then.

I saw her again when she was thirteen, and too old to see who I really was. I hadn't expected to see her, and when I did I moved back into the shadows so she wouldn't notice me. She was angry, rebellious, storming out of a store in front of a woman who was praying loudly and calling upon Jesus to spare her such a worthless, ungrateful daughter.

I'd wanted to grab the woman, slam her against the wall, and inform her that Jesus was far more likely to spare the daughter such a harridan of a mother; but I didn't move, watching as they got into a car, the mother tearing off into traffic, her bitter mouth still working as Allie looked out the window, trying to shut her out.

That's when she saw me again. Even in the shadows, her young eyes had picked me out, and for a moment her face softened as if in recognition, and she lifted a hand.

And then the car sped around a corner, and she was gone.

I should have known then. Instead, like a coward I'd blotted it out of my mind. I'd been shown her early on so that I could look out for her, keep her safe, but I'd been too determined not to fall into that trap again, and I'd turned my back on her.

I should have come for her when she was ready. My instincts would have told me—it might have been when she was eighteen or when she was twenty. Instead I'd wasted all those years, when she could have been here, and safe.

"What the hell are you talking about?" she said.

"Or thinking about—whatever. Why would I want to be here? I want to go back to my old life. I want to write books, and go out to lunch, and have lovers, and wear my own clothes. I—don't—want—to—be here," she enunciated. "Is that clear enough for you?"

I moved past her, climbing back into the apartment, knowing she'd follow. I didn't bother checking to see if the door was locked—no one, not even Azazel, would climb the stairs and interrupt us.

She came after me, of course. She watched, silent, as I found a bottle of wine and opened it, pouring us each a glass. I handed her one, and she took it, and for a moment I wondered if she was going to throw it in my face in the kind of dramatic gesture she was fond of.

"No," she said, reading me, and went to sit on one of the sofas. "But I won't say I'm not tempted."

It had been so long since anyone had been able to read me that it was going to take some getting used to. She was already far too adept at it, considering how little sexual congress we'd actually indulged in. And I hadn't fed from her.

I wouldn't feed from her. Once I did, there'd be no going back, and there was just enough resistance left inside me to hold out that hope. At least for a little bit longer. Besides, she was still weak from Tamlel's clumsiness, though I could sense her strength returning. That was one more sign that she was the Source. Her ability to bounce back from blood loss.

"You can't go back to your old life, Allie," I said wearily. "How many times do I have to explain this to you? You died. It happens to people all the time. You don't get a happy-ever-after with a prince, riding into the sunset. You don't get a house with a white picket fence and two-point-three children. You won't have any children, ever. You died too young for all those things."

I heard her quick intake of breath, a sound of pain that she tried to hide from me. I would have thought she wouldn't care about being a mother. I was wrong. About this, about so many things.

"So instead I get to be the meal plan for a bunch of vampires? Whoopee. Do I get weekly transfusions?"

I felt the now-familiar flare of anger at the thought, but I tamped it down. "You won't need them. The Source provides blood for those who are unbonded, but the amount is minimal, the occasion is surrounded by ritual, and you won't be called upon to serve more than once a month." The moment I said it, I knew it was a bad choice of words.

"Serve?" she said. "Like a waitress with a hearty meal?" ·

She was doing her best to anger me, and she was succeeding. "No. Like someone with a higher calling."

"Feeding blood to vampires is a higher calling?"

"Giving life to the Fallen is a higher calling. And the term is *blood-eaters*."

"I don't care what the term is, you're vampires."

I ground my teeth. She really did have an extraordinary ability to get under my skin, when I'd managed to be impervious to everything and everyone for so long. She was bringing me back to life, and reanimating the dead was always painful.

"Fine," I said. "We're vampires. Get over it."

"What did you do in the past when the Source died? Did one of you have to quick find a willing sacrifice?"

Beneath her hostility I could sense a real concern, and I decided to answer her. "Azazel has been the only one married to the Source. The Source has never died suddenly—it was always natural causes and there was plenty of warning. The healers . . ." I wasn't sure how I was going to phrase this, but Allie filched the image out of my mind.

"They take blood from her at regular intervals and store it," she supplied. "How charming. So how long does Azazel get to mourn? How long before Sarah is replaced by some nubile young thing?"

"He has always had enough time to grieve. With Sarah it will be a problem. I don't know how long it will take him to recover from her loss."

"He's had enough practice," she said, her voice

brutal. "So why me? And don't give me that crap about being bonded mates—you and I both know that's impossible. We don't even like each other."

I resisted the impulse to smile. She was putting so much effort into keeping me at a distance. She didn't want me anywhere near her. She didn't want me pushing her down among the pure white sheets, moving down her sweet, gorgeous body, tasting her, my hands on her thighs, my mouth—

"Don't do that!" she said, shaken. She was searching for some way to stop me, some kind of insult. "After two nights ago, I thought you didn't believe in foreplay."

"Was I too fast for you?" I said, unruffled. "It seemed to me you were right there along with me. Are you telling me you didn't like it?"

"Of course not!" she snapped. "I'm just saying that women like to be wooed, slowly and respectfully."

I laughed. "So those orgasms were faked? You're able to control your body that well? I must admit I'm impressed. And clearly my information was incorrect—it said you only climaxed by yourself. Which, by the way, is considered a sin by some scholars, but which we embrace enthusiastically."

She was blushing, and I couldn't resist her. "Come to bed with me," I said, rising and holding out my hand.

She just looked at me, mutinous. "So you can feed on my wrist? You may as well do it here."

"No." Again I felt that little growl that seemed to come from nowhere. The growl I knew she sensed, and which frightened her. I struggled to control it. "I won't take your blood. If I did, it would be from an artery, not a vein."

"Ew," she said, wrinkling her nose. "What if you screw up your anatomy lessons?"

"I can hear the difference," I said. "But it's not going to happen."

"Why won't you take my blood? If I'm your supposed mate, what's stopping you? Everyone else will be having a go at me."

"It's not a good idea."

She looked at me, long and hard, and the conclusions she was jumping to were a mishmash in her brain. "Fine," she said, rising. "You can sleep on the couch." And she started for the bedroom.

TWENTY-TWO

I WASN'T GOING TO SLAM THE DOOR. I was going to close it quietly and forcefully, indicating dignified displeasure, but he was already there, his hand yanking it open. "I'm not sleeping on the couch."

"All right," I said. "I will." I started past him, but he caught me, spinning me around and pulling me against him, his strong arms imprisoning me.

I didn't like being controlled. At least, not really. There was a tiny little shiver of erotic reaction as my body was clamped against his, and for a brief moment I took that pleasure, even though I knew I shouldn't. I looked up at him, so close, so damnably, deliciously close.

"You're not going anywhere," he said, and bent his head and kissed me.

So, okay, I liked kissing him. I know I should have

stayed still, and I tried, I really did. But he cupped my chin, his long fingers gently stroking my face, and his mouth was soft, damp, and really, how could I resist? Because the brutal truth was, I felt more for him than I'd felt for anyone in my entire life. He was mine, even if I was afraid he still wanted to wiggle out of it. He was mine.

I softened against him, and he released my wrists, knowing I wasn't going to hit him. I slid my arms around his waist, pulling him closer, and rose on my toes so that I could reach him better, so that I could press my breasts against his hard chest, so I could sink into the heat of him.

He picked me up effortlessly. Yes, I knew he was supernaturally strong, but I still loved it, loved feeling delicate and weightless when I'd always felt clumsy. He thought I was luscious. I knew that, even as my doubts tried to discount it. He thought my soft, rounded body was irresistibly erotic. And I felt my blood heat, flowing through me like a river of pleasure; I wanted his touch, wanted his mouth on me, wanted everything.

He carried me into the bedroom. The light was muted through the bank of windows, and the awful stench was gone. Instead it smelled like cinnamon and spice, like Raziel's warm flesh and something underneath it, something hot and rich. He set me down on the bed, and this time I didn't try to jump up again, didn't try to argue or to fight, with his hands on me, unfastening the white tunic and pulling it over my head. He kissed my mouth, he kissed the swell of my breasts above the lacy bra, he let his tongue dance across my lace-covered nipple before fastening his mouth on it. I let out a quiet moan of delight. I'd never known my breasts were so sensitive. When other men had touched them it seemed simply part of the process, but when Raziel put his mouth on me—

He lifted his head, and his eyes were dark and glittery. "Stop thinking about other men," he said, his voice close to a growl. I wondered if I was supposed to be afraid of him.

"No," he said. "I won't hurt you. I would never hurt you."

I caught the strain of guilt and regret. He'd thrown me away from Tamlel, and I'd been knocked unconscious. I said nothing. His deep sorrow over what had been an accident was enough to assure me that I was safe. Whatever rage lived inside him, and I could feel it simmering, it would never be turned on me.

He pushed me back on the bed and I went, letting my eyes drift closed as he pulled the loose white pants off. He took the underwear as well, a little sooner than I was comfortable with, and flicked off the bra with a practiced hand. Well, of course he was practiced—he'd had thousands of years—

"They've only had bras for the last hundred years," he murmured against my skin, and his voice was thick with longing.

"Stop reading my mind," I protested, though my languorous voice was far from harsh.

"It's half the fun," he said, and I felt his mouth on my stomach, moving downward. I knew where he was going, and I knew I shouldn't mind. He thought he'd be doing something nice for me, when in actuality it had always left me unmoved. I sort of hated having him go to all that effort when I didn't particularly like it, but I didn't want to discourage him—

"You'll like it," he said, his long hands on my thighs, parting them, and he put his mouth on me, his tongue, and while I was telling myself to humor him the first shiver of reaction hit me by surprise.

I squeaked, and I could sense his amusement, but he didn't stop what he was doing, thank God, and I reached down and threaded my fingers through his hair, caressing him as he let his tongue flick across my clitoris. I let out a low, mewling noise, arching my hips, and his hands were there as well, long fingers sliding inside me, a gently thrusting promise of things to come, as his tongue worked its wicked magic. And then he used his teeth, gently, and I exploded.

Oh, he was a very bad man. He wouldn't let me

savor the first rush of climax; instead he had to draw it out, to keep touching me, licking me, biting me, so that wave after wave swept over me and my body went rigid, every nerve ending spiking, and I think I must have cried out, begging him to let me alone, begging him not to stop, begging him . . .

I collapsed against the bed, breathless, trying to control the sobs that were in my throat. He wiped his mouth on the sheet and moved up beside me, still fully dressed, and I wanted to put my hands on him, strip the clothing away, but for the moment I couldn't move.

He laughed, a soft, enticing sound. "That's all right. I know how to undress myself." He stripped off the black T-shirt, then reached for his jeans.

He was so fucking beautiful. But then, angels were supposed to be, weren't they? Long, graceful limbs, beautiful pale skin stretched over taut muscles. He was already erect, and I wanted to touch him, wanted my mouth on him where I'd never put my mouth on anyone.

The last stray shudders were finally ebbing away, but I still felt weak, exhausted, strangely on the edge of tears when I never cried. "Take your time," he said, stretching out beside me, letting his hand trace the plumpness of my breast. "We're not in any hurry."

"Maybe you're not," I managed to mutter. "You're eternal. I'm not."

It was the wrong thing to say. The playful expression on his face vanished, and darkness closed down. He started to pull away, but I shook off the last of my malaise and grabbed his arm, drawing him back. "Look, it's just me. There's no need to go all broody about it. It's not like I'm the great love of your life."

I could feel his anger again, but this time it didn't frighten me. He caught me, rolling me underneath him. "You idiot," he said. "Don't you understand anything about this?"

"That you go through women every century or so? Sure, I get it. And you said Azazel and Sarah were an anomaly, so I assume once I hit my forties or fifties you'll be turning your attentions elsewhere, and—"

"You don't know anything," he said brutally. "We're bound together, you and I. It's not casual, it's not until you grow old. It's not 'just you.' It is *you*. Why do you think I've fought it so hard? From now on, you're the most important thing in my life, whether I want it that way or not."

It still sounded to me like he didn't really want me, that some cosmic jester was playing a game with him, tying him to me when he would rather have been with someone else.

"No," he said, reading me again. "You're missing the point. I didn't want to care about anyone this way, ever again. The loss is too hard. If I think about losing you, it makes me crazy with grief and pain. I can't lose you."

"Just because someone put a whammy on you—" I began, prepared to argue my point.

"No one put a 'whammy' on me, whatever the hell that is. We were destined, and I was a fool to try to fight it. If I hadn't been so determined to stay alone, I would have saved us both a lot of trouble. Look into my eyes, Allie. Look deeply. You know me."

He was making me nervous, and I skittered away from the memories I was afraid to face.

"You *know* me," he said again, and I looked deep into his black, striated eyes, and remembered.

Sitting alone in the yard, listening to my mother scream at me from the living room, hugging myself, and he was there, and I didn't feel alone. And later, when my mother dragged me from the drugstore where I'd been looking at makeup, I saw him again. And remembered him, even when he wasn't there, and somehow I managed to withstand the rage and the lectures, knowing he was there. And my throat burned.

"I should have come for you sooner, Allie," he said gently. "If I hadn't been fighting it so hard, I would have been there. As it was, I didn't even recognize you."

I wasn't going to cry. "But you still want to

escape," I said. "You still want to break this . . . connection."

He hesitated, and that hesitation was enough to tell me I was right. "It's not that simple," he said finally. "You've been through a lot. I don't think you're ready."

"Don't tell me what I'm ready for," I said. "I know what I feel. And all I want to feel is you." And I moved up and put my hand on his chest, pushing him back on the bed.

He was warm, almost hot, and his skin was smooth and taut. I leaned over and kissed him, just the briefest brush of my lips against his mouth, and when he would have deepened it I moved away, letting my mouth trail down the side of his neck, kissing him where he'd tasted me, where he would have bitten me if he'd really wanted me forever.

But he wasn't going to sense that. I kept my mind filled with images of him and me, images and words and all the reactions of the senses, taste, touch, smell as well as sight and sound. I could hear his heart pounding, the blood pouring through his body, and there was something unbearably erotic about it. I moved my mouth down, down, not quite sure how to go about it. I'd seen porn at Jason's insistence, so I knew the mechanics, but I didn't want to follow that energetic example. Instead I wanted to explore him, carefully, using my tongue, tracing the blue veins, the thick, hard weight of him, closing my mouth around the head and sucking it gently, until I heard his moan of such blind surrender that waves of sexual delight danced through me, and I wanted more of him, wanted to pull and suck on him, wanted all of him in my mouth, and his groan sent shivers of pleasure through me.

He pulled me away, breathless, hauling me up to look at him. "Not that way," he said. "Not this time." And he pulled me under him, his mouth closing over mine.

I was shaking again by the time he moved his mouth. Could I come just from kissing him? Could I come from simply putting my mouth on him? Climaxes were there, just out of reach, almost ready, and my hands were trembling. It was too much. Panic was suddenly beating around me, and I tried to scramble away from him.

"I can't," I said in sudden fear. "I really can't." And I tried to get off the bed.

He caught me at the edge, pulling me back underneath him so that I was facedown on the bed, my mouth against the linen sheets that smelled of lavender and spice and something even more elemental. "Yes you can," he said with simple truth, and he slid his arm under my stomach, pulling me up to my hands and knees.

I knew what he was going to do, and I was past the

point of having expectations. I wanted whatever he wanted, and if he was going to take me this way I would revel in it. I could feel him against my sex, hot and solid and still wet from my mouth, and even at that angle he slid in smoothly, filling me, and I let out a strangled cry at the thick invasion that twisted at my heart. The different angle made it feel new, strange, incredibly powerful, and almost more than I could bear.

He took one of my hands and pulled it behind me, placing it on his cock, and I realized to my dismay that even though I felt completely filled, there was a goodly amount still waiting. I let my fingers wrap around him, and I wanted more. I wanted all of it. All of him. Everything.

"Allie," he breathed, a sound of regret and longing. "I don't think I can stop if you need me to."

"I don't need you to," I said, trying to push back at him, trying to get more of him. "I won't break, you know. I just need you."

He groaned, and pushed in, deeper, harder, and he felt huge, almost more than I could handle. Almost.

"More," I whispered, and he thrust.

I let out a little cry, a mixture of pain and surprise, as he somehow managed to sheath himself all the way inside me, and I could feel him against my womb, and I wanted his child in there, wanted it so desperately.

But I could never have it. No children, no family, no cottage with a white picket fence.

But I could have him, all of him, and I let out a soft grunt of satisfaction as I took him. He was mine, I reminded myself. Even if he was looking for an escape clause, I had taken him, everything, inside me. He was mine.

He pounded into me, a heavy dark rhythm that was like drumbeats from the heart of Africa. The drums of the gods. And I couldn't stop the shudders rushing through me, mini-climaxes that were building, and his hand went between my legs, his fingers touching me, and I screamed, putting my head down, my face into the sheets as I gave in to the wildness and power, the animal need washing through me. I gave myself to him with complete trust, no longer thinking, no longer doubting. He would keep me safe, he would stop when I had more than I could handle, he would know.

Again. And again. And again, he thrust into me, and each hard push made me shatter, over and over, until I couldn't think, couldn't hear, couldn't see, I was nothing but a seething mass of sensation.

He pulled out and I raised my head and cried out from the loss of him, but he simply turned me underneath him, pushing inside me again, deep, so deep. "I want to look at you when I come," he said, his voice a low growl, holding very still inside me.

My voice had vanished. I couldn't think, couldn't doubt; all I could do was feel. I was his completely, but he was holding back. "Take me," I whispered. *"Take me."* And reaching up, I took his head and pushed it toward my neck, so that his mouth was there, hot and wet, and I felt the scrape of his teeth, and I wanted more. "Take me," I whispered again. "Take everything."

He tensed, froze in my arms, and for a moment I was terrified that he'd pull away from me. He lifted his head and looked at me, and there was such sorrow in his eyes, a sorrow I didn't understand. "Allie," he said softly.

But I was inexorable. My body was aching with need, a need I neither recognized nor understood; but I somehow knew I had to have his mouth on me, drinking from me, for me to finally feel complete. "Please," I begged him, when I'd sworn I would never beg. "Feed."

He kissed my lips, so gently I wanted to cry. He leaned down and kissed the side of my neck, with the same feathering sweetness. And then I felt the sharp, sweet, piercing pain as his teeth sank into my skin, felt the draw of him sucking at my neck, drinking from me, drinking life from me, and I felt tears running down my face, as I was finally made complete. Filling him as he was filling me.

His cock inside me seemed to swell, and I cradled

his head against me, running my fingers through his thick, curling hair, whispering to him, soft words, love words.

And then he pulled away, rising up, and I could see my blood on his mouth, see the glitter in his eyes. He stared down at me, not moving, and I felt his climax deep inside me, giving me back what he had taken from me, and I joined him, flinging myself into the darkness with only him to guide me.

I MIGHT HAVE SLEPT MINUTES, hours, days. It didn't matter. I was wrapped in Raziel's arms, and neither of us was moving. I felt his hand brush my cheek, so gently. "You're crying," he whispered. "I hurt you. I knew I shouldn't have."

"You didn't hurt me," I said, rubbing my face against his hand like a hungry kitten. "I'm happy."

He moved a fraction so he could look at me, and his expression was bemused. "Do you always cry when you're happy?"

"I don't know that I've ever been happy before," I said simply.

He was about to argue, then stopped as he remembered my life, the life he knew almost as well as I did. "Maybe you haven't," he said finally, and kissed me.

I wondered if his mouth would taste of blood, but it didn't. It just tasted like Raziel, and I kissed him back, then let him tuck me against his warm, naked body. I didn't really want to move.

I ran my hand up his arm, my fingers delighting in the feel of him. "What does my blood taste like?"

His hand was at the back of my neck, his long fingers kneading the lingering tightness there, but at my words they stilled for a moment. "To me? Like honey wine, sweet and rich and intoxicating. Not like blood would taste to you."

"So can you bite people and turn them into va— into blood-eaters?" I asked.

"No. Why would I want to? It's a curse put upon us for disobeying God. Why in the world would I want to spread that curse, even if I could?"

"Because it would give eternal life, wouldn't it?"

He knew what I was getting at, and he sighed, pulling me even closer. "No, Allie. It can't be done. Humans are not made for the sacrament, and the one time one of the Fallen gave in to temptation, his mate died. It's forbidden."

"I was just curious," I said.

"Of course you were." His voice was wry.

"Are you always going to be able to read my thoughts?" I asked with a trace of asperity.

"I can try not to. When you're feeling strong emotion, it will come to me, and it will go both ways. In day-to-day life, I can shield you."

"And in bed? I'm assuming we're going to do this

again?" I held my breath, waiting for the answer. Was he still fighting it? Should *I* still fight it?

It was a long moment before he spoke, an endless one. "As often as possible," he said.

I know his thoughts, knew what he wanted. Now. Again. "Yes," I said. "Yes."

TWENTY-THREE

I SHOULD HAVE FELT GUILTY. I HAD tried to resist, but in the end she'd just been too much for me. I'd fed from her, drunk deeply, and in doing so I tied her to me forever.

It was something I swore I would never do again. I had my choice, aeons ago, and I paid the price. There was no escape for me or the others, but for Allie it was different. As long as I had kept away from her vein there was still a chance she could eventually leave.

Not anymore. And having taken her blood, I was going to find her serving as the Source even more difficult. Dangerous. Not for me, but for whoever dared approach her. They might have to restrain me for the first year or so, until I learned to control my possessive fury.

I should have known I couldn't stop myself. Not when she was pleading. And I should have known she would plead. A bonded mate needs that ultimate joining. Without it she never feels complete, and I'd accepted that she was, indeed, my wife. Once I'd taken her to bed it was a foregone conclusion, and it was remarkable I'd fought it for so long. I wasn't usually so thickheaded.

I'd lied to her, shielding my mind so she wouldn't know. There had been rare occasions when a mate had fed from her partner, but it was very dangerous. Four out of five times the woman would die. The fifth time she'd gain hundreds of years of life, as long as she continued to feed.

Morag had finally died when her mate had fallen beneath the Nephilim; she'd been well over eight hundred years old. I knew what Allie would do if she heard about it, and I couldn't afford to let that happen.

I wasn't going to worry about that now. I'd done my best to protect her—by taking her blood I'd made her escape impossible, and I was sorry for that. But sorry for nothing else.

I left her sleeping. I would have preferred staying with her, but I had to find Azazel. I knew him well enough, could feel his energy, and I knew things were very bad. Sarah had been his soul. He would be empty without her.

I found him perched on the top of the ledge, looking down over the compound and the sea beyond it.

The funeral pyre of the Nephilim had burned down to a few live coals, and I shuddered as I saw it. Our fear of fire is so deeply ingrained that it haunted me. Like us, the Nephilim were terrified of it, but we were too vulnerable to use it as a weapon.

I folded in my wings and sat down beside Azazel. He was staring at the boat that had hastily been built, the boat piled high with the bodies of our women and our dead brothers. Sarah would be on that boat. It would be set afire and then sent out to sea, a Viking burial to suit brave warriors, men and women alike. It was our ritual, one we couldn't avoid, the only time we willingly embraced fire.

"I'm going to leave," Azazel said in a quiet voice.

"I know." We had been together from the very beginning, from before we fell. I knew him as well as I knew myself. And for the first time in millennia, he was no longer going to be there.

He turned to look at me, and there was a ghost of a smile in his dark eyes. "How are you and the woman getting along? Are you still fighting your destiny?"

"My destiny? What exactly is my destiny?"

"You're married to the Source, or will be. It only makes sense that you should be the Alpha as well."

"No. You're the Alpha. You always have been."

"I've always been married to the Source, and I suspect you're not about to hand her over."

I said nothing. There was nothing I could say.

"Besides," he added, "I won't be here."

I knew there was no arguing him out of that one. "I will serve in your place while you're gone," I said. "The moment you return, you get it back."

He shook his head, his eyes bleak, staring into an empty future. "I may not make it back. The Nephilim are growing stronger, and there's nothing Uriel would like more than to bring me down."

"Then why go?"

"I have to." He looked back out at the boat. "I can't be here without her, not right now. This will heal, it always does, even if I don't want it to. But for now I can't stay in our rooms, sit at our table, be in our house without her."

I nodded. The loss of a mate was the most devastating thing that could happen to us, and Azazel's passion for Sarah had been deep and strong. I could only hope he'd survive beyond our safe walls. Walls that were not so safe anymore.

"I understand," I said.

He glanced at me. "Are you going to be able to watch when the others take the blooding sacrament?" he asked. "You seemed to be having a hard time controlling yourself earlier today. It might be better if you waited until you feed from her. Until you do, your possessive anger will be hard to control."

"I've already fed from her," I said.

Azazel looked at me. "So soon? You surprise me.

I thought you hated her. You certainly fought hard enough to get rid of her."

"She's mine," I said.

He nodded. "I suspected as much. But I should warn you. Even though you've fed from her, the first two or three occasions when others take her blood will be hard for you. Gradually you'll get used to it and see the difference between the sacrament and when you feed. But it will be difficult. Do not let your jealousy get out of control. The woman is besotted with you. Even if she were able to look at other men, she wouldn't—I've known that from the very beginning."

"Did you know she'd be the Source?"

Darkness shuttered Azazel's face. "No," he said. "If I had, I would have killed her." He rose, and I rose with him, watching as his wings spread out around him. "I haven't found the traitor. I'd planned to wait until we discovered who let the Nephilim in, but I find I . . . can't." He looked toward the funeral boat, and his face was bleak.

"You won't be here for the ceremony?"

"No." It was a simple word that conveyed everything. "Good-bye, my brother. Take care of that harridan you brought among us." And then he left, soaring upward into the night sky.

I watched him until he was out of sight, then sat again, not moving. This was the change I'd felt coming, the end that threatened us all. Azazel had led us from the beginning of time—he'd never left us. I had no gift of prognostication—but even I had known the end of times was upon us. It was no wonder I'd fought it.

Would the Nephilim have broken in if Allie hadn't been here? Had that been part of Uriel's plan? Had he known I would hesitate, recognizing her from our earlier meetings? Anything was possible.

There was nothing he wanted more than to distract us from our main goal, and he had succeeded. Lucifer still lay trapped, farther away than ever, and for a long time we would be busy mourning our dead and rebuilding our defenses. The monsters would have broken through sooner or later, but had Allie's arrival, the fact that she was unquestionably mine, somehow pushed things up? I would never know.

Uriel was winning. I knew it, so did Azazel. It was little wonder he hated Allie. Her arrival had signaled Sarah's death.

I thought back to the Source, her gentle smile, her wisdom. Allie was a far cry from Sarah's serenity. I wasn't even certain she'd agree to the sacrament. She'd insisted she wasn't going to provide blood for the Fallen. Once they started to weaken she'd change her mind, of course. Allie wasn't the kind of woman who'd stand by and let anyone suffer.

Except, perhaps, me, if I annoyed her. I liked peaceful women. Gentle, obedient women whose only reason in life was to love me. Allie was too much of the new world. Already she'd been a pain in the butt, and I knew she'd continue to be. I would have to get used to it.

I should go back, tell the Fallen that Azazel had left us. Most of them would already know—the unspoken bond among all of us was very strong. I could tell them, and then head back upstairs and wrap my body around Allie's and wake her slowly.

I'd tried to be careful, afraid I'd hurt her. She was small, unused to me, and the thought of causing her pain was enough to slow the raging tide of my hunger for her. But I hadn't been able to stop, any more than I'd been able to keep from feeding from her. Yet she'd been able to take everything with no more than a slight wince. More proof that she was made for me, when I'd refused to believe it for so long. No ordinary woman could take me as she had, not without pain that would preclude pleasure.

I'd felt her tighten around me in helpless response, felt her give everything to me. She was mine, and I was hers.

I was no longer alone. I turned to see Sammael land beside me, light as ever, his light-brown wings folding down around him. His face was set, emotionless, and I greeted him without rising. He'd lost his mate as well. His grief had to be very deep indeed. So deep that he didn't allow it to show.

"Azazel has left?" he said.

I had watched over Sammael after he'd fallen. Helped him with the huge adjustments, listened to him, advised him when he'd asked for counsel, stayed with him when the terrors hit him. If Azazel was an older brother, Sammael was a younger one. Someone I protected, guarded against evil.

I looked at Sammael and I saw the emptiness in his eyes. And I knew the truth.

I REACHED OUT FOR RAZIEL, but he was gone. The bed was already cold where he had been, though mostly he'd been on top of and beneath and behind and around me. I should have slept for days after all the things we'd been doing. Instead I was awake and wondering where he was. And when he'd be back, beside me, inside me, again.

I didn't want to get up—the evening air was cool and the covers were deliciously warm. Hadn't someone told me I wouldn't have to use the bathroom as much? They'd lied.

I got up, noticing with lascivious amusement that my legs were shaky. I staggered to the bathroom, understanding for the first time the term *relieving oneself*. Washing my hands, I looked at my reflection in the mirror and laughed.

He'd left his marks on me. The bite mark on my neck, two pale puncture marks that looked like something out of *Buffy the Vampire Slayer*. The whisker burns on my breasts. The tiny bites and scratches and even faint bruises all over my pale skin. Tentatively I let my hands slide down my body, caressing all those marks, and I closed my eyes, letting out a soft sigh of pleasure. "More," I whispered. What had the man done to me—turned me into a nymphomaniac? I'd had more sex in the last two days than I'd had in years.

I headed for the shower, stepping beneath the warm spray that was always at exactly the right temperature. Just another one of the perks of the afterlife, I thought. I'd always hated fiddling with showers to make sure the water temperature was right, particularly in a prewar apartment building in New York City with antique plumbing. The lovely perfection of the shower in Raziel's rooms was joyful indeed.

Not to mention that there were seventeen different sprays, ranging from the rain-forest shower overhead to the myriad massaging sprays coming from the silver pipe, each aimed at a strategic part of my body. I reached for the liquid soap and almost swooned. It had the same spicy scent that clung to Raziel's golden skin. I closed my eyes and slathered myself with it, letting the water sluice it away from me.

The bathroom was filling with steam, and I sat

on the shower's teak bench to enjoy it; a moment later I heard the door open, and my pulse leapt. He was back, sooner than I expected. I'd never shared a shower with a man. Sharing one with Raziel would be . . . delicious.

"I'm in here," I said unnecessarily. "Why don't you join me?" It was astonishingly bold of me—while shyness had never been my particular failing, sexual openness was equally foreign. But I had looked into his eyes and known how much he wanted me, and no foolish misgivings would get in my way. He wanted me, and for now I could let myself accept it, revel in it. He was mine.

I could see his outline through the heavy mist in the bathroom, moving toward the shower's doorless opening, and I rose in one fluid gesture, ready to move into his arms, when something stopped me. I froze, tilting my head to listen to him, but there was nothing but silence from the man who stood there.

It wasn't Raziel. This man was shorter, broader. Dangerous. I'd already called out to him—there was no chance of pretending that I wasn't there. No chance of slipping out of the open shower and hiding behind the bathroom door. I was trapped.

I left the shower running, on the off chance that whoever was in here had an aversion to getting wet, even as I realized how foolish that was—it wasn't the Wicked Witch of the West who was threatening me.

He moved closer, and the overhead spray beat down on his blond curls, his well-modeled face, and I felt relief wash through me. It was Sammael. Raziel must have told him to bring me to him.

His expression was odd, almost vacant, as he reached past me and turned off the water. He paid no attention to the fact that I was naked, but that didn't surprise me. I was hardly the type to inflame the passions of most men, and Sammael had just lost his beloved wife. He was probably barely aware of me.

He took my arm, not gently at all, and pulled me from the shower, tossing a towel at me. "Dry yourself," he ordered in his expressionless voice. Something was wrong. With Sammael, with the situation, and fear sliced through me. Had Raziel been hurt?

I turned to him, about to demand an explanation, when something stopped me. He stood so still, waiting for me, his face blank, his eyes dead. Mourning his wife, I thought. But I still couldn't rid myself of the belief that something was terribly wrong.

I didn't waste any time, though toweling off and dressing while Sammael watched wasn't one of the most comfortable things I'd ever done. I kept my back to him, turning around once I'd done up the white shirt and loose black pants I'd once more filched from Raziel. I still couldn't face bright colors, but plain white seemed too mournful. "Are you taking me to Raziel?" I asked.

"Of course." There was still that strange disconnect going on, as if he were in shock.

"I'm so glad you survived, Sammael," I said. "I know the loss of Carrie must be so hard for you."

He didn't blink. "He's waiting for you," he said.

Where? I didn't say the word out loud, though I'm not sure why. Feeling unsettled, I let my mind reach out, delicately, searching for Raziel.

There was no answer. Not even the muffled consciousness I'd been able to reach when he was deliberately closed off to me. Was he asleep? Had he gone somewhere to rest after the energetic hours we'd spent?

But he wouldn't have done that. When I'd drifted off to sleep the last time, I'd been folded in his arms; in his repletion he hadn't held anything back. He'd wanted nothing more than to sleep like that, his body entwined with mine.

And now he'd vanished. I jerked my head around to stare at Sammael. "Where is he?" I asked again. "Why isn't he here?"

"He wants you to join him. He's in the caves."

A cold, creeping sickness filled my belly. He was lying to me. Raziel had told me never to come to the mountain again, and there was no reason for that to change, even in our recent rapprochement.

I began to back away slowly. I had no idea whether I could run faster than one of the Fallen, but it was certainly worth a try. "Let me just get a cup of coffee," I said brightly, turning toward the kitchen.

"No."

I raised an eyebrow, feeling haughty. "No? If I want a cup of coffee, I'll get one," I snapped. "And if what Azazel said is true and I really am the Source, you're going to be relying on me for blood for the next little bit, however long it takes you to find another mate. So don't piss me off."

"I won't need your blood," he said. "The curse will be lifted, and I'll be back where I belong."

Oh, crap. "Just you? Or all of you?"

I didn't need his expression to verify what I already knew. "You let the Nephilim in," I said in a sick voice, remembering the sound and the stench of them, the hideous tearing of bodies, the screams of the dying. His own wife torn apart and devoured. I wanted to throw up.

"There is no new life without the end of an old one. The Fallen should have been wiped from this earth aeons ago. Once the Fallen have been destroyed, the new order can come to pass, and I will ascend to my throne in heaven."

"Ascend to your throne? Do you think you're God? Jesus?"

He gave me a look of withering disdain. "You know nothing of these matters. I will join Uriel as the guardian of heaven and earth, and wickedness will be burned out. The Fallen will be entombed in the middle of the earth as Lucifer has been, there to suffer eternal torment—"

"I get the picture." There was a messianic gleam to his eye now, and I'd learned at my mother's knee that there was nothing worse than a zealot. "And what happens to me?"

"You are the whore of a fallen one. There is no mercy or forgiveness for you." He took my wrist, his hand grinding my bones together, but I bit my lip and didn't say anything. "He awaits you."

He dragged me out onto the narrow terrace, and I gave up all dignity and shrieked for help, prepared to fight like hell before I let him throw me over.

Instead he put one beefy arm around my waist and soared upward, into the moonlit sky.

I stopped struggling. He could easily have dropped me, and I'd never liked heights. Yes, I know I was supposed to be over all my phobias, but there were a lot of things that were supposed to be true that so far had failed me.

I hadn't been afraid when I flew with Raziel. But Raziel was my mate, my soul, everything to me. Since I was probably going to die, there was no need to try to talk myself out of it. It was completely unoriginal of me, but I was desperately in love with my beautiful fallen angel, and thank God I was going to die before I told him. At least I'd be saved that embarrassment.

Except that he knew. He had to have heard me, known me, during those endless, blissful hours of taking and giving. He knew I was in love with him, and had been since . . . I could no longer remember when I didn't love him. It was so much a part of me that I couldn't separate it into time or space. Loved him so much that I could die for him, leap into hell for him. Whatever I had to do.

I had a choice. I felt dangerously close to tears, but I wasn't going to give in to weakness. If I was going to die, I was going down in flames, and I'd take Sammael with me if I could.

We landed hard on the side of the mountain, and he released me as if my touch were something unclean. I landed on my butt, and as I looked up into his face I managed to muster clear disdain. "So where's Raziel? Did you kill him already? And what are you going to do about all the others?" It wasn't over until it was over, and if I could get him to do the Evil Warlord shtick and reveal his wicked plans, I might just possibly have a chance to stop him. Particularly if he turned into a snake, which, according to Number 666 of the Evil Overlord Rules, never helps.

No, he couldn't do that. I was getting a little giddy—too many things had happened to me, and I was tired of being buffeted around.

"The others will be no problem. Their women are dead or dying. If there is no Source, they will weaken and die. The next time I let the Nephilim in, they will devour the rest, and I will ascend to heaven."

"Unless they devour you too," I pointed out, trying to be practical. "So I get to die because I'm the Source. Lucky me. Why kill Raziel? Why not let him weaken and die like the others?" It would take a hell of a long time for Raziel to weaken enough that Sammael or a whole host of Nephilim could take him, and before that happened he'd figure out who the traitor was. I had absolutely no doubt about that.

I'd be dead, though. And I didn't want to die. I wanted to spend as long as I could with Raziel, no matter how bossy he was.

"I can't kill you without killing Raziel. If he loses his mate too soon, he'll be very dangerous."

Yeah, right. For some reason I couldn't picture Raziel losing it over my untimely demise. For him, I was simply a matter of destiny. It wasn't as if he really wanted a mate. If I died, he'd have a get-out-of-jail-free pass.

I got to my feet slowly, feeling bruised and cold. He'd flown me up high, where the air was thin and icy, and I still felt chilled. "You know," I said in a conversational tone, "I don't want to die. Couldn't we work something out?" If Raziel wasn't dead yet, there was still hope. I couldn't believe that Raziel could be bested by a little shit like Sammael.

"What you want means nothing to me," he said.

I ignored him. "I spent the first part of my life with a religious crackpot. I'd rather not be killed by one."

Sammael was unmoved. "He's waiting for you. And I have things to do. Start walking."

I looked at the great yawning maw of the cave, and a cold sweat broke over me. "Is he still alive?" Because if he wasn't, I decided I'd just as soon die outside, beneath the clear night sky, as down in some dark hole.

"He lives," Sammael said grudgingly. "He waits."

"I go," I said, matching his terse language. And I started up the pathway.

TWENTY-FOUR

H E WAS LYING ON HIS BACK AT the far side of the huge stone cavern, and for a moment I thought he was dead. Raziel's color was always a pale golden, but right now he looked ashen, and he was absolutely still. He looked like he had that first night in the forest when he was dying from the poisoned burn.

"What have you done to him?" I whispered to the man whose hand was clamped onto my arm. I yanked at it, but I was no longer trying to escape. I was desperate to get to Raziel.

He released me, and I stumbled forward, almost falling to my knees. I ran across the hard rock floor, ignoring everything in my haste to reach my mate. I sank down on my knees, throwing my arms around him in a way I would never have dared to if he'd been conscious. I could hear his heart beating, more faintly than usual but still steady, and his skin was cool. I wanted to hide my face against his chest, but it would do no good. Sammael wasn't going to change his mind, walk away. God save me from zealots.

I rose, looking down into Raziel's still face. His tawny hair had fallen back, and he looked starkly beautiful, from his high cheekbones, his chiseled features, to his pale mouth that could do such lovely, wicked things. I let my hand brush his hair back from his high forehead, gently. "What did you do to him?" I whispered, unable to keep the anguish out of my voice.

"I thought you didn't care for him," Sammael said. "Why are you mourning him?"

I looked back at him. "You know perfectly well why," I said, irritation breaking through my despair. "I'm in love with him. I'm his bonded mate, his soul, whether either of us likes it or not."

"You both like it," Sammael said with an ugly twist to his mouth. "I know these things. You rut like animals. You are what caused them to fall in the first place."

"Hey, I wasn't even there," I protested, looking around me for any kind of weapon.

"Silence!" he thundered, like some kind of cartoon monarch.

Raziel stirred next to me, his arm twitching for a moment, and I wondered if he was waking up. As long as he was unconscious, there was little I could do. The cavern was devoid of weapons.

I looked down at him, and he opened his eyes, his vision sharp and clear. His hand caught mine, out of the sight of Sammael's mad eyes, and squeezed it tightly in reassurance.

I wasn't reassured.

He was lying on a strange sort of dais—bedding made of twigs and grasses and larger branches—and I looked down at him in confusion at first, then in dawning horror as I realized what Sammael had planned.

I whirled around, trying to shield Raziel from his view. "You—you can't! You can't be planning on burning him!"

"He will die by fire," Sammael said placidly.

I felt Raziel move behind me, and I tried to stay between him and Sammael, vainly trying to protect him. "Over my dead body." Yes, it was melodramatic, but I was past trying to be cool. I wasn't going to let him die.

But Raziel had struggled to his feet behind me, and I felt his hands clamp on my arms. "Stay out of this, wife," he said in a rough voice, trying to push me out of the way.

I wasn't moving. I did my best to dig in my heels, but of course my strength was pitiful next to Raziel's, even moments after he'd regained consciousness.

He shoved me, hard, and I went sprawling onto the ground, the breath knocked out of me. I lay there for a moment, pissed off enough to forget the danger we were both in. You couldn't breathe when you were dead, could you? Was it going to be like this? I didn't want to die.

"Leave her alone." Raziel's voice sounded almost bored. "She has nothing to do with this—it's between you and me."

"It isn't," Sammael said. There was a brief softening in his face. "I do not wish you ill, Raziel. But if I am to regain redemption, the Fallen must be vanquished."

"She's not one of us."

Sammael's brief smile was almost sorrowful. "She is the Source."

"If you kill us all, she'll be no threat."

"She must be punished. All the Fallen and their human whores must die."

"She's not human."

My breath came back with a sudden, gulping whoosh. "Don't," I managed to choke out. "You don't want to do this." I was ignoring Raziel by this point, just as he was ignoring me.

But Sammael had drawn a huge sword, a weapon that looked like it had come from some medieval painting of an avenging angel. It had appeared out of nowhere, like some damned *Star Wars* light saber, and I ground my teeth. How could you fight a supernatural being, when the rules didn't apply to them?

"You have to give him a weapon as well if you're going to fight," I protested, slowly getting to my feet. If I survived this, I thought, I'd be battered and bruised. Right now I could only wonder why it was taking me so long to rise to my full, fairly insignificant height.

"He's not going to fight me," Raziel said. "There are only two ways he can kill me—he can burn me, or he can cut off my head. But he's too much of a coward to come close enough to strike me. Therefore it must be fire, and he has the right weapon."

"But how—" I demanded, then saw Sammael raise the sword over his head, more like a medieval avenging angel than ever, with a—

Christ, a flaming sword of vengeance. Flames were licking along the blade, kept from Sammael by the broad hilt and nothing more.

"You know that whoever wields the sword will die by the flames as well," Raziel said, seemingly unmoved by his imminent demise.

Sammael shook his head slowly. "Uriel has granted me redemption. I have followed his orders, and I will ascend to the heavens once more, cleansed of sin and the stench of mortals."

"Don't be a fool, Sammael. We are cursed by God. Even Uriel can't change that."

"I have faith," Sammael said simply, and he slowly lowered the sword, pointing it toward Raziel and the funeral pyre.

It was enough. All I knew was that I couldn't let this happen, couldn't let the forces of ignorance win, not this time. "No!" I shrieked, diving across the floor, throwing myself at Sammael to stop him.

At the sound of my voice he automatically turned, the flaming sword between us. I felt it slice into me, and it was curiously painless, just heat and pressure as I stared into Sammael's startled face. The flames were licking toward me along the shining metal of the sword that impaled my chest, and I reached up, grasping the blade, and pushed the fire back at him.

I could feel the heat but the blaze didn't burn my hands as it moved back over the protective hilt, onto Sammael, onto the rough fabric of his clothing, erupting in flames.

He screamed, and yanked the sword free. I collapsed like a marionette whose strings had been cut. I was lying in a river of blood, and if I'd been able to speak I would have told Raziel to find something in which to bottle it. I was dying, and there would be nothing for the Fallen who counted on the Source for sustenance.

But I couldn't speak. I was so tired. It seemed as if I'd been battling forever, and I needed to rest, but there was too much primal satisfaction in watching

Sammael thrash and struggle in a conflagration. He was dying in hideous pain, and I guess there was enough Old Testament in me after all that I reveled in it.

"Allie. Beloved." It was Raziel's voice. I was probably already dead—there was no way he would call me *beloved*. After all, I'd been speared by a sword the size of Excalibur—even if it had missed my heart, it had to have done irreparable damage.

I felt him pull me into his arms, and I struggled, able to summon up a dying panic. "No," I said. "There are sparks. . . ."

He ignored me, pulling me against him, and he put his hand over the gaping wound in my chest. I saw the last remaining spark jump to him, and I moaned in despair, even as the pressure in my chest grew harder, sharper. "This is ridiculous," I said weakly. "Now we're both going to die, and we aren't cut out for Romeo and Juliet—"

"We're not going to die." I heard the pain in his voice, and I wanted to scream at him.

He pressed his hand against my chest, and the sudden pain was blinding, so powerful that my body arched, jerked, and then collapsed in his arms again. The bleeding had stopped, and I knew he'd healed me—somehow managed to close the wound, seal the tear.

But I was dying. He couldn't stop that.

"No," he said. "I won't lose you. I can't." He pulled me against him, and his face was hard, cold, bleak. He reached out a hand and stroked my face gently, and I knew he was saying good-bye. And then he yanked his own shirt open and tore into his skin, ripping across the flesh so that blood spurted out.

I knew what he was going to do the moment before he did it, and I opened my mouth to protest. Opened my mouth as he pressed it against his wound, and the blood ran into my mouth, hot and rich, and my cold, cold body turned to fire as I drank from him, deep gulps of the sweetness of life, his life's blood becoming mine.

He was trembling, his arm burning beneath my head. He pulled me away, and I could feel the wetness of his blood on my mouth. He leaned down and kissed me, full and hard and deep, the blood mingling between us, and the last barrier dropped away. "I love you," he said, the words torn out of him.

"I know."

He rose then, in one fluid movement, but I could see the weakness in him. "If I don't make it," he said in a low growl, "promise me you'll live. The Fallen will need you. You're the Source, even without me."

"No. You live or I won't," I said, stubborn and angry.

He didn't argue. His wings spread out, a gloriously iridescent blue-black, and a moment later we were soaring out of the cave, up and up into the night sky. I could feel his strength failing as he carried me. The ocean was ahead—he just had to make it that far, but heat was spreading, much faster than it had that first night, and I knew that giving me his blood had quickened the poisoning, and I wanted to hit him.

I did the only thing I could. "Don't you dare drop me," I warned him. "We didn't go through all this to have me splattered on the cliffs like a drunken seagull."

He laughed. It was only the faintest tremor of sound, but it was enough. He pushed, managing to rise higher, and then the last of his strength left him, as well as consciousness, and I knew we were too far from the ocean, we were going to crash like a modern Icarus.

I wanted to die kissing his beautiful mouth. His arms had gone limp, and I clung to him, turning my mouth to his, and the movement angled his winged body into the wind.

A breeze caught us, slid underneath us, and suddenly we were gliding, moving ever faster on the wind, crossing the night sky at a nightmare speed, and then falling, falling, spinning, my arms wrapped around him, my mouth on his, the blood between us, as we plummeted . . .

Into the sea. We plunged deep, the icy water a shock, tearing me away from him. It was so dark, so cold, and I'd lost him, gliding downward through the churning water. You could only cheat death so many times, I thought dazedly, and this time I closed my eyes against the saltwater sting, let my breath out, knowing I had nothing left to fight with. Raziel would survive; the ocean water would heal him, and he would find what he needed.

> Full fathom five thy father lies:
> Of his bones are coral made;
> Those are pearls that were his eyes:
> Nothing of him that doth fade,
> But doth suffer a sea-change
> Into something rich and strange.

This time I would drown. I had already suffered a sea-change of such magnitude that there was nothing left, and my bones would be coral, my eyes pearls. Shakespeare in my ear.

Someone was there, a hand brushing mine as I floated, and I opened my eyes to see Sarah, serene and beautiful, smiling at me. All I needed was a bright light, I thought, smiling back at her. There was no one else I wanted to meet on the other side, and I reached out for her.

She shook her head. Her mouth didn't move, but I heard her words clearly. "Not yet," she said. "Not for a long time."

I shook my head. I was so tired of fighting.

"Wait for him," she said. "He's worth waiting for."

A strong hand grasped my wrist, yanking me upward, and I went, bursting up into the cold air endless moments later, coughing and choking in Raziel's arms as he struck out toward shore.

We collapsed on the beach, exhausted, both of us gasping for breath. Raziel rolled onto his back, and I could see the blood on his wet clothes. My blood.

I was facedown in the sand, and I knew I should roll over, but I didn't have the strength to do anything but lie there and struggle for breath.

His hands on my shoulders were gentle as he turned me over to face him. He brushed the wet sand from my face, my hair, and looked down at me with impatience, with annoyance. With love.

"The first thing you do," he said in a rough voice, "is learn how to swim."

And he kissed me.

TWENTY-FIVE

FIVE YEARS LATER

Sarah lied. I swear to God I somehow did the impossible and managed to gain ten pounds since living in Sheol, most of it in my ass. Fortunately, Raziel had a weakness for Renaissance women, and he still found my slightly overripe body irresistible.

The Nephilim were gone, vanquished, at least from this continent. A few were scattered into the wild, but since they survived on small animals and the flesh of the Fallen they would eventually starve. Unfortunately, Raziel told me they could live centuries without feeding, so this would take a while. I refused to consider the idea that that explained their foul, ravening hunger.

Small groups would remain on other continents—a handful in Asia, a larger group in Australia, sent there by Uriel in search of renegade Fallen and then abandoned. That wasn't my worry. I had no intention of ever leaving Sheol again.

Raziel taught me to swim. Of course, with Sammael gone and the Nephilim effectively routed, there was no need for me to get into the icy-cold ocean, but Raziel had a bossy streak. Not that I put up with it, but if I could see common sense behind his autocratic announcements, I tended to give in, after as much delaying as I could manage, even if it was my idea in the first place. Raziel did better when people weren't kowtowing to him, and I considered it my duty to keep him off balance.

He didn't like being Alpha. And he hated me being the Source, though after the first few bloodings he managed to keep his jealousy in check. Tamlel and Gadrael sat on him the first two times, just to make sure he didn't tear anyone's head off. I could read his thoughts, and knew it was a close call.

I have no idea whether the fact that I loved being the Source made things easier or harder for him. If I was to have no children, I could at least nourish and nurture the Fallen, and I welcomed the chance as a way to alleviate some of my mourning. I never spoke of my longing for children to Raziel, and he never spoke of it to me. But we knew each other's thoughts, and shared the pain.

There was no word from Azazel. Most thought he was dead, including me, but Raziel believed otherwise. He would return, Raziel said, when the time was right. There would be a sign, and he would be back.

I might have been getting fatter but I wasn't getting any older. My face was unchanged—no crow's-feet forming at the corners of my eyes, no laugh lines, though I found I could laugh a lot in the hidden mists of Sheol. I never fed from Raziel again, even though he knew I wanted it. Instead I gave him my body, my blood, and he gave me ecstasy, annoyance, and the deep abiding love that I'm not sure exists in ordinary life.

I had no idea how long I would live, and I didn't worry about it. In the timeless world of Sheol, you had no choice but to live in the moment; and if I couldn't live up to Sarah's gentle example, I did well enough.

Until the day she turned up. Lilith, the demon wife.

And all hell broke loose.

TURN THE PAGE FOR A LOOK AT

DEMON

BY KRISTINA DOUGLAS

THE NEXT EXCITING BOOK IN THE FALLEN SERIES

COMING IN JUNE 2011 FROM POCKET BOOKS

H E WAS FOLLOWING ME AGAIN. I knew it, instinctively, even though I hadn't actually seen him. It was as if he was just beyond my vision, on the outer edges of my sight, hiding in shadows. Skulking.

Not stalking. There might be huge gaps in my memory but I had a mirror and absolutely no delusions about my totally resistible charms. I was determinedly average—average height, average weight, give or take ten pounds. Anyway, totally average. I had short hair, the muddy brown you get when you dye it too often, and my eyes were a plain brown. My skin was olive-tinged, my bone structure average, and there was no clue to who or what I was.

Here's what I knew: my name was Rachel. My current last name was Fitzpatrick, but before that it was Brown, and the next time it might be Montgomery.

Average names with Anglo-Saxon antecedents. I didn't know why, I just went with it.

I'd been Rachel Fitzpatrick for almost two years now, and it felt as if it had been longer than usual, this comfortable life I'd built up. I was living in a big industrial city in the Midwest, working for a newspaper that, like most of its kind, was on its last legs. I had a great apartment on the top floor of an old Victorian house, I had an unexciting car I could rely on, I had good friends I could turn to in an emergency and have fun with when times were good. I was even godmother to my coworker Julie's newborn baby girl. I kept waiting for the other shoe to drop.

It was November, and I thought that probably I had never liked November. The trees were bare, the wind was biting, and the darkness closed around the city like a shroud. And someone was watching me.

I didn't know how long he'd been there—it had taken me awhile to realize he was back again. I'd never gotten much of a look at him—he kept to the shadows, a tall, narrow figure of undeniable menace. I had no wish to see him any better.

I was very careful. I didn't go out alone after dark, I kept away from secluded places, I was always on my guard. I had never mentioned him to my friends, even Julie. I told myself I didn't want them to worry.

But I didn't go to the police either, and it was their job *to* worry.

I spun any number of possibilities out of the big gray blank that was my memory. Maybe he was my abusive husband, watching me, and I'd run away from him, the trauma of his brutality wiping my mind clean.

Maybe I had been in the witness protection program and I'd gone through some kind of horror, and the mob was after me.

But it didn't explain why he hadn't come any closer. No matter how careful I was, if someone wanted to hurt me, to kill me, there was probably no way to stop them, short of . . . well, there probably *was* no way to stop them. So my watcher presumably didn't want me dead.

I was working late on a cold, rainy Thursday, trying to get a bunch of obituaries formatted. Yup, doing obituaries late at night was not my favorite thing, but with the Courier on its last legs we all put in overtime whenever asked and worked on anything that was needed, though I drew the line at sports. I was ostensibly the Home and Health editor, *editor* being a glorious term for the only reporter on the beat, but I generally enjoyed my work. With obituaries, not so much. It was always the babies that got to me. Stillbirths, crib deaths, miscarriages. They made me feel like crying, though oddly enough I never cried. If I could, I would weep for those babies, for days and weeks and years.

I didn't bother to wonder whether I'd lost a child myself. Instinct told me I hadn't, and besides, grieving for lost babies was a logical, human reaction. Who wouldn't feel sorrow at the loss of a brand-new life?

The wind had picked up, howling through the city and shaking the sealed windows of the new building the Courier had unwisely built less than five years ago. I logged off my computer, finished for the night. I glanced at the clock—it was after ten, and the office was deserted. My car was in the parking garage; there had to be someone there. And I could have my keys out, make a dash for my reliable old Subaru and lock myself in if anything loomed up out of the darkness.

I could always call Julie and see if her husband could come and escort me home. While I hadn't told them about my watcher, I had explained to them that I was extremely skittish about personal safety, and Bob had come to the rescue on a number of occasions. But they had a brand-new baby, and I didn't want to bother them. I'd be fine.

I grabbed my coat, heading for the elevator, when the phone at my desk rang. I hesitated, then ignored it. Whoever it was, whatever they wanted, I was too tired to provide it. All I wanted was to get home through this blasted wind and curl up in my nice warm bed.

The elevator was taking its own sweet time considering the entire building was practically deserted. My desk phone stopped ringing and my cell phone started. I cursed, reaching into my pocket and flipping it open just as the elevator arrived.

It was Julie, sounding panicked. "Rachel, I need you," she said in a tear-filled voice.

Something bad had happened, and my stomach knotted. "What's wrong?" And like a fool, I stepped into the elevator.

"It's the baby. She's . . ."

The door closed, the elevator began to descend, and I lost the signal.

"Shit," I said very loudly. We were on the twenty-second floor, and I'd pushed the button for the second level of parking, but I quickly hit a lower level floor to stop the descent. The doors slid open onto the dark and empty eighth floor and I jumped out. I pushed the call-back button as the doors slid closed, abandoning me in the darkness, and a shiver ran over me, one I tried to ignore. I had nerves of steel, but I was never foolhardy and there was no reason to feel uneasy. I'd been in this building alone on numerous occasions.

But I'd never felt so odd before.

Julie answered the phone on the first ring.

"Where did you go?" she said, her voice frantic and accusing.

"Lost the signal," I said. "What's wrong with the baby?"

"I'm at the hospital. She couldn't breathe, and I called an ambulance. They've got her in the emergency room and they kicked me out, and I need you here for moral support. I'm terrified, Rachel!" Her voice was thick with tears.

"Where's Bob?" I said, trying to be practical.

"With me. You know how helpless men are. He just paces and looks grim, and I need someone to give me encouragement. I need my best friend. I need you. How soon can you make it?"

Odd how we became such good friends in so short a time. It felt like an enduring bond, not an office friendship, almost as if I'd known her in another life. But she had no clues about my past any more than I did. "Which hospital?"

"St. Uriel's. We're in the emergency waiting room. Come now, Rachel! *Please!*"

St. Uriel's, I thought. *That's wrong, isn't it? Was Uriel a saint?* But I made soothing noises, anyway. "I'll be right there," I said. And knew I had lied.

I mentally reviewed the contents of my desk. Nothing much—a copy of *House & Garden*, the latest Laurell K. Hamilton book, and the Bible, which was admittedly weird. I didn't understand why I had it—maybe I'd been part of some fundamentalist cult before I'd run away. God knows. I only knew I needed to have a Bible with me.

I would find another, as soon as I checked into a hotel. There was no need to go back. I traveled light, and left as little impression behind as I could. They'd find no clues about me if they searched my desk. Particularly since I had no clues about myself.

My apartment was only slightly less secure. There were no letters, no signs of a personal life at all. I had a number of cheap pre-Raphaelite prints on the wall, plus a framed poster of a fog-shrouded section of the Northwest Coast that spoke to me. It was large, and I hated to leave it behind, but I needed to move fast. I'd have to ditch the car in the next day or two, buy another. It would take Julie that long to realize I'd gone missing. She'd be too busy hovering over baby Amanda, watching each struggling breath with anxious eyes.

But Amanda wouldn't smother. She'd start to get better, as would any other newborns with mysterious flu-like symptoms, and soon the hospital would be full of them. All I had to do was get far enough away and they'd recover. I knew it instinctively, though I didn't know why.

I pushed the elevator button, then paced the darkened hallway, restless. Nothing happened, and I pushed it again, repeatedly, then pressed my ear to the door, listening for some sign that the cars were moving. Nothing but silence.

"Shit," I said again. There was no help for it; I'd have to take the stairs.

I didn't stop to think about it. The time had come to leave, as it always did, and thinking did no good. I had no idea why I knew these things, why I had to run. I only knew that I did.

It wasn't until the door to the stairs closed behind me that I remembered my watcher, and for a moment I freaked, grabbing the door handle. It was already locked, of course. I had no choice. If I was going to get out of town in time, I had to keep moving.

In time for what? I had no clear idea. But baby Amanda wouldn't survive for long if I didn't move it.

I tripped and went sprawling, slamming my shin against the railing. I struggled to my feet, and froze. Someone was in the stairwell with me. I sensed him, closer than he'd ever been before, and there was nothing, no one between him and me. No buffer, no safety. Time was running out.

I had no weapon. I was an idiot—you could carry concealed weapons in this state, and a really small gun could blow a really big hole in whoever was following me. Or a knife, something sharp. Hell, didn't I hear you could jab your keys into an attacker's eyes?

I didn't know whether he was above me or below

me, but I had no choice. The only doors that opened from the stairwell were the ones on the parking level. If I went up, I'd be trapped.

I had no choice but to keep going. I started down the next flight, moving as quietly as I could, listening for any matching footsteps. There were none. Whoever he was, he made no sound.

Maybe he was a figment of my paranoid imagination. I had no concrete reasons to do the things I did, I acted on instinct alone. I could be crazy as a bedbug, imagining all this power. Why in the world should small, insignificant Rachel Fitzpatrick have anything to do with the well-being of a baby? Of a number of babies? Why did I have to keep changing my name, changing who I was? If someone was following me, why hadn't he caught up yet?

What would happen if I simply drove back home and stayed there? Joined Julie at the hospital?

Amanda would die.

I had no choice. I had to run.

AZAZEL MOVED DOWN THE STAIRS after the demon, silent, scarcely breathing. He could sense its panic, and he knew it was going to run again. He had taken longer to find it this time; it must be getting better at coming up with new identities. If the demon vanished this time it might take too long to track it down.

It was time to take it. He had no idea why he'd hesitated, why he'd watched it without doing anything. His hatred for the creature was so powerful it would have frightened him, if he was capable of feeling fear. He was incapable of feeling anything but his hatred for the monster. That was what had stayed his hand. Once he killed it, he would feel nothing at all.

He had no idea how easy the demon would be to kill. It looked like a normal female, but he felt its seductive power even from a distance. It didn't need any of the obvious feminine wiles to lure him. It didn't wear makeup, didn't dress in revealing clothes. It tended to dress in dark-colored, loose-fitting T-shirts and baggy pants. There was nothing to make a man think of sex, and yet every time he looked at her—at it—he thought about lust. It wouldn't do to underestimate her power.

It. Part of the demon's power was to make him forget that it was nothing but a thing, not the vulnerable female it appeared to be. It was so easy to slip, to think of it as a woman. A woman he would have to kill. Maybe it had been once, but not anymore.

He could catch her in the parking garage, break her neck, and then fly up into the sun till her body burned in his arms. He could bury her deep beneath the earth in the belly of a volcano. Somehow he thought he would need fire to eradicate her completely, her and her evil powers. Only when she was dead would the threat dissolve.

The threat to newborn babies. The threat to vulnerable men who dreamed of sex and found only a demon possessing them.

And the threat to him. Most of all he hated her for the connection that was to come, with him of all people. And the only way to make certain that never happened was to destroy her.

He was standing in the corner of the stairwell on the bottom floor, watching her. He'd pulled his wings around him, disappearing, and though she searched her surroundings, she saw nothing, and moved on.

More proof of her power, the power she was trying so hard to disguise. No one else sensed him when he cloaked himself. But she did. Her awareness was as acute as his. And he hated it.

Tonight, he told himself. Tonight he would kill her. Whether he'd present proof to Uriel was undecided. He might simply leave him unknowing. He could finally return to Sheol, take the reins back from Raziel if he must. And see Raziel's bonded mate in Sarah's place.

No, he wasn't ready. Surely there must be something else he had to do before he returned.

She'd escaped into the garage and he followed

her, the door closing silently behind him. The place was brightly lit, but there were only a handful of cars still there. She was already halfway to her dark red Subaru.

He knew then where he could take her. As far away as humanly possible from this place. To the other side of the world, one of the only places where the scourge known as the Nephilim still thrived.

What better place for a demon?

He waved his hands, and the parking garage plunged into darkness, every light extinguished. He could feel her sudden panic, which surprised him. He wouldn't have thought demons would feel fear. She started running, but her car was parked midway down, and he spread his wings and took her.

I SCREAMED, BUT MY VOICE was lost in the folds that covered me. I couldn't see, couldn't hear, could barely move. I was so disoriented and dizzy that I felt sick. I could feel the ground give way beneath my feet, and I was falling, falling . . .

Something tight bound me, but I couldn't sense what. It felt like irons bands around my arms, holding me still, and my face was crushed against something hard. I breathed in, and oddly enough I could smell skin—warm, vibrant, indefinably male skin. Impossible. I smelled the ocean as well, and we were at least a thousand miles away from any salt water.

I squirmed, and the bands tightened, and I couldn't breathe. My chest was crushed against whatever thing had done this, and I was helpless, weightless, cocooned by the monster that had grabbed me. I tried to move once more, but the pain was blinding It was as if my heart was being crushed, I thought, as consciousness faded and I fell into a merciful dark hole.

Fantasy.
Temptation.
Adventure.

**Visit PocketAfterDark.com,
an all-new website just for Urban
Fantasy and Romance Readers!**

- Exclusive access to the hottest
urban fantasy and romance titles!

- Read and share reviews on
the latest books!

- Live chats with your favorite
romance authors!

- Vote in online polls!

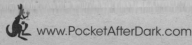
www.PocketAfterDark.com

26119

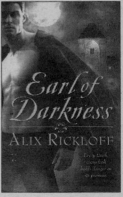

Passion is stronger
after dark.